COLD RUN

COLD RUN

RACHEL A. BRUNE

Charlotte, NC

FALSTAFF
BOOKS

WWW.FALSTAFFBOOKS.COM

This book is for my sister, Jennifer

1

The phone rang when I was into the twelfth beer of the afternoon, catching me with my pants down. Literally. Out here in the middle of Vermont, no one was looking, and the full moon was on the rise. The first time I hung up, the asshole called back. The second time, my fumbling fingers accidentally answered the phone instead of turning it off. I hate cell phones.

On the other end of the line, a series of numbers were repeated mechanically, followed by a beep and a pause.

I belched, not bothering to cover the receiver.

"Wolfhound?" The voice on the other end sounded almost familiar.

I hadn't received one of these phone calls in a long time. Thinking through a variety of responses, most of which contained some creative German swear words, I opted for silence.

"Saturday morning." A sharp rasp to the man's tenor voice gave it that thick Brooklyn squawk you didn't hear much anymore now that everyone had moved out to Jersey.

I finished the beer, opened the back door, and threw the empty bottle into the darkness. It sailed off the porch, chunking into a tree on the woodline and falling into the snow. Might be a new record.

"There will be a ticket reserved for you out of BTV."

"I'm on the no-fly list."

"Not a problem."

"Where am I supposed to be going?"

"New York."

"Uh-huh." I closed the phone, then took out the battery and stomped on it, cracking the little chip in two, just in case anyone tried to call me back. I knew one thing for certain: any car waiting for me at the airport would be waiting for a long time.

Tossing the phone on the counter, I grabbed another beer and walked barefoot onto the back porch. The cold didn't bother me. In fact, the phone call ignited an adrenaline burn that, I had to admit, I almost missed. There was something in the back of my brain bothering me, something that had to do with the phone, but I couldn't remember what it was.

The night smelled clear and cold as only New England in early November can, the air so raw it burned going down. A half-inch of snow had fallen over the leaves I never bothered to rake. Shadows patched the mottled ground. Underneath the scent of wind through the pines, something was tugging at my senses. Something metallic, corrosive. It lingered, but like the thing with my phone, I pushed it away. In an hour or so, it wouldn't matter. It would be a good night for a run.

The neighbor's cat paused at the edge of my property. He was a big gray tom, and I often caught him trying to sneak through the backyard in search of the moles I couldn't seem to kill off. I would have invited him over the property line, but I imagined he'd get offended if the sneaking were allowed. Out of principle, I growled at him. He snarled at me, and then, happy our mutual understanding remained intact, he slunk off into the undergrowth.

Shaking my head, I drained the bottle and tossed it after the others. It was an old family recipe, brewed with ingredients that were impossible to get in the States, and I rationed them for these nights. That reminded me; I was down to the next to last shelf in the basement. A twinge in the lowest part of my spine also reminded me that tonight wasn't for making to-do lists. It was for answering the call that the moon would bring with her.

The first twinge was followed by a massive cramp that started deep in my torso, folding my body in on itself, a promise of the pain and wrenching to come. I let myself fall to the floor, the electric needles jabbing their way up my arms and legs from within, coaxing the change from my willing human form.

The full moon rose behind the trees, silhouetting starkly the bare branches of the line of paper birches that bordered the deeper pine forest beyond the clearing. My senses expanded as my limbs contracted. From several kilometers away, my neighbors were burning trash and weed, the sweet scents of smoke and earthy skunk. In the pines before me, small creatures darted away, scrabbling and diving through the dark loam.

Winter wind through the pines on a cold moon night. It always had been my favorite scent. It brought with it that comfortable, invigorating rush of pure energy and curiosity that had me chomping and eager for the crest of the change to roll over me.

My vision widened and brightened at the same time, my normal monochrome deepening into a razor focus. In my periphery, each leaf and stone and crawling thing popped into sharp relief. As the light from the sun bled out, the full moon replacing it brought out the sheen reflected off the snow. The sharp cold air brought a thousand scents to me, flooding my senses and overwhelming the ability of my brain to process them. My intellect would get in the way of my instinct for another hour or so until it finally shut down and let things change.

Something was off. Some scent in the final throes of the change had me coughing and hacking, trying to rid my nose and tongue of the offending flavor. It was the taste of heavy cotton and nylon, metal and gun oil, face paint and the sweat of men who were comfortable with an elite level of physical activity. I hadn't scented that in over two decades.

Stumbling, I lurched to my paws, panting, flanks heaving. The human part of my brain was quickly sinking into the wolf's instinct-driven id. Still, I hadn't lost all the harshly wrought control the agency had forced into me, and I strained to keep my awareness above the call of the change, like a drowning man searching for an air pocket under the ice.

Where were they? I forced myself to calm down and scent the air, but I couldn't get a fix on their position. A cracking sound came from behind me, somewhere in the front of my house. My head whipped to the side as an accompanying grunt came from the left, deep in the woods. That answered the where, even as more sounds of stalking pursuit came from my right, about fifty meters past the tree line. Better question—who were these humans who trespassed into my sanctuary on this night of all nights?

Some answers were worth outrunning the question. Growling, I gathered my legs under me and sprinted forward, heading into the woods where I had to trust that the night and the cold would shelter my path.

WHEN I FIRST BOUGHT THE property, I spent long weeks building, shoveling, and scraping together various obstacles and traps I figured would keep whatever came after me at bay. One of the first things I learned in my training was to analyze the terrain—the topography, natural obstacles, avenues of approach, and places where I did not want the enemy to establish a foothold or overwatch. I put this training to work and bought a lot of guns to back it up if they made it past the fortifications.

After a few years, when nobody came after me, I grew sloppy. Weeds clumped thick in the trenches I dug at random intervals. I grew tired of re-emplacing various explosive devices and then having to explain the loud noises and fires to my neighbors. They didn't live too close, but when a deer trips a grenade line, they reasonably wondered why their windows shook. I sold most of the guns for beer money.

Running, I didn't regret the guns. Whoever these men were on my heels, they knew which night of the month to come after me. I did kick myself mentally for not maintaining at least one or two of the tripwires. My day sight gradually blended into shades of gray as the twilight faded from between the trees. The snow and shadows left ghostly patterns against the white birches and dark pines. The nascent night and the chill of the ground created an energy that could not be described or duplicated, and it charged my steps as I loped along. The full moon had barely cleared the trees, but I was fully in her grasp.

A shot rang out, zinging as the bullet ricocheted off an exposed rock and kicked up the dirt in front of me. A second later, I ran over the place where it hit, smelling the sour sharpness of silver on the bullet. Another round cracked past, and I poured on the speed, jerking and zigzagging through the dense pines.

The worst thing is to know you are short on time and unaware of how fast that time is slipping by or when your time will be up, but I ran as if somehow I could beat the odds. The stitch in my side sent out feelers of pain, traveling up and down my body, tapping into the energy from the night, and spreading to my chest and legs.

Twenty, even thirty years ago, I would have been more in control, able to keep things from getting out of hand before I reached the culmination of the change, but that had been a long time ago, and I lost the habit of limiting the transformation. These days, when the full moon came up burning silver, I was wholly wolf.

I drew up, out of breath from the full out sprint, and stopped short on the path as the uncanny silence weighted my ears. A light snow began to fall, filling the woods with light, white mist. I couldn't see anything. Couldn't hear anything. My senses were a riot of overstimulation. Still, any wolf knows the bounds of its territory, and I was approaching the edge of mine.

At the small creek that marked the end of my property, I looked around warily. My first concrete clue of something wrong lay at my feet. This path, an unused spur of a forgotten WPA forestry project, never saw more traffic than the tracks I laid once a month. But here on the ground—a brightly-colored wrapper, the candy scent overlaid with the aroma of gasoline and cordite. I chuffed at the scent, the sharp tang itching my nostrils, and leapt forward, the men at my back and their approach lending panic and fear to my flight.

Branches of mountain laurel whipped my snout, leaving welts on my flanks where the branches slapped back against my passing. Growing so long, they appeared wild and un-traversable. I'd planted them to become so. Even in the barren winter snow, they kept their leaves. I crept slowly through them, ears and nose alert to the men behind me, the path I knew by heart, as it long ago grew to obscure its secrets even from its creator.

I stopped short on the other side, brought to a halt by the wires lying unraveled on the path before me, and blinked against the pain. What had once been a sturdy wire laced through the bushes and trees, a perimeter to defend and protect, now lay in separate, useless pieces on the ground. Some substance coated the ground, something that smelled of salt and silver. I backed away from it, trying to find a way around, cursing whoever had laid this trap and then cursing myself for falling into it.

A step behind me, soft but still detectable, whirled me around. Snarling, I leapt for the man who had crept up behind me. His weapon fired, but I was already in the air, teeth bared, aiming for his throat.

The weight of my attack bore him to the ground. His throat was protected with a thick layer of some kind of armor, but he still screamed and beat at me, trying to get me off of him. I snapped and growled, latching onto anything I could.

The silence in the forest, so unnatural, echoed around the buzzing in my ears, as did the grunts of the man under me. The crack of a rifle was like a knife driving into my ears, immediately followed by an actual blade that the man drove into my side. I flinched back, and he heaved me off him, scrambling to his feet, knife at the ready.

I darted at him. He circled, not allowing me in his guard. Something was wrong. The flesh where the knife had entered was knitting together already, but something was trickling down my left haunch. My back leg didn't want to listen. Now that I had become aware of the pain, it intensified, a deep, stinging furrow along my side that a silver round had ripped open.

This man in front of me was dead; he just didn't know it yet. The change overrode the human part of my mind that screamed out to pay attention, that there was something coming up from the woods. The wolf demanded that I attack, and with the final pull of the moon, that's what I did. Leaping, less forcefully than before, I launched myself at him again.

Another shot rang out. Something punched me in the side and knocked me to the ground, where I drew a long, bloody furrow in the snow.

"Keller."

The man behind the weapon was a ghost, a black tactical suit concealing his form, expensive scope mounted on some sort of rifle. I howled again and tried to lurch up at him, but the pain in my side had me flailing, four legs trying to find purchase on the slippery ground.

Another man appeared to the side, shining a bright, piercing strobe light at my eyes, disorienting me as I tried to turn to face the new threat, my traitorous body rendering my reactions unreliable. The man with the knife backed up, cursing as he limped. I'd at least left my mark on him.

"Stay down, asshole." The man with the gun raised it, crouching as he aimed through the sight. I don't know why. It wasn't like he needed to take cover from the attack phalanx I'd hidden in the woods.

No, the only troops in the woods belonged to these two interlopers. Three more men approached from the wood line, stalking softly. I barely noticed them, my attention focused on the barrel pointing at me.

I growled again, weighed my options, and let the wolf take over. Ignoring the pain in my side and the imminent promise of death, I attacked the man with the rifle, my rusty instincts ignoring the man with the knife who crept closer.

Instead of the soft viscera of the rifleman's throat beneath my teeth, the next sensation I felt was intense pain, which slowed and disjointed my movements. I raised my head, snapping and gnarling in vain against the folds of the net suddenly enveloping me. Ignoring the knife man—stupid mistake. From the burning the lines of the net raised against my hide, I could tell the wires were laced with silver filaments.

The man with the rifle scrambled away from me. I let him go, rolling on the ground, trying to escape the clutching net.

"He's a big one." The man holding the light spoke the words, looking down on me from an impossible height as the pain began to outweigh the panic, the silver working against my struggling.

"He always was." The rifleman hocked and spat. It smelled of Copenhagen. "It's going to be a bitch dragging him down to the truck."

The words made no sense. I could hear them but didn't understand what they meant.

"If we let you up, do you promise to be a good doggie?" The man with the rifle prodded the barrel into my side.

The growl I leveled at him was mostly wishful thinking, the energy from the night and the change suddenly sapped by the silvered net. I lay on my side and simply lolled.

"Good boy." The man kept his rifle trained at me as his partner with the light knelt down and fiddled with the edge of the net. Grasping a loop from the edge, he pulled. It contracted the net into a small, compact circle around my neck.

"Come on." The man jerked at my neck, holding the line as a leash. "I'm not carrying you down this hill in the dark."

The net continued to burn against my neck as he dragged me to my feet. Head hanging, I padded after him through the snow.

A BOX TRUCK waited at the bottom of the hill where the woods drifted down to meet the unimproved road. The falling snow dusted the oil and gravel surface. Both men slipped as they made their way down from the leaves to the back of the truck, tugging the silver at my neck tighter against my skin.

A large metal padlock secured the cargo compartment. The first man bent to unlock it, then grabbed the thick canvas strap protruding from the back and lifted the back door. It rolled up with a loud rumbling, revealing a cavernous interior, empty except for the cage secured to the interior by means of thick cargo straps.

"Go ahead, get up there, boy." The man holding my leash kicked me in the side to encourage me.

"Knock that off." The first man sounded almost bored. "Just let him get up there."

I tried. I really did. The pain and the change and indignity of crawling behind the unknown men with the silver and guns staggered me to the point of not caring.

I lunged upward, but my back legs didn't understand what my front legs were trying to accomplish and gave out under me. I landed on my back in the snow and yelped, bucking to try to regain my feet.

"Aw, hell. This isn't going to work." The first man lowered his rifle, slinging it behind him, so it hung from his shoulder by the strap, freeing his hands yet remaining available if I decided to try something.

"Grab his feet."

"What if he's faking us out?"

"Then jerk his chain, and he'll quit it."

The second man had nothing to fear. I wasn't faking anything.

I stayed limp as the first man grabbed me around the hindquarters, the second man grasping me around the chest and neck. Together they hoisted me up to the loading platform, pushing and shoving me over the ledge like a piece of canine freight. Still holding the leash, the second man jumped up into the truck next to me.

"Come on, get up." He tugged at the collar firmly, dragging me to my feet. I staggered the few steps and followed where he pointed, into the cage.

I sat heavily, head lolling, not resisting as he attached the leash to a loop on the cage and closed the door. He padlocked it firmly behind him and reached up to grab the door strap.

"Be a good boy." He smirked, drawing the door down against the last image of snow and moon on the road.

I circled around in the cage, avoiding the sides. The subtle pressure emanating from the enclosure told me the bars were predominately silver. Considering the density of the composition combined with my current state, contact with the cage would not be a pleasant thing.

The two men walked around to the front of the truck. The metal under me started vibrating as one of them turned on the engine. I braced all four legs as the blackness started to move, jerking me backward. My eyes tried to adjust, but no light remained for them to capture.

The unheated compartment added to the misery. The coherent part of my mind, the tiny part left still able to remember how to form promises, made one in the dark. I would find these men. I would leash them, cage them, and finally, I would kill them.

I howled, the sound echoing off the silver and steel encasing me in darkness.

2

G*uten Morgen, Herr Keller."*

The man squatting in front of my cage was short, blond, smirking, and smelled like aftershave and cream cheese. He was also kind of blurry, but I chalked that up to the fact that my eyes were still swollen and gritty from whatever had happened while I was out.

I was flat on my stomach on a cold cement floor. The aching cold and damp in certain sensitive parts of my anatomy told me no one had bothered to re-clothe me after dumping me wherever this was. My right arm, flung at an awkward angle across my back, tingled with pins and needles. I gritted my teeth against the prickling, put my hands on the floor, and pushed myself to a half-sitting, half-kneeling crouch.

"Fugam I?"

"A cage in the basement." It was the gravelly tenor from the mystery man whose call preceded my capture.

"Fugaryou?"

"Agent John Tell."

I rubbed my left hand across my face and scratched my jaw. With about three days' growth of stubble, it itched like hell. I had a burning need to urinate, but the cage was completely bare, as was I, and I would be damned to the last shreds of my dignity if I pissed naked in a cage in front of the smirking Agent John Tell.

"If I let you out of there, do you promise to behave?"

My fingers were still stiff and didn't move properly, but the intent of the gesture made it through.

"We can do this the easy way or the hard way." Tell stood, dusting off his tactical khaki douche slacks as he did so. "The difference is, you get to meet your new masters standing upright and with some semblance of cleanliness."

I stared at him.

"The other way is, I drag you up there naked by the chain around your neck."

No doubt he would do it. I shrugged. "Fine."

He bent down and opened the cage door. I half crawled, half staggered out into the dingy, mostly empty basement.

"Here." Agent Tell tossed me a towel. I grabbed it and wrapped it around my waist. It wasn't much, but I'd take what I could get.

"Bend over."

I flinched back, but apparently, the net collar remained attached to the line, and he jerked my head down.

"Try to hold still. This is going to hurt."

As I gritted my teeth, he slowly peeled the lines of the net off my neck. The individual wires of the device embedded themselves deep into the skin, fusing to the bone in the areas around my collarbone. I smelled burning in the air—the silver in the wires cauterized my skin as he pulled the collar off. The pain had me wavering, but I managed to stay standing, even if something like a whimper did escape from somewhere in my throat.

"Always have to do things the hard way." Agent Tell shook his head.

"Fuck are you talking about?"

"We tried asking nicely." He tossed something at me, and I went to catch it but missed. I watched as my cell phone fell onto the cement and cracked open.

"Bullshit. MONIKER never asks anything, let alone nicely."

"Next time we send for you, check your texts." He didn't acknowledge the guess, just shrugged. "Your phone might be an ancient piece of crap, but that didn't mean we couldn't ping the signal."

Of course, they could. That's what had been bugging me. The phone wasn't the only thing getting old and rusty. I knelt down and picked up the pieces. It wasn't the first time the abused piece of technology had been treated in such a way. I clicked the flip top back in its place. I could buy a new phone later. Or not.

"What's the big rush?" My neck burned. I tentatively poked a finger at the raw skin left by the net, recoiling as the touch burned worse than the removal. "Two for one sale on bondage wear?"

He shrugged. "Follow me and find out."

There didn't appear to be much of an alternative. I followed Tell out of the basement to a dark hallway. It smelled like something had died after living there a long time. Or it could have been me. A flight of wooden stairs led somewhere. A metal door opened into a small room behind the stairs, revealing a tiny, dark bathroom with a broken, stained sink and a toilet in worse condition.

Tell nodded at the room. "There's a bag in there. Take your time—we're going upstairs in five minutes."

He stood in the doorway, making it clear that privacy was not an option. I didn't protest. He seemed particularly oblivious to profanity and smartass comments, which was all I had at the moment. Fumbling for a light switch, I stepped farther into the dark room. Something brushed against the top of my head, and I waved my hand around until I finally found a chain. I pulled it, and a single light bulb turned on, revealing the rest of the concrete, industrial bathroom.

Without further ado, I took care of business. It took a few seconds after turning on the taps to wait for the dark water to clear itself out of the pipes.

On the sink, there was a disposable razor, shaving cream, washcloth, and a toothbrush still in its package.

A peeling, faded *Playboy* centerfold, circa 1983, covered the mirror. I pulled it down, tearing the paper and tape. Underneath, the mirror hung cracked and dirty, but I didn't want to get too good a look at myself anyway.

My reflection stared back, grim and blurred by the imperfections in the glass. I peered more closely at my neck. When Tell removed the net collar, he took large chunks of skin with it. A deep, wavy line of blood glistened around my neck, dripping in places. It would be a while before it healed.

I washed and shaved as best I could, using the towel to sop up the cold water and wipe away the worst of the grime. It wasn't much as far as hygiene went, but I would take what I could get.

The bag Tell mentioned sat under the sink. I rummaged quickly through but could find neither toothpaste nor soap. Just jeans, a long-sleeved T-shirt, socks, no shoes. Under the clothes, I found they did remember something useful. A box of gauze and a roll of medical tape. I washed out the open sore around my neck as best as I could, then taped the gauze to it. I looked like some kind of freakish clown, but when I slipped the T-shirt over my head, the collar hid most of it. At least the thin material didn't stick to the wound. Take the wins where you can find them.

The jeans were the right length but loose enough to have me wishing the fashion genius who put this ensemble together had the courtesy to remember a belt. I'm not a huge guy at the best of times, topping out about five-eight, or if you want to get picky about it, five seven-and-a-half. The change always takes it out of me, no matter how I binge eat beforehand. Looking at the hollows in my cheeks and the clothes hanging off me, I wondered if they'd bothered to feed me at all the past three days.

"Time's up." Tell held out a pair of cuffs and motioned me forward. "Come here."

I thought briefly about taking him out. He wasn't much larger than me and didn't move like he had a lot of unarmed combat training. I also hadn't seen a pistol, but that didn't mean he wasn't carrying—just that I was rusty at spotting concealed weapons.

A sudden wave of dizziness caused me to shudder and brace myself against the wall until it passed. With this organization, they were either going to feed me soon and tell me what they wanted or strap me on a lab table and call it a day. Either way, I didn't see myself making a break for it with my pants falling down. Better to wait and see. And maybe get something to eat in the meantime. So I turned around and let him snap the cuffs on me, wincing at the traces of silver that chafed the skin on my wrists. He kicked the back of my foot, and I headed up the stairs, hanging onto the waist of my pants and the last shreds of my dignity.

I DON'T KNOW what I anticipated when we reached the top of the stairs, but I didn't expect to find myself walking in a corporate wonderland. The richly carpeted hallways with dark wood baseboards, flanked by walls hung with tastefully framed prints, screamed executive chic. The few offices we passed, though dark, proudly displayed names of generic businesses in Lucida Sans.

All the shaving in the world wouldn't have saved me from feeling out of place, and the urge to bolt became overwhelming. The only thing keeping me in Tell's footsteps was the fact the hallways were deserted, and after three turns, I hadn't even seen an exit sign. It was also hard to make a getaway when you're wearing silver-laced handcuffs and no shoes.

Plus, I hoped they would at least feed me before they did whatever they planned to do.

He stopped by a bank of elevators and pressed the up button. When the lift arrived, he used a small key to illuminate the button for the tenth floor. The doors closed, and we started moving.

"Calm down, boy," he said. "It's only an elevator."

It wasn't the enclosed space that caused the trembling. I was starving, nervous, and trying to keep myself from bolting the hell out of this creepy corporate building. Yeah, okay, so the sudden movement and the shaking as we began to move *was* freaking me out. I hated elevators. I'd ridden in too many early versions of the technology not to freak out.

The elevator stopped, and we stepped out into another anonymous hall.

"Well, come on." Tell led the way down the corridor. I followed, hands cuffed behind me, feeling weirdly awkward and embarrassed. We turned a few times, each bend bringing another blank hallway. I wondered where the offices were, or if behind each of these walls, I would find just another long walk going nowhere.

After another turn, things started making sense again. Turned out that I had guessed correctly. On the frosted glass double doors before us, in the familiar art deco font, read the simple word: MONIKER.

The initials faded to obsolescence after the first world war, but I guessed the agency kept the name. Maybe for nostalgia. Maybe so assholes like me would have some sense of continuity.

I didn't realize I'd stopped in the hall until Tell grabbed my upper arm and pulled me forward.

"Go ahead." It wasn't a suggestion. "We're late."

I barely heard him. I was too busy staring at a ghost.

3

A well-coiffured receptionist raised her eyebrow at my appearance when I stumbled in the front door, followed by the helpful Agent Tell. She paused with her finger over an actual switchboard, an interesting anachronism.

I stared at her, my mind still on the tall brunette we'd passed in the hall. There was no way it could have been—but there she was, clipboard in hand, talking to a man in a flannel shirt. Neither of them had so much as lifted their gazes when we stumbled by.

"This is Keller?" The receptionist raised an eyebrow, and I realized my pants were drooping. "Ah yes, and Agent Tell." A smile for the man. "They're expecting you in Conference Room Three."

The foyer sported none of the typical corporate trappings—no logos, no stationery, not even a vision statement. Agent Tell took the lead, and I followed him down a hallway simply adorned with framed black and white prints. Any question about where we were going resolved itself when I saw the two men with automatic weapons standing outside what I figured must be Conference Room Three.

The guards flanking the door appeared bored and ornamental like in the movies, but I knew if they worked for MONIKER, they were anything but. They didn't ask for any identification but instead checked us both against a list, held the list up to us as if comparing our image to a photograph.

"Finally elevated paranoia to an art and a science." I tried to give them a wiseass grin, but even the effort to say something annoying had taken it out of me.

Agent Tell ignored me as he pressed his thumb to the pad. I'm never as funny as I think I am. There was an awkward moment when the larger of the guards grabbed my hand, spun me around, and stuck my thumb onto the device. I tried to flinch back, but his grip held me, iron-fast until the scanner beeped satisfactorily.

The guards nodded and stepped aside. I followed Tell into the room, tripping over the threshold.

For all the effort MONIKER expended to get me to this room, I thought I'd get more of a reaction when I walked in. Our appearance was not so much ignored as taken in stride by the twenty or thirty men and women milling about. Some had taken their seats, while some gathered in small, quiet conversations.

Others, and my stomach growled loudly to see it, were gathered around a table laid out with what looked like a tray of catered fruit and pastries and—sweet nectar of the Gods—coffee.

Agent Tell grinned. "Let's get you something to settle your stomach."

I would have wiped the grin from his face if I hadn't ceased thinking about anything except food the minute I saw the table.

———

THREE DANISHES, four plates of fruit, and a cup of coffee later, I sat at the table as people gradually took their seats around me. It was awkward trying to eat with my hands attached to each other, but I made it work. Agent Tell had at least switched the cuffs from my back to my front before he left me sitting there, the two door guards flanking my back. While he circulated around the room from group to group, people turned to look at me, to size me up. I stayed where he left me, hating life. Being on display raised my hackles, but there was no place to really hide. I settled instead for avoiding their gazes.

My own eyes wandered around the room, taking in the banal corporate décor, the inevitable projector, and the fact all the windows were double-paned and sound-proofed, covered by blackout curtains that could be drawn to protect the proceedings from prying eyes and ears—and long-range surveillance devices.

It didn't surprise me to see half the people around the table were women. MONIKER, like its original O.S.S. department, had never been squeamish about sending women into harm's way, a euphemism that sometimes—actually, *usually*—meant straight-up combat. For all the debate over the years by people who never heard a weapon fired with bad intentions or worn a uniform that took them to a place where they might be asked to fight and die for their country, I knew women were not only capable of handling combat, but also, all the excuses for not sending them were long ago nullified by the fact they kept going. The past thirty years were proof of that.

A voice, thick with a New York flavor, cut through the room and interrupted any further conversation. I bit back a growl and tried not to scratch where the silver in the handcuffs had already raised welts.

"Everybody, sit down. We're already running behind." We'd seen the speaker, a large man with a buzz cut and a ridiculous tie, in the hall talking with the woman I couldn't forget. He sat down behind a name plate on the table identifying him as "DIC Ramirez." Was it missing a letter, or was he the Director in Charge? Seemed redundant to me. He glowered down the table until everyone sat. As the odd man out in handcuffs when it came to this game of musical chairs, I kept my piece of the table.

"Everyone has read Mr. Keller's file," Ramirez began.

I was "Mister" Keller now. I wondered if the file included any information on what MONIKER did to get me there. Whatever they were planning, I wanted no part of it. I also had no idea how to avoid getting cast in the lead role in another MONIKER shitshow, so I waited to find out if they were going to shake the clue tree and send me a hint of why they'd expended so much effort, or if they were going to fire up the PowerPoint and add torture to ill treatment.

Sure enough, a lackey got up and dimmed the lights, and another turned on the projector. The image on the screen looked familiar—Eastern Europe, my favorite hunting grounds since I first came to work for the organization. Now it appeared to be the backdrop for a slide outlining someone's corporate agenda.

"Keep going." Ramirez waved impatiently. "Get past this shit."

The briefer, a tall, skinny man in his mid-forties, obediently advanced the slides to the heart of the matter.

"In the past six months, we've seen a huge increase in human trafficking in the Middle East and eastern Asia, particularly the former Soviet bloc states." The briefer looked at Ramirez, who nodded, and a slide flipped. "Mostly girls, some boys, they get sourced out of places like Kazakhstan, Afghanistan, and then they get sent through the pipeline to Russia.

"A lot of these kids are moved around by the various mafias, and the money they make goes straight into criminal organizations. Next slide."

My eyes adjusted to the dark, and I looked around the table, observing people's reactions. From the bored expressions, they appeared familiar with the subject matter. I guessed the only one who really should be paying attention would be me, and I'd already lost the gist of the presentation. I closed my eyes and rubbed the back of my hand against my eyelids. If a point existed around here somewhere, I couldn't find it with a map and a metal detector.

Ramirez stood, taking over the brief from his lackey, who obediently sat down, deferring to his boss. "We've gotten reports that some of the insurgent groups operating in these areas, namely southwestern Afghanistan and across the border into Pakistan, are funding and controlling these groups. Others, they're taking tolls to move people across the border for the purpose of sex trafficking and forced labor."

He looked around the table. "These operations have come to concern the people who fund our organization very much."

The cynic in me noted "the organization" seemed more concerned over the fact the trafficking operations were being implemented to fund insurgencies run by our ostensible "allies," rather than the fact the girls were being bought and sold like so many trinkets in a bazaar. But I've been around long enough that it wasn't really cynicism, just a complete and total lack of surprise.

I shivered. Something inside me still felt wonky, like I wasn't shaking off the effects of the last couple of nights as easily as I usually did. Maybe I was still hung over.

To my discomfort, the next slide featured me, a very different me. This image from the past wore the starched uniform of a proud member of the Office of Strategic Services. From the faded monochrome, I put the date at almost a century ago.

I got a couple of startled glances, but apparently, the only surprise in the room was how short I turned out to be in real life.

"Mr. Keller has been invited here today, given his expertise in this area of the world." This time Ramirez waved casually in my direction.

I laughed out loud. Not only was "invited" a stretch of the imagination, but an even further stretch was required to view me as an expert on anything except northern Vermont. Being out of the game in any part of the world for ten days put you hopelessly out of touch with reality. Ten years, and I might as well start from scratch, which, in covert counterinsurgency, happens to be a great way to die for your country.

I did not intend to make *that* offer.

One of the people around the table raised his hand.

"Yes?" Ramirez's tone held a bite. He was not a fan of being interrupted.

"Ken, I understand this guy was someone back in the day, but what the hell are we going to do with him now?" The speaker, a younger, dark-skinned man, spoke with an accent slightly tinged with first-generation Indian American.

"Find him a good cover story and start getting him read up on the situation." Ramirez shook his head at the table. "Listen, people; the money coming from this network is funding roadside bombs and martyrs that are killing our boys and girls overseas. We need someone who can observe and infiltrate, then hit them from a direction they won't expect."

"But, sir, he's been out of the game too long. You can't seriously expect he'll be ready in the time frame we were discussing." I didn't know the name of the blond woman who spoke so frankly to her boss, but I agreed with her. My head hurt worse than before, and as I stood there, everything grayed slightly around the edges. I needed more coffee.

"He's got experience, he adapts well, and he can speak the languages." Ramirez neglected to add I was also the most expendable non-agent currently on the roster. Put me in, Coach. Or not. "He's what we've got to work with, so figure out some way we can insert him in there."

Visions of doubt continued to regard him from around the table. I thought of another reason to doubt—so far, no one had asked if I would volunteer for this ridiculous mission. I opened my mouth to explain that I had no intention of doing so.

"Richard Keller?" The question came from someone standing in the periphery of my vision. I turned to see the dark-haired woman from the hall. She wore a tailored suit, holding her clipboard and a syringe.

She smiled, and her smile took me straight back to 1942. I flinched, bringing my hands up in front of me, my reaction stymied by the unyielding handcuffs. One of the door guards gave me a look of warning.

"Didn't mean to startle you." She held up a syringe. "Our records indicated you're probably familiar with our little technologies."

"Very." I tried to push myself back, but the door guard stopped me. Everyone around the conference table was staring. I couldn't tell if they knew what was coming or not.

"Hold out your hands—I need to roll up your sleeve." Her voice stayed polite, but I felt she would be undeterred by any reluctance on my part. "Left arm, please."

I tried to get to my feet and push myself away, but the two guards clamped down on my shoulders. Tell caught my glance from across the room. As if guessing my intentions, he shook his head slowly enough for me to catch his meaning. There was no place to go and no point in trying to get there.

The dark-haired woman used her teeth to tear open a foil package and removed an alcohol swab. Tucking the clipboard under her arm, she took hold of my bicep with one hand. With her other, she swabbed clean a small patch of skin. Without comment, she uncapped the syringe, expertly pinched the skin between two fingers, and plunged home the needle. The liquid stung as it went in, and a small bump rose immediately on the surface. I hoped it was some kind of freaky vaccine.

Her silence gave me time to stare—and be bowled over by the features at once so familiar yet uncanny in the younger face. I knew it couldn't be, but I couldn't stop myself from asking.

"Margaret?"

"Karen." She recapped the syringe and put it in her pocket. "Doctor Karen Willet."

"What the hell are we expecting to see here?" The blond woman who hadn't been impressed with me before spoke up. "Is this that guy's grandson or something?"

Most of the people around the table looked at me with boredom or a passive acceptance that this meeting would go past lunch. Except for Agent Tell. Anticipation burned in his eyes. He sat forward, expectant, on the edge of his chair as if I were a giant piece of torte, and he had a fork in each hand.

A sudden flash of rage blasted across my vision. I heard myself growl, and the bones in my fingers twitched with a familiar ache. A separate, more intense pain echoed in my stomach, doubling me over as I was wracked with the change that should have been tucked deep and dormant into my body. *What the hell?*

The guards behind me racked the slides back on their weapons and raised them to point at me. From the stink of silver as the bolt covers opened, I guessed the rounds in their magazines would be enough to put me down. Permanently.

Control. I was long out of practice. The change pulled me forward, and I clasped my arms to my sides, dug my elongated fingernails into my upper arms, tried to push past the pain.

"Rick." Dr. Willet spoke the words softly, keeping carefully out of reach. I lifted my head, bleary, unable to focus on her face. "You have to try to show you can still control it. Otherwise, they will shoot you."

Imminent death is more of a promise than a threat when your insides are crawling out of your skin by way of your spine. Inside me lurked a part focused on surviving long enough to share that promise with these arrogant children. That part snuck back into control. I flexed my hands, forcing my arms to relax. Stretching, I cracked my spine until I could stand up straight. I felt the change leaving me as I wrenched my neck until it popped on both sides.

Panting, I glared at the woman with the empty syringe. "What the hell did you just pump into me?"

She ignored me and made a note on the clipboard. I swallowed back against nausea and the food I'd crammed down my gut. Pins and needles danced along my arms and legs, jabbing under the skin, stretching in anticipation of the change. I felt numb, my head buzzing. I stood, shaking, silhouetted against the gazes from the table, some curious, some dubious, some completely blank. Ramirez shook his head.

"I'm sorry, Mr. Keller." Dr. Willet almost seemed like she meant it. "It was necessary."

Ramirez grunted. "Some of you may not have seen this before. Pay attention."

"What we've done, Rick, is pump you full of minute specks of silver." Agent Tell's voice was pitched low and full of menace and yet, a note of triumph. "We needed a demonstration of the peculiar abilities you bring to this mission."

What they had done was destabilize the change, crashing through the barriers of nature, and it came back on me with the force of a freight train. For long years I left the change to itself, not seeking to call it to me—to take it on at a whim. I'd left it to rest in the regular cycles of the lunar seasons. Now, I felt each bone in me crack under the weight of the tiny virus as my control slipped viciously away under the onslaught of the silver in my blood. If they'd wanted to know if I could still control the change, there were less dramatic ways they could have gone about it.

"Rick? Mr. Keller?" The voice was Willet's, but I turned and snarled, snapping at the sound, tangled in the clothes wrapped around my twisted limbs.

"He's losing his grip." Agent Tell stood up, shaking his head.

I felt myself slipping away, arching toward the claws and the blood, conscious thought gone, my superego subsumed into mere teeth and intentions—pure id. I gathered myself on my back legs, aching with the change, and launched myself at Tell.

A muted pop came from my left, and then I was sliding on the floor, face burning against the carpet until the pain faded to black.

4

I did a lot of drugs in the seventies, but my bitch of a metabolism wouldn't cooperate. The most I ever got, even from the most hardcore designer drugs, was a serious case of the giggles. Mostly, I would pass out and wake up wondering why I didn't just stick to alcohol. With the right supply laid in, I could ride a good beer buzz for days and the hangovers never really lasted past noon. Based on what others told me about their experiences, MONIKER could probably make a lot of money if they figured out how to bottle the shit they'd pumped into my veins for the mass market.

The tide I was currently riding tore me back and forth through a cacophony of pain exploding in random parts of my body, accompanied by the light show I felt in my brain more than saw with my eyes. Pure, intense feeling ripped through me in irregular streaks of lightning, half pain and half a sensation of pure ecstasy looping back through my nerves, rubbing them raw as gravel under skin.

Every time the waves subsided, a new landscape of sensation rode up and flattened my struggling ability to separate the threads of reality. The smells of the sterile area, making up in power what they lacked in variety, flooded in, and I could taste and see them inside my head.

The more I fought for control, the harder whatever they added to my blood fought back. There had to be more in that cocktail than silver. Something kept the metal poison from dissolving and purging. I wasn't surprised. When I first came to the organization, they spent almost as much time studying me as training me—and I had let them. The toys and potions they cooked up were as useful to me as I was to them, and I had participated in my own biochemistry experiment.

After all, it was the age of science in the service of war, and they had tried to break down the secrets of my blood as they had the atom. They hadn't known then, even after years of painful—for me—lessons, that the change was more than science. It was a deeper part of me than what could be charted in medical files. It went far deeper than biological fact.

I felt my awareness crest once more, and as my consciousness rose for a moment above the pain, I exploded my control outward and grasped at the straws of my focus. For a second, my vision resolved into clarity, and then the muddle of the change pulled me back down. I kept struggling against the pain even as I sank back down into the black.

WHEN I WOKE UP, the worst of the bad trip seemed over, and all that remained was to ride out the pain. I found myself curled on the floor of a room about nine by ten feet, drenched in sweat. The T-shirt and jeans had disappeared and been replaced with a set of threadbare scrubs. A cot with a mattress and blanket sat untouched in the corner; I guessed whoever had dumped me in there hadn't even tried to get me onto it. The door was made of bars laced with silver, and I clenched down on a host of unpleasant flashbacks. I almost would have preferred the cage.

The intrusive memory stirred the change below the surface, but with an awkward and overly heavy touch, I rearranged things and sent it back down. I could feel the change hovering just below my conscious awareness, a gentle pressure. It brushed up against my focus every once in a while, but for now, it remained dormant.

I tried to remember how I used to finesse the control, but my muscle memory stayed little more than a whisper tucked somewhere deep in my brain. Every time I reached for it, the pain and the anger and the hunger to rip and tear and shred got in the way, so I let it go for now.

I growled softly in my throat and pushed myself into a sitting position. Using a hand on the wall to steady me, I stood. My legs trembled.

A noise outside the cell startled me, and I turned with a snarl.

"Terrible." Tell stood outside the bars. "You used to have much better control."

"Let me out of here."

He smiled. "You'll have to ask more nicely than that."

Another spasm brought me to my knees.

"And you're going to have to get that under better control." Tell shook his head. "You're not going anywhere until you can keep the old boy locked up tight."

Closing my eyes, I ignored him. The surge passed and subsided. Panting, I staggered back up, slipping a little on the tile floor, and wished someone would get me some fucking shoes.

"You left this downstairs." Agent Tell held my phone up. "I think you and my grandfather have the same phone."

His voice grated, raising hackles on my neck and back. I lurched forward on unsteady legs and leaned against the bars, one hand clutching a crossbar to make sure I didn't slide down again. My mouth felt like I'd chowed down on some dryer lint.

The dizziness faded somewhat. I started to recognize the change pulling back, tucking deeper into dormant tissue, waiting but impatient.

Tell set the phone down outside the bars, just out of reach. It didn't stop me from launching myself at the bars. I wasn't sure if I wanted to go for the phone or for him.

This wasn't a change reaction. This was my normal reaction to an asshole doing his thing. I used to have better control, but my filters were crap by now.

Something buzzed on his waist. "We searched your house." Tell pulled his phone out and checked something on the screen. He paused to tap back some sort of message and send it, then put the phone back on his belt. "Didn't find much. You've been living rough. Some of the boys were most impressed with your porn collection. How many years you been working on that?"

I growled, turned, and sat down against the wall as another supernova kaleidoscope burst behind my eyes and faded quickly away.

"Some of those defenses were a little outdated, though." Tell watched me almost disinterestedly. "Almost a little—I hope you don't mind me saying this—amateurish? Yeah, I think that's the right word."

"What is the point here, Tell?" I wondered how far I would get if I could just get out of this cage. "Are you here to give me some kind of pep talk to get me to sign up again? You're wasting your time."

He laughed. "We don't need you to sign up for anything. We just need you to start remembering what it is you do."

"I remember just fine." I probably should not have gone that far; I was still pretty shaky. "And I remember why I left and why you can rot in hell before I join any MONIKER crusade any time soon."

"Rick, the first rule of negotiation is understanding your position." Tell fiddled with some change in his pocket. The clanking of metal on metal drove me as nuts as the sound of his annoying voice. "Yours right now is in a cage to which we hold the key."

I wondered if this was his version of psychological manipulation, getting me completely bored and pissed off before tempting me with some sort of great adventure. Just one problem with that—I'd had a century full of grand adventures. It's why I lived by myself in Vermont.

"You guys made your pitch by kidnapping me and locking me in a series of cages." I wondered if they would feed me again soon. Maybe another dozen pastries would shore me up. "Then you shot me up with something that's got me wandering in and out of reality. You could offer me a magic carpet and a harem full of tall blond tennis players, and my answer would still be no on principle."

He laughed again, a sort of high-pitched giggle that set my teeth on edge.

"We want you to work for us, so obviously, we're not going to wave a magic wand and send you back to the middle of nowhere simply because you don't want to."

He leaned closer to the bars. "Until you say yes, we will ensure your life remains untenable. Even if we unlock this door and let you walk out of here in your bare feet, we will follow close behind. Whatever new life you try to carve out for yourself, we will be there to make sure it falls apart."

He smiled. "And it won't really be going out of our way. There are a lot of people in this organization who still think you were too dangerous to let retire."

I smiled in return. Finding the bed, I crossed my hands behind my head and settled back.

"Fine, asshole. Do your worst." I had a lot of time for them to follow me around and get bored. The threats didn't bother me, although the idea of seeing this jerk over and over for an extended period of time wasn't the most pleasant thought.

"In all reality, that part will probably happen anyway, no matter what you decide." Tell pulled a quarter out of his pocket and was now flipping it across his knuckles. Even that gesture hung on my nerves. "But three weeks from now, you *will* be on a plane because you *will* be joining this mission."

"Yeah, I don't think so," I said, and I was mostly very sure of myself.

"What's really amusing is how you think you have a choice." He dropped the quarter. I expected him to pick it up, but he simply kicked it away and folded his arms. "You will be going, or you'll spend a very long time here as our guest. The cage in the basement is usually vacant, and the rent is cheap." He shrugged. "And it's been a long time since our lab geeks had someone like you to put under the microscope."

He shut up for a minute and let me digest his threat. He opened his mouth again, but the door opened, interrupting whatever other boring conversation he planned on making.

DR. KAREN WILLET WALKED IN, and at first I thought they were going to stick something else into my body—let them try; my feet were back under me now. But she just carried a clipboard and a thin Manila folder.

"Good afternoon, gentlemen."

"Karen." Tell nodded, acknowledging her.

She nodded to the door. "Do you mind?"

He shrugged. "You sure? He seems to still be having some aftershocks."

"Yes." She checked her watch. "As long as he's maintaining for more than forty-five minutes at a time, he's fine."

Tell shrugged. "All right, then." He tapped something into a pad somewhere on the side of the wall, and the door sprang ajar.

Dr. Willet walked into the cell, and I smelled rosemary. It wasn't a scent applied to her body, more like something that grew where she lived until it became part of her.

Tell noticed my reaction. "Down, boy."

The faintest hint of a flush appeared at the high collar of her sweater. "Not helpful, Agent Tell."

She stepped near me, and I flinched back.

"Relax, Mr. Keller."

"Last time you got this close to me, I ended up here."

"Yes, I'm sorry about that." She seemed almost embarrassed, so it might have been true. "But we are on a shortened timeline, and reports indicated that you had lost about twenty years of control."

"Reports?"

"Surveillance." She turned up one corner of her mouth. "Very, very long-range surveillance." She held the folder out to me, and although I made up my mind to be my naturally unhelpful and surly self, I reached out and took it.

"Take a look at that." Tell smirked. "Karen, I've got to step out. I'll be right back." To me: "Keller, you try anything, and you'll find we have worse cages than the one downstairs."

I waited until he left, then handed the folder back. "Take it." I dusted my hands off on my pants. "My answer is no."

"I didn't ask a question." She took the folder and placed it on the bed next to me. "I'm not here to make you any offers. I'm here because we'll be working together."

"Working together?" I raised an eyebrow. "Have a lot of experience with cages, do you? Because apparently, that's where I'm going to spend the next couple of years."

To her credit, her composure didn't crack. "Sit still," she said. "I'm going to make a few observations."

She placed one hand firmly on my shoulder, tilted my head to one side, then another. She paused and made a few notes on the clipboard. She scrutinized my eyes, took my pulse, and I half expected her to pull out a microscope and start combing my scalp.

I sat still for about five seconds before the close inspection made me squirm.

"So, what's your story, Dr. Willet?"

"What do you mean?" She noted down however fast my heart was beating.

"How did you start working for MONIKER?"

"Family business."

I froze. It's one thing to have suspicions. It's another to have them suddenly confirmed. A lightning stab of hope exploded in my chest. I swallowed it down.

She went to put her hand on my head again, and I put my arm up to block her. I didn't want her to touch me.

"Rick…" She trailed off. She cocked her head, and I wasn't sure if her look indicated puzzlement or scientific speculation. "Do you recognize me?"

"How's our boy?" I hadn't heard Tell come back and wished he would go away again. "Clean bill of health?"

"Mr. Keller seems fine." Karen jotted a few notes on her clipboard then clicked her pen shut, hooking it on the front of her blouse. "Dehydrated, malnourished, and angry, but otherwise fine."

She turned to leave and glanced back at me. She kept her expression neutral, but her shoulders were tense. I recognized the signs of uncertainty.

Tell crossed his arms and leaned against the door. He waited until she left to speak again.

"She's a great kid, right?"

"Whatever." I shrugged. "Can I get out of here? And maybe get some lunch?"

"You can eat after you look in that folder."

I turned and saw the folder where Dr. Willet had left it on the bed next to me. I really didn't want to look inside and see what was in there. These people had a good track record of knowing which buttons to press. I wasn't going to like what I found inside—or what it would make me do.

"It's simple." Tell saw me hesitate and gave me a verbal push. "Look inside, and we go eat. Or be a stubborn jerkoff and stay here and starve."

If he thought simply looking at the contents of the folder would change my mind, then I was pretty sure the last thing I wanted to do was look inside. But I also knew, for all my attitude, I really, truly wanted out of this cage. One part of me—the same part that had been living happily in Vermont for several decades—wanted to use Tell for a chew toy, steal his keys, and blow this popsicle stand. But the traitor part of me—the part that could smell the faint bit of rosemary lingering on the folder when I picked it up—really wanted to look inside the damn folder.

I opened the folder. A divider in the middle kept several sheets of paper neatly fastened to the top by a two-hole punch. The left side of the file looked like a medical chart. It could have been mine, but the papers were so old they had thinned and cracked, and the typewriter someone used to fill in the blanks used a spotty ribbon to begin with.

On the other side were several more sheets of paper. On the top, I saw my own face staring up at me. From the shaggy lack of haircut, they must have taken it sometime during the 60s, or what I liked to think of as my Scooby Doo phase. A lot of running around thinking I was saving the world from evil... A lot of watching beautiful women in miniskirts and thigh-high boots. In other words, a good decade. What I could remember of it.

I skipped those pages. What I didn't remember about my own life I had forgotten on purpose and didn't want to be reminded. Under my profile, I found another photograph.

The picture smelled new. A glossy, shiny wallet photo. Karen Willet—Dr. Karen Willet, apparently, a former Army psychological operations officer with a Ph.D. in sociology and language competency in multiple eastern European dialects. She looked younger than the number on the page, having recently passed the questionable milestone of thirty-five. Already, she was older than the other woman I had known with her face.

I looked up from the file. "What's her part in this?"

"She'll be your partner." I heard a peculiar undertone when Tell spoke the word. "She's got the experience and the languages."

"And she'll keep me in line?" Tell said nothing, simply leaned against the open door and smirked. I glared. "I'm not a fucking moron, Tell. You don't think I noticed the family resemblance?"

"Keep reading."

I flipped the center divider.

The pictures on the other side showed a woman in hell.

5

The photos were arranged neatly with a little label on each one precisely stating the date, grid location, and a short descriptor. The visuals were oversaturated and a little grainy, like someone attempted to blow up a digital picture past what the pixels could handle.

My brain noted this even as it shied away from the damage displayed mutely in the eight-by-ten rectangle. I wasn't sure if the woman—no, more like the girl; she couldn't have been more than fourteen or fifteen—was screaming in agony or if the picture captured her death contortions. It wasn't my first time viewing a digital relic of what men do to other human beings in the name of criminal profit. Hell, I had seen it in living color so many times. I flipped the photo.

The violence spilled off the page and inserted itself into that special place in my subconscious, where I harbored all the sights and sounds I hoped one day would disappear from my nightmares. I didn't need to see it to know it existed. I didn't need to look further. MONIKER did, indeed, still know how to pull my strings.

But because I'm an asshole, I closed the folder, tossed it on the floor, and said, "Fuck off."

Tell took it in stride. "So, I guess you will relearn the comforts of the cage, and Karen and I will be heading to Eastern Europe."

"You're going to send her without me?"

"She's going in." Tell shrugged and straightened, one hand hovering over the door controls. "You can go with her, or she'll go alone. Your choice."

I was going to take the job. I didn't have a choice. I knew that the moment Dr. Willet looked at me with her grandmother's big brown eyes.

And yet, I had left for a reason. For a whole bunch of them. For years, the agency had been venturing farther and farther into the gray territory of covert operations, making decisions that had more to do with ego and mission creep than national security and any sense of honor. I'd grown tired of losing people. Tired of being their pet supernatural nuke. After the wall fell, all sorts of ad hoc organizations rose from the ashes of the 90s, and MONIKER was deep in the mix of things. The underground world was wide open, and everyone was feeding at the trough. I'd finally seen too many things—things that made it hard to decide if we were the good guys anymore.

Or if we had ever been.

I rubbed my eyes with the heel of my palm. "I'm rusty. You said it yourself. Outdated."

"We'll fix that." For all Tell seemed trying to convince me to join this little adventure, something under his tone smelled almost apathetic. "For now, concentrate on getting back in control of yourself. Otherwise, you won't make it out of that cell, let alone back to the hole you live in."

I felt something shift in the black when I blinked, something smooth that rolled over before settling back down. A sudden sharpening of the pain, and I could feel the change drifting back. Only when I looked up at Tell from all fours did I realize I had fallen off the bed. I blinked back the change and the pain.

"So, you're sending me where?" The folder contained a lot of very fine details except the necessary ones that might hand me a clue about where and when we were starting. "Afghanistan?"

Tell laughed and hit the controls that closed the door. He spoke through the bars. "No, we have people there."

"So where then?"

"How's your Russian?"

"Rusty."

"We'll fix that, too."

With the eternal smirk, he left me alone in the dark.

THEY DROVE me up to Vermont to give me the chance to gather some things. I may be a bastard, but I am a superstitious bastard, and there were a few things without which I would not go behind the wire.

The first being my Smith & Wesson .38 Special. I found it not far from my back porch, nestled in my jeans where it had slipped from my body with the change. It would need cleaning, some scrubbing to make sure the snow hadn't started up any rust on the steel, but the weight hung familiar and comforting at my waist. Yeah, a pistol would give me more rounds faster, but what I lacked in quantity of firepower, I made up in the fact that I had used it for so long. I barely needed to sight down the four-inch barrel to hit whatever bothered me. The wood grip showed small indentations, slightly worn from years of handling, but it wasn't time to replace it just yet. I would need to purchase more ammunition, as the only rounds I had were the six I kept in there for home defense on the off cycle.

The other object I found in the top drawer of my dresser under a few of the more recent magazines still wrapped in their coarse plain covers. The St. Jude medal was slightly tarnished where the metal had rubbed against the wood of the drawer. It hadn't seen the light of day since I had moved in and taken it from around my neck. The small bit of ancient metal had belonged to my grandfather, and if people thought it strange how someone like me would take the Catholic saint for his guardian, that was their problem.

I kissed the medal and put it around my neck. The chain was sized just large enough to stay in place through a change. The damage from my adventures with the commandos was almost healed, but I winced as the shirt material caught on the rough edges of my scabs. I looked out the bedroom window one last time. Snow had fallen again, and the trees were heavy with it. The neighbor's cat picked its path gingerly across the snow crust that gave way at unexpected intervals. I threw him a salute and then turned to go.

I didn't expect to see this place again.

IT TOOK LONGER than I expected to get to the training center, located in an abandoned steelworks an hour outside Albany. The natives refer to the area as Upstate New York, but it's actually only a couple exits north of the Jersey border on the Thruway. By the time we reached the place, restlessness had kicked in, and I found myself fidgeting in my seat. The confines of the long ride south, then west, had stiffened me, and I needed to stretch my legs and shake out the kinks.

We took an exit off the highway and followed a series of increasingly deserted roads until we reached the old mill on the banks of what used to be a canal. In the industrial heyday of the state, the waterway had linked the mill to the Erie Canal, funneling steel and barges into the maw of capitalism. Now, it appeared as dead as the economy, and our car was unaccompanied by any others as it turned off the final road and drove up to what used to be the main office.

There were subtle signs that MONIKER had prepared this place. A hint of silver in the door as we passed through—a scent of it at the windows. One door in the hallway, I gave wide berth as we passed. I did not want to go past that door, with its silver inlay in the scrollwork decorating the surface. The same metal raised a sheen on the handle. If people didn't want me in there, wherever it led, I wouldn't be going inside. Or—uncomfortable thought—getting out.

Tell and Willet waited for me. No one else appeared to be around except the men who drove in with me. They stood in the kitchen. Willet cradled a cup of coffee in her hands. Tell cradled a sandwich. I could have used both, but apparently, there was no time for things like eating.

"Put your things upstairs in one of the rooms and come back down," said Tell. "We'll wait for you here."

My stomach growled, and I clamped down against hunger and restlessness. I promised myself a good long run, ready to stretch muscles stale with lack of use.

I found a room at the end of a long hall of what looked like old offices converted into living spaces. The one I chose was small and had perhaps once been a broom closet, but I didn't have a lot of stuff, and it worked for me. I dropped my bag, but I didn't go downstairs. I'd had enough of following orders—I'm not really good at it to begin with. I stripped down and threw my clothes on the bed.

The one window in the room was small but large enough for me to wriggle through without any sensitive parts getting hung up on anything. I swung, suspended for a moment with the ledge cutting into my hands, then let myself go limp and drop to the snow below. I fell about twelve feet, but I had survived longer drops.

I stood up and shook myself off, dusting snow from my fur, the change flowing through me easily now with just a hint of my prior disuse. The night shone clear, the waning gibbous moon still casting enough light off the snow to bring a monochrome clarity to the grounds. In the years of neglect, the forest had crept up to the walls of the house, and I bit back a howl as I loped into the woods.

The air tasted crisp and smoky, the piquant surrender when autumn has fully ceded the ghost to winter. I felt flavors of wood smoke and leaves, underbrush, and snow on my tongue. A thousand different scents vied underneath for attention.

In the brushes, a rabbit startled, darting away as it sensed my running presence. I bolted, giving chase, flying around the thick black trunks of trees. I howled my intentions to the night as I slipped and doubled back, chasing the thin line of energy and fear scrambling ahead of me.

The rabbit knew its territory, and I did not, but hunger lent an edge to my rusty chase, and I caught up with the furry missile seconds before it disappeared into its hole beneath a fallen log. I bowled it over, breaking its neck, and ripping its throat before it even became aware it lost the race. The heat of its blood on my tongue and my teeth were ecstatic, amazing, and I crunched happily away until all that remained was some fur and blood spotted black on the snow.

For a moment, I felt myself drifting away into the mindless euphoria of the change I had surfed for the past ten years, but I dragged myself back from the brink. I needed to start recapturing the control I once mastered. I paused, cocked my head, and wondered if I should head back. There would probably be some more harsh words directed my way if I went back now. But nothing about that would change if I headed back a little later, so I bounded off once again into the night.

I EVENTUALLY TURNED my steps back to the building, a little earlier than I felt ready for, but just later enough to really piss off Agent Tell. I didn't bother sneaking in. The front door worked fine.

I thought maybe one or two hours had passed, but the clock in the kitchen when I walked in said it was closer to dawn than midnight. Agent Tell and Dr. Willet—or was it Agent Doctor?—were still up, waiting at the table, deep in discussion. Their looks when I walked in were worth whatever price the run would cost me.

There's a certain practicality I hadn't mentioned when it came to the advantages I brought to the team, partly because I wanted to see their reaction, but mostly because they were going to eventually have to get used to me coming back from missions naked and covered with various grime and gore. I licked my chops as my human form settled back into a chair and patted my neck to make sure the St. Jude medal was still there. I may have crossed my legs for modesty. Or not.

"Really, Keller?" Tell smirked.

To Willet's credit, she neither looked away nor made a big deal about things. She blushed ferociously under her collar but merely arched an eyebrow and said nothing.

"Hope you enjoyed your run, Keller," Tell said. "It's going to be a long day."

THE NEXT THREE weeks brought a lot of pain but very few surprises. The moments when I wasn't locked in a room shoving Eastern European dialects back into my head and polishing my pronunciation, I read through stacks of files, attempting to memorize all the small details of our cover, playing catch-up on learning ten years of tradecraft, and poring over maps. One of the lessons included learning how to use a smartphone with a GPS, which by the way, is probably one of the most annoying gadgets I've ever encountered. After I broke the first one and somehow managed to set fire to the second, Willet and I mutually decided she would be the one to work the infernal device. Anyway, I never got lost. Slightly distracted, yes, but never lost.

The dull pain that came from the headache of cramming all this crap into my head was easy to remedy. Whenever I got bored or restless or just so damn itchy I couldn't sit still, I would slip away for an hour or two. I tried to time these breaks for when Tell and Karen were asleep or ready for a break themselves. They each indulged in their own vices. Tell smoked pretentious French cigarettes on the back patio, and Karen set up a chin-up bar and a heavy bag she used with such ferocity I wondered if she was picturing my face or Tell's on the leather.

Yeah, somewhere in there, Dr. Willet had become Karen, and I had become Rick, but Tell was still an asshole.

The pain from staring at a book all day and then having to look at Tell during meals and right before bed, I could deal with easily enough. The sharper pain, the one breaking straight through my bluster and giving me the shakes, took place behind the heavy silver door I had noted when I first arrived.

The fortified door led to a short wooden staircase that, in turn, led to another basement. This one didn't contain a cage; rather, a set of manacles attached to a strong cement pillar served as the control mechanism. They were laced on the inside with silver, but in such a way the metal didn't touch my skin. They didn't burn to the touch, rather were unresponsive to my every attempt to break through.

Believe me, I attempted as hard as I could. The other part of my training involved regaining the lost control I had given up in ten years of solitude and twenty years of letting the change go wild. The initial measure came in the form of the liquid Karen had first injected to spur the change and destabilize my physiology. She gradually increased the dosage every other night, injecting the nano-silver into my bloodstream. Sometimes she waited as the dosage took effect and I began the long night of trying to remember how to be what I should never have forgotten.

Other nights, she left quickly, turning the light off at the top of the stairs before the cocktail kicked me gyrating off my foundations and left me to swim back through the murky depths of my subconscious.

The first night they had put me down there, it had taken a lot of persuading in the form of harsh words from Agent Tell and a silent threat from one or two of the stooges with machine guns who lurked around the periphery of the building, and who came running when it seemed I intended to be difficult.

I had managed to keep hold of myself until the time came for them to put the cuffs on me, at which point instinct overcame dignity, and I bolted, or tried to bolt. A silver-tipped trank from the guard at the top of the stairs, and I had woken up securely fastened to the pillar.

"What the hell is that stuff for?" I glared at Karen as she swabbed my arm.

"We're building your tolerance."

"Tolerance for what?" I squirmed as she pointed the syringe at my vein.

"Don't move, or this will bleed a lot," she said.

I didn't listen. I tried to pull back but Tell grabbed my arm, and she pointed the needle—the tip ripped my skin and I ended up bleeding a substantial puddle. The nano-silver went in with predictable results.

"The Balkans." Tell watched as I flinched back, starting to roll once again with the lights bursting behind my eyes.

"What?" I choked out the word.

"One of your last missions before you left us." Tell seemed unfazed by my struggles. The bastard might have even been enjoying them. "You got sloppy."

I remembered that trip. I remember freezing my ass off in the middle of the summer, shivering through the nights on the borders of a country that had been a war zone for the past century or so. The trenches where lime seared the dead when the living didn't have time to bury the bodies or to do anything except try to stay alive themselves.

I did get sloppy. I also got caught, rolled up for a day or two until the other side overran the area and killed more people, and I slipped out in the fighting.

"One of those mercenaries noticed your special, shall we say, qualities?" Karen capped the needle and put a gauze pad on my arm to stop the bleeding, although it mostly stopped on its own. "About six months later, one of MONIKER's operatives raided a special weapons lab somewhere and found this little recipe."

By this time, I was fading away, trying desperately to hang on to whatever she was throwing out.

"They had weaponized the silver mixture." It seemed she held the last little bit of light in the room in her face, and I held onto her outline as the rest of the room faded to black. "We're pretty sure they've passed the information on to others in the region."

After that, her mouth kept moving, but the rushing in my ears drowned out any more words. I wanted to ask why they had been weaponizing it, who they had been weaponizing it against, but my brain lost the train of thought as the wave of pain and darkness crashed into me, pulling me under. Then, I fell beyond caring, really, as the destabilization took me on another fantastic journey of light and sound and pain.

IN THE MIDDLE of the second week, we had a guest, the first sign being the unfamiliar pickup truck parked in front of the building. I came in from a run—clothed, as Karen had accompanied me—to find Ken Ramirez looking out of place in jeans and a flannel shirt with another loud tie under a fleece-lined leather jacket. I put on the brakes and hung back as she greeted him. They knew each other well, judging from the fact that she let him hug her. She didn't go in for much touching, guarding her personal space with a clinical eye and a wary stance.

Tell wandered in from outside, followed by a cloud of noxious smoke. It stung my eyes and I hacked, trying to clear my throat.

"We didn't expect you until some time next week." Tell field stripped the butt and stopped to toss it into the sink.

"Our timeline got moved up unexpectedly," Ramirez replied. "We need to validate your team early so we can move you out a week ahead of schedule."

"What's the rush?" I didn't trust random changes in the plan, especially unexplained ones.

"Contrary to popular belief, Mr. Keller, international criminal organizations do not trouble themselves to move on our convenience." Ramirez eyed me, and I felt like a recalcitrant child sent to time out. "Thus, you move your ass out early."

"What's happened?" Karen wiped her eyes with the palm of her hand. Now that we were back inside, she sweated freely. It sounds gross, but it smelled amazing, like a freshly-mowed lawn in summer. She swiped her forehead with the arm of her long-sleeved running shirt and gave me a look telling me to quit being an asshole.

"You'll get a full brief on the situation when you get back to the city," Ramirez said. "We have a surveillance team monitoring it right now. We'll let you know the details then."

He looked around. "Can I get a cup of coffee?"

Tell nodded at me. I gave him the finger. Karen rolled her eyes and got Ramirez a cup of coffee.

"The specs for your validation mission are in that folder," Ramirez said, accepting the coffee. He used the mug to gesture at the table before taking a sip, grimacing, and setting it down next to the large Manila envelope.

"What do you want us to do?" I knew MONIKER had more in store for me than one lousy mission. Once again, I both regretted not tearing the throats out of the men who came for me and, at the same time, found myself oddly eager to get back out in the field.

"Mostly make it back alive." Ramirez tried the coffee again, with the same result. "Thanks for the shitty coffee."

He left, and we heard the roar as the F350 engine came to life. The huge truck disappeared down the road back to the highway. Tell reached over and opened up the packet.

"Looks like you'll be practicing your Spanish," he said, handing a thin sheaf of paper to Karen. He handed a similar one to me. "You *habla* any *Espanol?*"

"*Nada* word." I looked down at the papers. They included a boarding pass, a passport, and what looked like a biographical data sheet. A small photo clipped to the top caught my eye, and I pulled it off to look at it more closely.

A small girl, about eight years old, stared up at me. It was a typical school photo, but she wasn't smiling. She merely looked solemnly out of the picture, as if the photographer had made a joke she didn't find particularly funny.

"Kidnapping?" Once again, MONIKER knew just which of my buttons to press, and hard.

"Looks like," Tell answered. "Family vacation in Mexico, outing on the beach, daughter runs ahead and gets lost in the crowd, the mom and dad lost sight of her."

Karen looked at her papers. "Does it say if they've been contacted by anyone? A ransom demand? Something like that?"

Tell shook his head. "Just one call with a date, location, and amount." He frowned. "And a threat. Apparently, they sent a lock of hair and a baby tooth in the letter."

I grimaced, baring my teeth. "So when they come to pick up the drop, I'll be waiting."

Karen looked at me. "This isn't your usual op. Even before you took your extended vacation."

I shrugged. "I was always good at improv." Folding up the papers, I put them in the pocket of my sweatpants and turned to go.

"Where are you going?" From the tone of Tell's voice, I could tell he had something planned.

"Upstairs to shower and go to sleep." I wiped the sweat off my forehead. It trickled down into my eyes, and I blinked back against the salty sting. "Check the boarding pass. We're going to have to leave early if we're going to catch a seven o'clock flight out of Newark."

"So, where are you going again?"

"Upstairs, asshole," I said, suspecting I was not going to bed just yet.

"Ah," Tell said. "No."

"What do you mean no, John?" Karen kept her usual poker face, but her tone sounded as pissed as I looked.

"There's one more thing we have to do before we go." Tell grinned. "I think we could stand to try one more time through the Gauntlet."

6

The Gauntlet was Tell's pet name for the natural obstacle course presented by the abandoned millworks. The organization had strung closed circuit cameras through the structure, but that was about the only thing they had done before declaring it an open training course. Before starting, one of the guards, with the assistance of flashlights and safety wires, would place a tattered, triangular flag somewhere in the building. When the time started, Karen and I would head into the building, unassisted by such things, with only Agent Tell as the voice in our earpieces, attempting to guide our movements. MONIKER set it up as a facility to simulate our team roles in unfamiliar and tricky situations.

The last three times we had attempted it, we hadn't found the flag. Karen ripped her shin open on a piece of protruding metal and needed to get twelve stitches. I ended up with one massive bruise down the right side of my body, and a couple cracked ribs from falling through a rotting staircase and down two stories. I really hated the Gauntlet.

The moon rose burnt and stark behind the black skeletal trees, looking for all the world like some spooky horror movie scene. Beside me, Karen shivered as the wind whipped along the ground, raising dead leaves in little whirlwinds. The decaying steel and brick walls of the old mill rose before us, mutely reflecting the mottled light.

Tell's voice crackled in my ear, buzzing against the membrane. I flinched slightly.

"What?" My tone sounded as sour as I could make it. Karen and I paused outside the building, taking cover behind a low brick wall long overgrown with vines and weeds. I carried my .38 out and at the ready. There weren't any pop-up targets at this range, but it was always a real possibility some sort of wildlife had wandered in and made itself at home.

Karen held her M4 at the ready, night-scope sighted, the rifle on a sling around her neck and attached to her vest by a carabiner. The first time I saw her weapon of choice, I made a joke about the rifle being overkill. I quit joking when I saw her use it at the live fire range. She was lethal with that thing, day or night.

"Five minutes until go." Tell's voice sounded in my ear again, and I resisted the urge to dig out the bud and smash it.

"Just start the damn clock," I growled. "Who the fuck cares if we go now or in five minutes?"

A screech of feedback came through the earbud. I could swear he did it on purpose. It felt like my ears were bleeding.

"Fine, jerkoff." Tell paused, then continued. "In that case—get your ass inside. The clock starts now."

Karen and I rose from behind the wall. I led the way on an angle to the main entrance. She covered the rear, slipping soundlessly along the broken concrete path.

At the door to the old mill, I paused. I cocked my head and listened for the sound of anything inside, sniffing the air to confirm the first room was empty.

I looked back at Karen, who nodded, face masked by the dingy glow of her night vision optics. I pushed the door open and slowly moved in, crouching to avoid any low-hanging wires.

My feet splashed through shallow puddles in the concrete as I navigated the hallway. We'd made it this far before, and I knew where the broken desks and uneven tiles were. Karen followed behind, close enough to maintain visual contact but not so close as to be ambushed by someone attacking me.

At the end of the hall, the moonlight filtered dimly through a large window. The glass, made of the thick squares people used decoratively in the thirties, refracted the moonlight in thick waves. A few of them had been broken, and the missing squares let in just enough illumination for me to see the stairs at the end of the corridor.

Pistol at the ready, I started up the staircase. Halfway to the top, I paused. Half-hidden in the murk, a gaping hole waited. Two steps were missing—the ones I had plunged through before. I had no desire to repeat that experience, but who knew if the stairs above were any sturdier?

"Crap."

"What is it?"

"Nothing." I gingerly stepped forward, drawing my foot back when it met only empty air. "Watch the hole. Wait until I get to the top. I'll signal you to follow."

"Roger." She set her back against the wall and pointed her weapon down the stairs. There wouldn't be anyone coming up after us—it wasn't that kind of exercise—but as usual, her reflexes were there. I found it reassuring.

"When you get to the top, make a right."

My answer was to growl slightly at the peremptory tone coming through the mic. Looking up the stairs, I could barely see anything. I closed my eyes and widened my control for just a moment. Opening them again, my natural night vision flattened out to a slightly lighter, grainy black and white. I could just make out the shadowy lines leading up to the second floor.

Blowing out my breath, I gathered my legs beneath me and, taking a two-step running leap, launched myself over the gaping maw. I landed, trying to keep myself as light as possible. The steps let out a distressing creak, stopping my heart for a moment, and then I was scrambling up the last five or six steps to reach the relative safety of the second floor.

I paused a moment to catch my breath.

"Karen," I whispered down the stairs, hoping her hearing was as acute as her aim.

"Here." The voice came through my ear, and I remembered belatedly we were tuned to the same frequency. Sometimes I'm a dumbass. I try to minimize that in life-or-death situations.

"There's going to be a gap of about two steps," I said, keeping my voice low and trusting the mic to pick it up. "You're going to need to make that jump, and then you'll have about five or six steps to go until you reach the top."

"Roger."

The comm went silent, and I held my breath, trying to listen hard in the darkness. All I heard was my breathing and the blood rushing in my ears until something broke the silence with a thud and a creak. I froze, afraid my partner was about to crash through two stories of brick and steel.

A few seconds later, I heard her step on the stairs. A breath later, and she stood next to me in the hallway. She tapped my shoulder.

"Here."

"All right." I looked ahead again, squinting to resolve the shadows in front of me. "Follow me."

I took a right and started heading down the hall. The roof was broken in several places, and the light filtering in made it slightly easier to see where we were going. I stepped gingerly over a pile of something that could have been old rags or could have been some decaying remains. It smelled like more than one creature had lived and died there.

The hallway came to an end at another long corridor, and I stopped.

"We're at a T," I said. "The hall leads either way."

"Left will take you toward the stairs to the upstairs offices," Tell said. "Right will take you out over the main floor."

"That's great news, Geraldo. Which fucking way do we go?"

"How the hell should I know?" Tell's tone remained even, belying the frustration I could sense under his control. "All I can tell you is where you're going."

"Jesus—"

Karen laid a hand on my arm. "Let's try the floor."

"Might as well." I turned right and started moving down the hall.

A few feet down the corridor, I stopped. The roof remained intact in this area, and the lack of windows plunged the hall into full darkness. I tried to peer into where the outlines disappeared, but my eyes found no light to capture. I moved forward as blind as anyone else.

Karen tapped me on the shoulder. "Can you see anything?"

"I can't see shit," I replied. "Hold this for me." I handed her my pistol. She took it without a word and slipped it into the cargo pocket of her tactical pants. "Stay here. I'm going to scout ahead."

"If you can't see, what's to stop you from falling through another hole?"

She had a point.

"I'll take it slow. If I figure a way through, I'll come back here and guide you." I hoped.

"All right." Karen settled herself, again watching our rear. "I've got your back. Watch your step."

I winked at her as I shucked off my clothes before walking into the dark. I shuddered and twisted. When my front paws hit the floor, I felt the cold through the pads of my feet. This close to the full moon the change flowed easier—I no longer had the sensation of being jerked off my feet, holding the leash on something I couldn't control.

I wasn't going blindly into the hallway. As I padded along, I caught the faintest scent lingering in the corridor. It smelled of grease and licorice, and it wasn't a scent that belonged in this place.

I lost it for a moment when I passed through a couple of puddles left from the snow melting through the building. I had to double back and sniff around. The temperature was dropping rapidly, and where my nose and paws passed through the water, they were now freezing. I shook my head and went back to the business at hand.

At another intersection, I picked up the scent again, this time strong and clear. I bit back a howl—letting loose was emotionally satisfying but never very smart, tactically speaking—and began loping down the corridor to where the hall met a swinging door. With more haste than I probably should have made, I pushed through the door and attempted to apply the brakes. The door opened onto a metal grating that served as a catwalk above a vast, empty area.

My momentum carried me over the narrow walkway, and I scrabbled with panicked limbs to gain purchase in the open grating. The only thing saving me from hurtling into space and probably finally succeeding in killing myself were regularly spaced supports along the walkway. My body slammed into one of those, cracking a couple more ribs but saving me from a long drop and a sudden stop.

Leaving the change was harder than usual, but I twisted myself out of it. I got my feet under me and stood up shakily. I stood all the way up, hands gripping the railing. I looked out over the floor. The scent had ended, but I could find no sign of the stupid tease of a flag we were supposedly tracking.

"Fuck."

"Where are you?" I had almost forgotten Tell was there until his voice came through again. That was one hell of an earbud design to stay in place through the change. It hurt the inside of my ear.

"I'm on a catwalk." That didn't sound right. "Um, I'm above the main floor."

"You see the flag?"

"I can't see anything; it's fucking nighttime."

"Look up." He sounded like he was eating something, and my stomach growled.

I looked up. On the ceiling, almost indistinguishable amongst the mottled grays of the dark expanse, hung the skeletal remains of large industrial fans. "Oh shit."

"What is it?" Karen's voice came in my ear.

"Could they have put this thing in a more annoying place?" I stared up at it, cursing on the inside.

"Probably." Karen again.

"All right, I'm on my way back to you." I shivered, the cold leaching in through my skin. "Wait for me."

"I'm not going anywhere."

I shifted down and headed back to reappear silently at her side. To her credit, she simply placed her hand on my neck and let me guide her.

We made it back to the walkway without incident. I stepped back up out of the change, feeling slightly light-headed from all the back and forth.

"Where is it?" She looked around, but in the dark, even I had trouble finding it again.

Shivering a little, wishing she had thought to bring my clothes from the corridor, I pointed to one of the ceiling fans, the farthest from our position.

"Oh shit." She finally noticed the fluttering pendant hanging from the fan. She looked even less enthused than I felt. "How the heck did they get it up there in the first place?"

"I have no clue." I looked around for something we could use, coming up empty. "Did you bring some sort of rope or something?"

In the gloom, I could still see the withering glance she directed at me. I suddenly felt even more naked.

"Do you see a rope?" She shifted her weight, gripping the rifle more firmly. "What, do you think I stuffed it in my bra?"

I opened my mouth for a wiseass remark but Tell cut me off.

"Focus, you two." He coughed and cleared his voice. I could see him sitting at the table, his monitoring equipment set up before him, windows wide open so he could smoke in the kitchen and pretend we couldn't smell it.

"I am focused," I said. "I'm focusing on the fact that unless Karen suddenly develops the magic ability to fly, there's no way we're coming back with that."

I turned to her. "You're not some kind of crazy shapeshifter, are you?"

"You're not very helpful." The dryness of her tone could cut diamonds into glass. "I thought you were supposed to be good at improv."

That hurt my feelings. Or would have if I wasn't going slowly numb from standing there in the cold without fur. Or clothes.

"Do you mind?" I asked, motioning to her rifle.

"Yes, actually I do." She moved it away from my reach.

"Give it to me anyway." I held out a hand.

"Go fuck yourself." She made it sound like an actual invitation.

"What the hell is going on?" Tell, not privy to our nonverbal gestures.

"We're having a discussion about tactics." I held out my hand again. Karen shook her head, matching me glare for glare. "Unless you have something helpful to get us up there, shut up."

"Look around," Tell suggested. "Are there any long poles or pieces of metal?"

"No." I gritted my teeth. "Karen, my apologies. May I please borrow your rifle?"

I felt rather than saw her glare.

"Fine." She unslung the weapon and handed it to me. I think she guessed what needed to be done and figured it best if I got my ass ripped for it.

"Thank you." I took the rifle and flipped the cover off the night scope. Raising the rifle to my eye, I set it on burst and fired off three rounds at the ceiling fan. I waited half a second and then let loose another three-round burst.

The noise of the shots ricocheted around the empty steel mill, deafening us temporarily. The bullets struck sparks that leapt and faded instantly.

The ceiling fan creaked dangerously, rocking and swinging back and forth. Karen and I watched, waited, and finally expelled our breaths together as the whole thing came crashing down.

"We've got it." I spoke the words aloud for Tell's benefit. "We'll be back at the base in ten."

7

The sun shone hot and hard, heating the dust in the air to unbearable levels. Sitting in the back of the white Toyota pickup, I kept choking on it through the bandanna wrapped around my face. I pulled my Yankees cap down lower to shield my eyes. I hate the heat, I hate the sun, I hate the dust. Avoiding all three was why I lived in Vermont.

I found myself in the back of the truck by default. Tell had the keys, so he was driving, and Karen had simply looked at me as if to ask if I really intended to do something as immature as call shotgun. Of course, I did. Sadly, by the time I thought of it, she was already sitting inside. On the other hand, did I really want to spend the hour and a half ride from the airport stuck in the cab with Tell?

I shifted position, trying to get comfortable as the truck bounced on the dirt road. I hadn't stopped being pissed that we were being shunted to a validation mission before getting cut loose to get this shit over and done with. The sooner we were finished, the sooner I could get back to not working for these people. I should have known there would be sudden changes in the plan before they sent us on to the main mission. They had me, they were going to use me, and there wasn't much I could do about it except follow along for the moment.

On the other hand, this job had its perks, and one of them was riding shotgun.

I rapped on the glass of the cab.

Karen turned around and opened the sliding window. She yelled to be heard over the noise of the truck. "What is it?"

"How far out are we?" I yelled back.

"Map says twenty minutes." She held up two fingers to illustrate.

"So, about a half hour?"

"Yeah."

Tell said something I couldn't make out. She replied. I tried to listen but couldn't hear anything.

"Anything else?" Karen grasped the sliding edge, ready to close it against the heat.

"Yeah, tell that asshole next time I drive."

She shook her head and closed the window. In the rearview mirror, I saw Tell glance up briefly at me and smile. I gave him the finger and sat down again with my back against the window. I coughed and hacked some more. The dust burned straight down my nose and throat, muting my senses until all I could smell was the sunbaked dirt we drove over.

The Mexican countryside rolled by, burnt sere and dead in muted gray tones. We passed a couple of cars on the road, old Chevys and Ford trucks, and even a couple of 1980s model Japanese sedans. Our beat-up pickup fit right in. I sat back in the truck and wished I had a cooler with a couple of longnecks to make the drive more comfortable.

Amid the things bugging me, the biggest remained the fact my team hadn't gelled and still showed no sign of doing so anytime soon. MONIKER hadn't changed its basic tactical team structure in a long time. The men and women with the organization worked mainly in independent three-operative sets, one handler and two field personnel. Typically, these teams would go into the area with little to no overhead support and rely on their training in language, culture, and tactics to make it through to the flip side. I didn't mind this setup—in fact, I preferred it.

For all of our good times at the mill, though, our team showed every sign of heading for disaster. For Tell, well, I hungered for the moment when I could rip into him and scatter the body around the backwoods.

Karen was excellent—a competent operative and someone I would have chosen to work with if they actually gave me a choice, but she thought of me as an arrogant little shit. She was polite enough to say it when she thought I couldn't hear, primarily in the aftermath of my unique solution to capture the flag. It wasn't the first time someone referred to me as such, and to be honest, I had spent some time cultivating the asshole in me, but it felt uncomfortable coming from someone I respected and actually cared about. But then, at least I was consistent. Her grandmother had said pretty much the same thing to my face.

Although I admit I felt a little bad about being called out, the truth stuck. I wasn't a team player anymore. I had chosen to leave the organization, and instead of throwing me a carrot, they went straight to the stick the moment they thought they needed me back. The only part of me I could honestly say gave a crap about this whole mission was the part that kept thinking about a scared little girl wondering if she would see her parents again. Another part of me, the part much larger and truer to any form I would choose for myself, spat, disgusted to have been bought so cheap, manipulated so easily based on nothing but a tenuous link to a glorious past. And a girl.

But the rest of me—the part most closely linked with the change and the hunt—slavered. I was eager, more alive than I had been for many years, even before I had quit MONIKER for a backwoods Vermont sabbatical.

———

THE TRUCK GROUND to a halt outside a crappy little motel with fake decorative palm trees drooping sadly in the sand out in front of the office. Karen spoke the best Spanish compared to my complete lack of it, and Tell's accent made him sound like one of the Three

Amigos, so she got out of the truck. She stopped a moment to stretch the kinks out and almost caused a traffic accident. In the white linen pants, tight tank top, and movie star sunglasses, she looked like a rich urbanite meeting her lover at a beachside slum. It worked.

She stepped into the office and after a moment, reappeared with a set of keys.

"Ready for some afternoon delight?" I hopped out of the truck.

She ignored me and let us into the room furnished in depressing, crappy chic decor.

I helped Tell carry in his gear. It wasn't as much as I expected—electronics had gotten smaller and lighter since my last round in the game. He fired up his main computer, fixing the position of local law enforcement and testing the long-range wireless mics and cameras.

"The first order of business will be to set up surveillance of the family and their contact with the local *federales*." Tell fiddled with the dials.

I'd hoped the first order of business would be lunch. "We haven't made contact with them?"

"No," Tell answered, pressing one side of a headset to his ear. I could hear the squeal of the frequencies as he tuned through the channels. "And we're not going to. Our presence here is strictly under the radar."

"The last thing we want is to spook the kidnappers," Karen added. "Or the cops they have in their pocket."

The gadgets might have been new, but the plan was what I expected from MONIKER. Use the shadows to conceal action, and then strike unexpectedly and hard.

"We'll wait until the family makes the drop." Karen dropped her bag on the floor. "Mr. Keller follows the money home and takes out the kidnappers?"

"That's the plan." Tell didn't look up from his gizmos.

"Wonderful." I didn't bother to hide the sarcasm. "How is your craptastic plan going to deal with the fact that they'll probably kill the girl once they have the ransom?"

"There's no guarantee they'll do that," Karen said. "These are run-of-the-mill kidnappers, not *narcotraficantes*."

"Says who?" I waved my hand at Tell's jury-rigged gear. "The intel they handed us on this is lacking, to say the least."

"All right, genius." Tell put down the headset and crossed his arms. "How would you do it?"

"Can you get access into police systems down here?"

"Yeah." Tell looked insulted I'd even asked. "Radio scanner will give us an ear into what the cops are saying. But if we want to know what's going on in the house, we're going to have to set up and run surveillance."

"That would take time." Karen frowned. "Time we don't have."

"Can you get me inside the house?" I mentally kicked myself over and over. Why was I here? Oh, yeah. Kidnapped little girl. "Or better yet, I'll get myself inside."

The eyebrow went down. "What are you thinking?"

"I'm thinking there's no way the kidnappers have taken the girl outside the city," I said. "If I can pick up her scent, then it's possible I could scout around down by where she was taken. See if I can track her down before they go to make the drop."

"Do we know when that's supposed to happen?" At least Karen seemed willing to give my plan a shot.

"No." Tell needed more convincing. "But with the short time hack getting down here, I'll bet it's soon."

"Then let's split up," I offered. "I'll get in there and see if I can get something with the girl's scent on it. Karen can set up surveillance on the house and let me know if the drop starts happening."

Tell turned to Karen. He seemed to be coming around. "I can set up a mobile ops center with you on the surveil."

"That's okay." Karen pulled a jacket from her bag and shrugged it on over her tank top. "It's better if you run it from here. Gives us a place to draw back to."

"Are you sure?" Tell didn't seem overly enthusiastic about the two of us going without him.

"Yes." Karen settled a concealable holster onto the waistband of her pants, hidden by the jacket. She picked a small pistol from the gear and snugged it into the holster. "Besides, here you can smoke those vile things all you want and leave my lungs out of it."

Tell paused, a cigarette half out of his pack. He looked at her, then at me, then finished pulling it out and stuck it in his mouth.

I didn't care about the smoke, as long as we were gone before he lit up. "You got an address on the house?"

"You don't want to grab something to eat first?" Tell's attempt at smartassery failed miserably.

"I'll go now and try to keep my sense of smell intact."

Karen grabbed a small bag and followed me out the door.

THIS WAS how I remembered working. Coming in fast and flexible, maybe not knowing every detail going down, but working as a team, we were able to make things come together on the fly.

This wasn't my area of geographical expertise per se, but it felt familiar, and I had a lot of experience coloring outside the lines. The slow burn of adrenaline started inching its way through my system, and I literally itched with the need to start moving. If I were furry at the moment, I would have been scratching behind my neck, but in my skin, I wasn't so flexible, so I settled for fidgeting like a mad beast.

Karen met me outside the motel room, and we got into the truck. I let her drive, or rather, she let me ride in the cab.

I pulled out a map from the glovebox.

"You got a plan on how to get in there?" She started the truck and shifted into reverse.

"I've got about four miles to think of one." I grinned at her.

"You are not really that funny." She pulled out and then accelerated quickly out of the parking lot, shifting expertly into the heavier traffic. It was getting on into the afternoon, and people were heading out and about.

"The parents were staying at the Espejismo, a couple blocks from the beach." I checked the map. "Nothing to indicate they've moved, so I suggest we check out the hotel. See if I can make it inside the room."

"Any other buildings around?"

"I have no idea." I showed her the paper. "This is a street map, not Google maps."

"Don't be an asshole." She laid on the horn at an intersection. "I meant, does it look like there is someplace I can set up?"

"It looks like that section of the beach is mostly residential. Could be difficult to do outside the hotel."

"Hmm." Karen went to say something, but a shiny Jeep trying to beat the traffic light jumped out in the street in front of her. She cursed out loud, slammed on the brakes, and extended her hand out the window, followed by a few choice words in Spanish. It was very impressive, even if I had no idea what she said.

I waited for her to continue her thought, but she didn't speak until after the light turned color and we started moving again.

"All right," she said. "I'll drop you off. If you make it into the room, I've got a bug you can drop. That will give us a line into what's going on in the room."

"I can do that."

"Do you need me to hang on to that for you?" Karen nodded to my waist.

"Nah." I didn't expect to change and didn't want to give up my weapon. "I might need it. Unlike ceiling fans, these guys will probably shoot back."

"Ha." She rolled her eyes. "You're still not funny."

THE HOTEL GLOWERED along the boulevard, a low-slung, two-story affair opening onto a deserted street leading down to a narrow path to the beach. Karen dropped me off a couple of blocks away, then parked unobtrusively in a lot across the road. I ambled down the street and sat on the curb just short of the building.

"I'm in position." Her voice crackled slightly but came through audibly.

"Got it." I dug in my ear to adjust the bud. Effective, but uncomfortable. "I've spotted the parents' room."

"You sure?"

"Pretty sure." The room was the only one in the hotel with a car parked out front with U.S. diplomatic plates. As I watched, two men in khaki suits came out. They paused briefly in the doorway to say something to the rumpled, middle-aged man who escorted them out. He watched them leave and then turned to go back inside.

"Shit."

"What is it, Keller?"

"Nothing."

But it wasn't nothing. If I were still any good at judging character, I would say the man before me had given up hope. I hoped there wasn't a reason to do so, but I recognized his look and, for a moment, sat there on the curb trying to find the motivation to get up and keep going with the mission.

"Rick?" Karen crackled again in my ear.

"I'm here."

"What's your status?"

"I need to find a way to get in there." The thought of weaseling my way in the front door seemed suddenly obscene.

"Heads up," she said. "You've got a possible delivery coming your way."

I looked down the street, and sure enough, a dirty sedan with a makeshift car topper advertising some pizza joint in Spanish trundled up the road. I rose to my feet and stepped out into the road.

The car swerved before it came to a stop before me. The kid driving it hopped out, puffed up his alpha male chest, and began to curse me up and down, loudly. I did my party trick where I let the change into my eyes and smiled with a hint of teeth, and he cowered with his tail between his legs like a good pup.

I ENDED up paying the pizza kid for the pies. I felt bad, and besides, I didn't want him to go back and get some more to try to deliver them again.

With enough of a pretext to get up to the front porch, I still needed a way to get inside.

"All right, I'm ready whenever you are." Karen's voice came through my ear.

"Hear anything in there?"

"I'm not picking up anything, just some kind of low murmur," she answered. "I think it's the television."

"All right." I steeled myself. "I'm going to go deliver their dinner."

I hefted the pies in their warming bag and headed down the street, trying to think of some excuse to intrude on someone's tragedy.

In the end, the father gave me my opening without realizing it. He didn't have money in his pocket and let me in while he searched for his wallet. His wife sat in a chair, watching television, staring straight through it.

The air smelled stale, and I tried to hold my breath against an underlying rank thread of something like despair. I tried to separate the various scents, but there had been so much pain and fear concentrated in so small a space in a short period of time that it was almost impossible.

"Here you are." The father handed me a stack of bills. "I'm not sure ... here, take these. Are these enough?"

As he handed me the strange money, I caught it. A faint unfamiliar scent, one that didn't belong to the man or the woman. It smelled of cherries and salt and sunblock, and I knew it hovered there, lingering, from their daughter.

"I can't take this," I tried to say, but he was no longer listening to me. He set the pizza on the counter and sat on the edge of the bed, staring blankly at the television. I waited, hanging, half turned to leave, half wanting to know the right thing to say. Nothing I said would matter in that room. I left the money on the desk as I walked out, closing the door gently behind me.

I HEADED out toward the beach, not so much following the scent as hoping to pick it up down in the sand. It wasn't much of a hope, but I followed more than a physical scent. I took the narrow path through the dunes out to where the beach opened up to the gulf. It was a strong, windy day with clouds hanging thick and low. They promised one hell of a storm.

I broke into a steady jog, more of a shuffle. Kenny Chesney's "No Shirt, No Shoes, No Problem" kept circling around in my head. I could only remember the part that talked about sun and sand and wind and something else, but like an echo, it chased its tail around and around between my ears.

"Rick?"

I had almost forgotten the earbud. "Yeah, I'm here."

"You find anything?"

"Parents look like they haven't gotten any good news in a long time."

"Well, maybe we can help with that."

I stopped a moment and sniffed the air. I wasn't getting much except the overwhelming sense of brine and undersea things coming close to the shore.

"Maybe." I took off the boots I wore, leaving me in just a loose T-shirt and shorts. Even with the storm coming, I felt warm enough, and I preferred to run barefoot anyway.

My stomach growled. The pizza smell had reminded me forcefully I hadn't eaten since dinner last night, and I was rapidly reaching the point where I either needed to eat something or beat the crap out of someone. Happily, my system had waited until I safely escaped the parents' room. That could have been embarrassing. Although truthfully, in the state they were in, I probably could have helped myself to a slice and sat down with them to watch television, and they wouldn't have noticed.

I headed down the beach. The sky had grayed over, and the wind whipped up slightly. With the heavier surf and the threat of rain, the snowbirds had mostly packed up their beach chairs and towels and gone to find something else to do indoors.

In the distance, a pier jutted out past the breakers. Tell had said the family had eaten at a restaurant, sitting at the end of the structure to look out over the waves, their last meal together. On their walk back from the outing, the daughter disappeared. I ran, and the pier grew larger as I got closer to the end of the beach. I enjoyed the run; it gave me a grim satisfaction to be back on the hunt. But I made it all the way there without catching even the faintest trace of my quarry.

I turned around at the structure and followed it up the beach. There were few places she could have gone, and all of them, the police canvassed multiple times. I closed my eyes and tried to let the wind pass over me. She wasn't telling me anything today, though.

"Karen." I held my hand up to my face to block the wind from blowing away the words.

"Here."

"Question." I looked around. "If you were a little girl, what would make you leave your parents for just a few minutes?"

"Be more specific, Keller." Karen sounded bemused. "What are you getting at?"

"A little girl walking with her parents on the beach." I tried to picture that afternoon, a different beach than the near-empty one before me. "She leaves her parents' side to run to something, maybe thinks they're following her... What is she running toward?"

There was a silent pause, and I could almost hear her thinking through the hypothetical.

"Well," she said finally, "what do you see?"

I looked around. "There's a couple of shops at the end of the pier."

"No." She sounded thoughtful now. Although it could have been my imagination, putting something into the crackle of the transmission that wasn't actually there. "Someplace farther down the beach."

I started retracing my steps, keeping close to the edge of the beach where the sand met the line of bungalows that bordered the area.

"Tell me what you see," Karen said after a longer pause. "Walk me through this."

"Mostly, I see some people sitting on the beach." I looked around again, sniffed the air. "A couple of houses along the beach."

"Is there something with bright colors? Something advertising a kid's event or something like that?"

"Um…"

"What?"

"I have some trouble with colors. Not one crack about dogs seeing in black and white. I mean it. I thought that was in my file."

"Oh. Sorry." She waited for a moment, and then her voice crackled in my ear again. "Okay, so look for something for kids, maybe with pictures on it of—I don't know, clowns or something?"

I never had kids, or been forced to confront what makes them tick and something told me, neither had Karen.

"Hang on." I spotted something that smelled like it might be color-ful. "I might have something."

I jogged toward a small stand, presided over by a bored-looking kid sweating through his T-shirt under the apron advertising ice cream in Spanish. There were no clowns on the cart in front of him, but there was a picture of a girl with a puppy. The cart sat on a square patch of broken asphalt, part of a path leading off the beach.

The teenager looked up with a total lack of interest as he saw me approach. He stirred himself slightly but then settled back into his slouch when I walked by him.

I stopped. The smell of cherries came from the cart. Or seemed like it did, mixed up with the chemical smells and "natural" flavors in the mix. I opened myself up again, conscious of the gaze of the ice cream seller. I set aside the acrid artificial chemicals that burned my sinuses like chlorine water, and then I dove deeper past the layer of salt and brine permeating everything on the little section of sand.

The kid's reaction was the first clue my attempt to finesse the change was about to go haywire.

"Dude." His voice cracked, and he stepped back, away from the cart.

I looked up at him as the first wave of pain shot through my body like electricity through a shorted fuse.

"Lobo..."

Then I knew the change came too quickly to hold off, the destabilization riding me again, crunching my body and my psyche into a small ball of pain and regret I had ever met the MONIKER fuckers who thought I was some giant high school science project with teeth.

I stumbled away from the beach, from the sand, from the ice cream seller. I sought someplace dark and quiet where I could get hold of myself, but the change rolled me too quickly. Staggering, I fell to my knees at the side of the road. The heat made the cramping of my muscles under my skin unbearable. My hands twisted the fastenings on my shorts, tearing the fabric as I writhed out of my clothes.

"Rick!" This time Karen's voice didn't come from the earbud. She had driven around the block and parked the truck between me and traffic. "Come on, let's get you inside."

I twisted and snarled. She backed off, pulling her weapon and pointing it in my direction as she slowly put the cab of the truck between us. I didn't blame her. In this state, I wasn't sure what I would remember and what I would forget of myself when the change took over. Or how far it would go.

I received my answer a minute later as the pain evened out into the monochrome gray of the November evening. I circled around once or twice in the street. My last coherent, and by coherent, I meant fully human, thought was the hope Karen would remember to pick up my clothes and my weapon and follow me.

Sitting back on my haunches, I howled, grabbing at the breeze drifting in off the ocean. I latched onto the girl's scent, sniffing the ground. Karen watched me warily, but I didn't care about the look in her eyes, somewhere between regret and disgust.

I began retracing the footsteps of the little girl. Somewhere in the next couple of blocks, the cherry and salt scent became underlain with hints of doubt, fear, and finally, full-blown panic. I reached a more populated area, back toward the pier and the shops that littered the end of the wooden pilings. There I lost the physical scent, overwhelmed with car leather and an American brand of cigarettes, lifting the girl from my awareness, but not beyond following.

"Keller?" Karen's voice came again through the earbud. I had no idea what she was doing or what she said, even if I'd had the ability to reply.

THE PATH I FOLLOWED, laid down by the scent of exhaust and the sense of the girl, took me away from the beach, down a short stretch of highway, and into the warrens of a dense residential area. This was one of those small towns, just a step above a shantytown, that eventually forms next to seaside towns when the native residents can no longer afford to live there and still need someplace to stay while they work for the tourists and rich foreigners who now live in and pass through their former streets.

A few blocks in, I picked up the girl's physical scent again, this time enhanced by the sharp smell of urine. The implications escaped my short-circuited brain, and I felt only gratitude at having a nice, strong scent to run down.

I hit the next block and stopped short, circling the scent, trying to block the new information it sent me. There was no help for it—I started to whimper, a trembling gut sound that grew stronger when I sat back and howled at the sky. A window slammed shut and a door locked. Voices muttered in Spanish. I smelled gun oil and bit back the rest of the howl, strangling on it.

My feet gathered under me, I took off down the street, no longer unsure of where I was headed, lured on by the sudden absence of being that vanished from the scent as surely as a flame is snuffed by the flood.

8

The little girl was a broken doll, cast forgotten on the dirty couch. After searching desperately for her scent, the room full of it overwhelmed me.

From the lingering scent of violence and the physical proof on her tiny body, she had died hard and scared, and I promised her those who had done this to her would face the same fate. They lingered in the room as well, the same smell of cigarettes and adrenaline, tainted by the cordite and grease reeking older and steadier in their scent path.

I circled the room, sniffing out the last bit of what I could find, then sat back and howled a promise of blood and death.

"Oh." Karen's voice came from the doorway. She had followed me and walked in, unprepared for what lay there, thinking I was the worst thing she would find in the room.

I turned to see her sag briefly, then recover. It might have been the worst thing she ever saw, but from her face and the sudden wave of familiar nausea emanating from her, I knew this wasn't the only bad thing she had ever seen.

I rubbed myself against her, nudging her with my shoulder to move her out of the way of the door. She groped for me with one hand, but I'm not a dog, and I don't wear a collar, so she had nothing to grasp. I paused for a second out of the door to catch the scent path again and then took off down the street.

"Keller! Wait, stop!" She followed me for a block, but I ran faster, and I needed to get away from her. I knew what I needed to do and that my team would be sure to try to stop me.

I darted into a narrow alley, pausing for a moment to look back. She had stopped and begun dialing her cell phone. Her pistol drawn, she looked in my direction as she spoke into the phone. As I watched, she closed the phone, turned, and went back to the room. I knew it was a good thing she stayed there for the girl. She would know the right thing to do. I didn't care about the right thing. At this moment, I cared only about expiating some of my guilt at getting there too late.

Following the men's path was easier than trying to tease out the girl's. For one thing, it smelled recent, fresher. For another, it was still heightened by the aftermath of what they had done. The two men who had been in there with her had left maybe an hour ago, but they had been living there for a while, and the scent drenched me with its rank bile. They felt no regret for how she had died; it had excited them, proved something to them, and they were looking forward to something else. Their excitement burned sour in my throat as I wolfed it down and ran for more.

I didn't get everything from the scent—their non-physical presence imprinted much stronger than simple tracking would need.

Sometimes I can follow a scent for days and wind up at the end of the week with a cold trail and no joy. Sometimes, I get lucky. Sometimes, other people don't.

The sedan was parked outside a convenience store, one of a row of dusty store fronts advertising meat and vegetables in playful lettering. By now, the gray light had mostly faded from the sky, and a few stark streetlights threw a nimbus around the mist starting to fall. Rather than cool off the streets, it caused a wave of humidity to roll along the asphalt, sending up all sorts of pungent distractions.

"Hey, perrito, que haces aqui?" A middle-aged man in an apron and a Phillies baseball cap greeted me, possibly thinking me some tourist's lost pet. I padded straight by him, deftly avoiding the broom and the sudden spate of angry Spanish he threw my way. I shouldered my way past a swinging door and followed the men's scent past the kitchen, down some narrow steps, and stopped short facing a wooden door.

I lifted my paw and scratched. The sounds from inside drifted off for a moment. I scratched again. Someone asked something in Spanish. A pause. I scratched again, and a different voice barked an order. Footsteps approached, and the door tumblers unlocked.

The inch of space for a questioning look and a Spanish cuss word were all the entrée I needed. I set my shoulder into the door and pushed it open.

The man's throat melted, soft flesh between my teeth. I didn't recognize his scent, but he stood between me and the table, where the two men I hunted sat. One of them pointed a gun at me, and I felt a short, sharp impact as one of the bullets found my side.

I lifted my head from the neck of the twitching corpse beneath me and growled. One man spoke in Spanish, and the only word I recognized was *Dio.* He screamed it again and again until my claws found his face, swiping through soft tissue and reducing his screaming to a whimper.

Turning, I snarled at his friend, who had crept closer. He pointed his gun toward me. It shook and trembled in his outstretched hand.

He fired again. The sound in the small concrete room echoed, deafening, and my ears rang with it as I launched myself at his legs. I tangled them up and bowled him over.

He thrust his hands and arms at me uselessly, trying desperately to keep me away from his face and neck. I opened my jaw wide and crunched. I relished the satisfying feel of my teeth on his skull. My cuspids caught, and I sawed my jaw back and forth until I could free his head from the grasp of my teeth.

I felt him screaming through the vibrations in his chest, but my ears were still ringing, and no sound came through. He mouthed words, but whether they were in Spanish or English or any coherent language other than a panicked babble, I didn't know and didn't care. I ended his pathetic movements with a slash to the jugular.

The first man watched me, slumped against the wall but still alive. The fear on his face twitched something in me, and I started to feel the carousel surf of the change rock through me again.

I found myself with one foot on each side of the border, my shadow cast crazy and upright against the wall by a single, swinging bulb.

I stalked him and found it fun to see the terror grow in his eyes. He tried to scream, but through his ruined face, it came out more as a mewling sound. He put his hands up to shield his face, but with his two friends dead on the floor, I didn't bother trying to go for the throat.

I was hungry.

"Well, isn't this a cozy scene."

Tell and Karen had come in behind me while I hunched over one of the men. There wasn't much left of any of them, but at least I wasn't hungry anymore. I licked my chops.

I caught Karen's look of utter scorn and revulsion, but in this state, I didn't care. I growled and turned back to the body before me.

"Keller!" Tell spoke sharply, in the sort of tone one would use to get their pet dog to drop some particularly tasty treat it found on a walk. It had about the same effect.

The next instant, I felt a sharp piercing in my side, and I jerked with the sudden shock of several thousand volts jolting through me. I found myself wrenched back into my own miserable skin.

Reaching down, I ripped the prongs out of me. Tell pressed the trigger mechanism again, and my hand involuntarily clenched around the metal. I rode the lightning for what seemed like an eternity until he let it go. My extremities kept twitching after he shut the current off, forcing my hand to let the prongs drop to the floor.

I staggered to my feet and stepped forward unsteadily, seeing my next target in Tell's wiry frame. My next couple steps were less unsteady.

The bullet impacting my shoulder was of a larger caliber and stung much sharper than the ones the men had fired, which by now my body had already rid itself of. Karen held her .45 aimed at me, center mass, the smoke drifting from the barrel. From the dark streaks immediately spreading out under my skin like a tarnished supernova, I knew she was packing silver. In the midst of my anger and adrenaline, it meant less than it usually does.

I hesitated, torn between the two, but turned back toward Tell. I wanted him. Unfinished business. I reached for the change.

The gentle prick in my skin felt so small as to be painless. I stepped forward one more time but suddenly found myself floundering.

"What was that?" I staggered and went down on my knees as the pain faded into numbness and black closed in on my vision.

"Something you're not going to get a chance to build a tolerance for," Tell replied.

My response was to try again to go for his throat, but I couldn't get my feet under me, and my arms refused to cooperate with the plan.

I felt him and Karen reach for me, pulling my hands behind my back, connecting the chain to my ankles. I spent the rest of the ride back to New York in a cage, shackled in steel laced with silver.

I WOKE UP GROGGY, achy, and thirsty, but at least I wasn't hungry, nor did I have to piss again. I was naked once more, but this time someone had thought to leave a blanket and some clothes in the cage. I found them by touch. Someone had forgotten to plug in a nightlight. I dressed quickly. My shoulder ached. I shivered in the cold, shifting as the damp cement leached away the warmth.

The basement was silent except for every once in a while when the heater ducts kicked on for a bit, did their thing, then rattled quietly back to sleep.

I settled back against the bars of the cage, wrapping the blanket around me. It felt scratchy and smelled of Simple Green, reminding me of Army barracks. It barely fit, but it was enough to make me comfortable.

My ears perked up when I heard footsteps coming down the hall. They stopped outside the door, and I heard a murmur of voices. The door opened, and the light flipped on. Karen stood in the doorway.

"Feeling yourself again?"

"Never better." It wasn't the truth.

"We need you upstairs."

"Let me out, and I'll be right up."

She walked closer to the cage, and I saw she held a pair of hand-cuffs in her hand. I felt the silver in them even from inside my cage.

"I'll need you to put these on."

"Really?" I twitched at the thought. "A little reminder of what you all actually pay me for, and I suddenly have to walk around sporting some bondage jewelry?"

"Put them on or sit down here in the dark." I couldn't guess which one she'd prefer. "But if I were you, I'd want to be around when people were talking about whether or not to put me down like a stray dog."

She was right. When she handed me the cuffs through the bars, I put them on like a good boy. She opened the cage, and I scrambled out, standing up straight, trying to work out the kinks. I cracked my neck.

"After you," I said, inclining my head. When I looked down, I realized my shoulder still ached with the bullet they had forgotten to remove.

I THOUGHT there would be more people in the room upstairs, but the only ones standing around when Karen and I got there were Director Ramirez and Agent Tell. I thought they would say something, but they barely acknowledged us as we walked in.

Karen pulled a seat out for me, and I sat down. It was a very comfortable leather office chair. In the sudden warmth of the upstairs, my body shivered involuntarily. I rested my hands in my lap, not quite sure what they wanted from me.

The discussion, or rather argument, between the two men seemed to center around the question of what to do now that the operation in Mexico had failed so miserably on so many levels. I agreed we had crashed and burned, but I thought, at some level, vengeance had successfully been extracted. A bitter compensation, but sometimes you take what you can get.

Alternatively, they appeared to be considering the possibility of killing me and burying my body under a block of silver somewhere or maybe keeping it for future study. They didn't state that particular option in so many words, but I heard what they were saying underneath the language they were using.

Obviously, I was a fan of choice C: let me the hell out of these cuffs and give me ten minutes in a room with Agent Tell. Sadly, I was the only one seriously considering this option.

"We need him," Ramirez said again. "He's got the skill set, the languages, and for Christ's sake, Tell, we need someone who can meet these people with the same taste for violence they've been dishing out."

"Ken, I just don't think—" Tell didn't seem to be on my side. Big fat surprise there.

"If we're going to go in there, we need to go in there fast, quiet, and in a hurry." Ramirez rolled right over him. "And preferably without a distaste for slaughter, or have you forgotten what they did to the last team?"

"Fuck you, Ramirez." Tell spat the words. "I haven't forgotten."

Karen looked surprised at the exchange. I wondered if she knew everything those two did.

"Then you know we need him," Ramirez pointed out.

"I know that he's unstable, dangerous, and rusty." Tell still wasn't voting for me for agent of the year. "And the only contact with the outside world in the last ten years was his *Playboy* subscription."

Tell was mistaken. *Playboy* wasn't the only reading material in the house, just what I kept in the bathroom. If Tell had searched the house, he would have seen a century's worth of books, mostly military studies and journals from the places I'd been or thought I was going. A man, name of Kilcullen, once wrote that counterinsurgency is adaptation. He was right, more than he knew. My ability—my value to the organization—was not just being able to react to what happened during a mission, but to change the rules of the game, to change myself, my habits, everything I'd ever learned or trained for. That's why I was so good at my job and why all MONIKER usually managed to do was get in my way, even when they still called it O.S.S. Anti-Partisan Branch and hadn't yet created its own little box it now couldn't think outside of.

I also had quite a respectable collection of the classics, thank you very much. Those books, as Mark Twain famously quipped, everyone praised and nobody read. During the time I grew up, they were a standard part of a child's education. As I got older, and older, I came to understand the passions behind the dry old words and felt fellow kinship with the ones who spoke familiarly of blood and death on the field. I had been there and found only their dry, distant words capable of defining these experiences.

"You have anything to contribute here?" There was heat behind Tell's words, and I opened my mouth to respond and then realized he had been talking to Karen. I waited to hear what she said.

She looked at me thoughtfully and then turned back to the men, almost as if dismissing me.

"We can do it without him," she said. I felt a momentary stab of panic. I know I'm an asshole, but I didn't want to get shot for it, carved up into little pieces, and left to become a distant MONIKER memory.

She wasn't done, though.

"We can do it," she said again. "But I won't go without him."

I looked at her, surprised.

"Don't look at me." She still eyed me as if she couldn't stop seeing me hunched over the kidnappers. "Personally, I think that what you are is disgusting. And what I saw in that room in Mexico I'll spend most of my life trying to forget."

I slumped in my chair. The faint ache in my shoulder where the silver bullet hadn't yet worked its way to the top of the skin stung harder. The longer I sat with my hands caught in the silver cuffs, the stronger the pain grew.

"But I've seen in person the reality of what they did," she said. "And they didn't have the excuse of being subhuman."

That smarted. But she wasn't the first person to put things that way, and she wouldn't be the last one to call me names. I shrugged.

"Maybe if you all hadn't dragged me out of Vermont and tossed me onto a team I have no desire to join in order to do a mission I don't give two shits about, things could have gone down differently." No one acknowledged my contribution to the conversation.

The pain in my shoulder was growing worse. That, plus the silver in the handcuffs, was starting to make me feel lightheaded. I knew I might be in trouble when the first dark spots appeared briefly in my vision. They vanished quickly, but I felt nauseous and entertained the possibility of vomiting on the nice corporate table.

Ramirez regarded me unhappily. "If this is the best we've got for this job, we are screwed." He shrugged and turned to Tell. I watched as the two of them grew somewhat hazy and indistinct.

"Is he all right?" Karen actually seemed concerned.

"He'll be fine once we take out the bullet." Tell shrugged.

"Holy crap, what are you waiting for?"

"To see if we're even going to bother keeping him around." I couldn't argue with Tell's logic, but I didn't agree with it either.

Ramirez broke in. "Karen, help him to the medic's office." He turned back to Tell. "You're the team leader. If you need him, he's yours. If not, they have something down there I'm sure the boys and girls in the lab are dying to test out."

At least, that's what I thought he said. It could have been the paranoia kicking in. I struggled briefly in the chair, but when Karen helped me to my feet, it was all I could do to stand without falling.

"You are one hell of a mess," she said.

I thought I might have said something in agreement, but I just tried to keep up as she walked me down the hall, hoping we were heading someplace they'd take the bullet out, not put more in.

9

The medics gave me something that stung going in but flooded cool and sweet through my veins, leaving the taste of candy at the back of my mouth. I hoped it wouldn't kill me, but at the same time, I didn't know if I would mind it all that much if it did.

The bed was so short my feet dangled over the edge. I was feeling good, a stupid grin plastered all over my face. My tongue might have lolled. Karen was bent over me, a look of professional curiosity in her eyes, which were all I could see of her face behind the surgical mask.

"You're a language doctor, not a doctor-doctor," I said, or rather thought I said. It might have come out in a long blurry mumble.

I felt pressure on the wound as she poked at it, but it was a clinical pressure without much pain. Whatever they put me on, it was amazing, and I wondered if there was any way I could get some more of it. Purely for reasons of scientific research, of course.

Just the scalpel in her hand unnerved me. I've always had a thing about knives, especially when wielded by women who did not particularly like me.

She bent over me again, and I tried to panic, but the anesthetic flowed more generously, and I couldn't stop my eyes from closing against whatever she was going to do.

KAREN'S VOICE faded into guttural syllables, which confused me because I hadn't heard those languages aloud in a long time. I spoke German and Russian like a native—maybe one who had been traveling outside the country for a few years—but a native because I wasn't born in the States. I'd followed several flags in my life before ending up wearing the red, white, and blue on my shoulder.

The forests in southern Germany were old and dark, and a wolf could find easy paths to run in the shadows against the deep, white snow. Even now, new-growth forests make me uneasy. There is too much light and not enough history.

The stuff pumping through me brought these patterns back to my eyes, and I heard a distant rumbling. It shook the black and broken asphalt beneath my feet, and I slowly got to my knees as the first vehicle in the convoy slowly appeared from around the corner.

The paint outlining the solid, lone star was muted and scratched but still stood out against the drab, military paint of the vehicle. The gunner in the passenger seat smoked a cigarette. As they approached, he shifted it in his mouth to blow out a lungful of smoke. His hands in their fingerless wool gloves never moved from off his weapon.

The forest road faded to dirt and gravel at the sides, and the heavy truck labored and left prints in the scuff. As it approached, I slowly lowered myself back into the deep snow so as not to catch any sharpshooter's eye with a fast movement. I trusted the pine branches camouflaging the defilade would do their work—and that the four members of my team would have the sense to stay put.

The scout vehicle passed slowly, and we knew they would be radioing a report to the next vehicles in the convoy. Sure enough, about fifteen minutes after the lead vehicle made it past our position, three heavily laden troop transports trundled down the road. They belched gray exhaust in the afternoon twilight as the drivers shifted gears coming down the hill and around the curve.

I waited as the transports passed by, almost holding my breath as the last one faded from view down the cold winter road.

"Fucking Bolsheviks." The voice was raspy, and spoke German with a thick Polish accent. It took all my self-control not to jump out of cover.

"Jesus Christ, Aleksy," I said in a hoarse whisper. "What the hell are you doing?"

"Hey, relax." He grinned at my alarm. "Nobody sees me when I move."

"Fuck." I glared. "All it takes is one Commie with a machine gun, and we're all dead."

"Fucking Russians." Aleksy added something in Polish and spat on the ground.

I was not truly mad at him. He had an uncanny ability to move in the woods, an ability matched only by my own, and that was saying something.

"And when are you going to learn some fucking Polish?" He scooted himself farther down in the ditch.

"If you don't like German, we can try Russian."

"I'd rather shit railroad spikes." Aleksy nurtured a deep and abiding hatred for both the Germans and the Russians who had in turn invaded, saved, and raped his country, relegating him to the life of partisan and probably, eventually, the death of a partisan. I felt sympathy, but I was still young and thought I knew something about lost causes.

"Shh." I motioned him to be still. A light flared once, then twice, about midway up the wooded hill sloping upward from the road. "All right, I'm moving. Cover my ass. Don't shoot me."

"*Da, Tovarisch Wolf.*" It was the name I went by. The follies of youth. Shoot me.

The team had prepped the barricades before we got set in place. We didn't have time to construct a full-scale impassable barrier, but we'd been working in the area for a while. The soldiers thought they recognized the signs of our work, so we used their paranoia against them. This time, instead of destroying the road, we had simply prepared fresh dirt to smooth in circles on the road, simulating freshly emplaced mines. I covered the ends of a few wires with dirt and laid them in a line disappearing into the trees. A sign in Cyrillic warning passing convoys of a destroyed bridge ahead put the cherry on the cake, or however that saying goes. English is my fourth language, and I didn't speak it in those days.

As planned, the real quarry traveled confidently into the downward curve, then squealed and screeched as the front driver tried desperately to stop his forward momentum. The trucks behind him followed suit, attempting to mitigate the domino effect.

Here came our true target, a nice fat supply convoy bearing enough guns, food, and ammunition—and hopefully warm clothing—to resupply my team and several others in the area. There were three trucks in the convoy, each open in the back, lightly guarded by a driver and a gunner, the contents protected by the tarp covering the back of the truck.

Using the glass lens of my compass, I flashed a signal back to the machine gun nestled on the hill, the same nest that first alerted me to the oncoming convoy. I took the first shot, rising from the defilade and spraying the tires of the first vehicle until it couldn't move anywhere except slowly. Ducking and bobbing toward the truck, I ran, spraying across the windshield until the driver and gunner were dead, and the vehicle effectively became a permanent obstacle.

At the same time, the machine gun opened fire, belching rapid-fire destruction down on the back of the trucks. They cut off retreat down the road, shredding tires and turning the drivers and gunners to so much fine mist.

Then, as fast as it started, the firing stopped. We waited for a few minutes. I crouched uncomfortably and hunkered down at the front of the lead vehicle, waiting to hear if they picked off any soldiers who had survived the ambush. At the same time, I kept an eye out for any vehicles returning, alerted by the gunfire. Stuck out there in the open,

I felt exposed. Hell, I was exposed. Finally, I stood and waved up the other members of the team.

"We've got to get this stuff out of here quickly." I hunkered back down as they came up on our position. "I'm sure there are going to be more where these came from, and they might have more guns."

The men smiled. Aleksy and his buddy Borys, who got a lot of flack from his name, hopped up in the back of the first truck. I took the back of the second truck with the last member of the team, a guy whose name I could never remember but who manned the machine gun with an almost religious fervor.

We emptied out the backs of the trucks pretty quickly. They were more lightly packed than we expected, and that should have tipped us off. But it was cold, and we were thinking about getting the supplies loaded up in the Jeeps waiting over the hill and heading back to camp where the weather might still be cold, but the vodka would warm us quickly.

Aleksy and Borys finished their truck before we emptied ours. They hopped down and came around the back where the machine gunner and I were wrestling with a crate of ammo. It was heavy, but after checking the shipping label, we found the rounds in it matched our weapons, every single caliber. He had brought the weapon down with him from the hill, heavy as it was. He never liked it to be farther than arm's reach from him. I would sometimes catch him reaching out to stroke it reassuringly.

"Hey, Wurst." Aleksy found my name as pretentious as it was and liked to tease me by calling me the German word for sausage.

"What is it?" I tried to glare harder, pissed at the nickname and the fact that the ammunition was so heavy.

"Take your time, brother." Aleksy paid no attention to the glare; in fact, he grinned ever wider. "We'll get that other truck; don't you worry your little German head about it." He chuckled, and I flipped him off. Shrugging, he headed for the other truck.

I didn't see what happened at first, but I heard the bark of automatic weapons fire and a scream, and then there were men pouring out of the back of the last truck. What we thought to be a cargo troop carrier covered with a tarp turned out to be armored with reinforced steel that concealed and provided cover to the infantry squad hiding there.

The enemy had gotten cunning. Tired of the constant plague of guerrillas interdicting their supplies and picking off their soldiers, they finally set a counter-ambush to trap us and rid themselves of the nagging partisan problem.

Aleksy and Borys were dead before they hit the ground. Aleksy fell to the side of the truck, and I watched as he twitched; his body expired without realizing it, eyes staring wide at the sky until they dulled to a pale gray.

I raised my weapon, and our machine gunner set his weapon right there in the back of the truck, covering himself behind a spray of automatic fire. But we were never flush with ammunition at the best of times, and when he ran out, the squad advanced around the sides of the truck, raining fire down on our position.

The machine gunner died quickly, three rounds from the lead soldier turning his face into unrecognizable shreds. His finger seized on the trigger, clenching it down in his death throes, an empty click of the trigger, his final contribution.

I retreated into the truck, hunkering flat on the floor, trying to keep out of the way of the bullets the squad kept sending into the back of the vehicle. One or two of them found their mark, but lead rendered as little effect then as it did now.

I fired and the gun clicked down on an empty chamber. The squad leader hesitated. I could see him torn between attacking or taking the prudent path to make sure I well and truly ran out of ammunition.

Using the butt of the rifle as a hammer, I broke open the crate the gunner and I had struggled with shortly before the attack. The shipping label only told half the truth. Nestled snugly in their cushioned packing crate next to boxes of belt-fed ammo sat the most beautiful sight in the world—a veritable cornucopia of devices designed to explode in various lethal ways.

I grabbed the closest one and pulled the pin. Peeking quickly out from behind the crates, I ducked back down just as quickly as the squad leader raised his weapon and sent a few rounds my way.

Counting to six, I tossed the grenade into the midst of the soldiers, targeting the squad leader in particular. I covered my ears, hoping for the reassuring sound of twelve infantry soldiers being converted to a bloody mess.

My luck held, which is to say that the grenade was a dud, and then I found myself tangled in the back of the truck with a dozen furious Russian soldiers who realized quickly the lead bullets were having no effect. A rifle butt came down on my head, and I was out for the count.

THEY DRAGGED me out of the truck and dumped me in the snow. The cold roused me enough to listen to their conversation. They were speaking rapidly in Russian, but I caught most of what they were saying—mostly whether or not to kill me there or take me back to someone named Dmitri. From the hushed way they said his name, I did not think either choice was going to be particularly salutary for my health.

Eventually, the squad leader cut the conversation short with a barked order, and the soldiers hauled me to my feet. They secured my hands behind my back with a piece of rope and marched me to the last vehicle.

Only one of the truck's tires had been damaged in the attack. They changed it quickly, and I found myself tossed in the back and kicked to the far end of the cargo area. I saw the reason for their survival—the thing had been lined with steel plating under the benches. The soldiers had simply lain on the floor and waited for us to stop shooting.

The ride was cold and bumpy. I wracked my brain trying to figure out a way to kill the soldiers riding with me in the back, but no clever plan presented itself. This was before I met MONIKER and their particular brand of change initiation—their experiments were not without benefits—but now the full moon wouldn't rise for several days, so I lay there and thought in circles. After about an hour, the truck slowed. I heard voices speaking in Russian, apparently granting access at an entry control point, and then we were in their camp.

The driver pulled out the latch on the end of the truck, and the soldiers piled out. They kicked me out onto the ground, and I curled around myself as best as I could when I hit the mud and gravel surface. I slipped getting to my feet, and went down hard on my knee. Something snapped in my ankle. I struggled up again. The soldiers surrounded me.

"He's the last of the team." The squad leader addressed a tall, thin, older man with major's rank displayed on his uniform. The major regarded me impassively.

"Did he say if there were any other teams in the area?"

"We haven't asked him anything." The squad leader frowned. "He was mostly unconscious since we picked him up."

That was one way to put it.

"Hmmm." The major rested his hand lightly on his sidearm. We stood in tableaux for a moment. He unsnapped the holster and drew the pistol, aiming it lightly at my face. He cocked the hammer back. I bit back the sudden surge of panicked adrenaline. I was ninety-nine percent sure I would survive a point-blank lead bullet to the face, but I wasn't so eager to test the hypothesis.

The major shrugged and released the hammer. He re-holstered the weapon. "Take him to Dmitri."

They took me to a room containing a table, a lamp, and something back in the shadows I could not quite make out. I guessed Dmitri's specialty centered around interrogation. If the Russians' treatment of partisans was consistent, I also guessed that he might be the last person I ever saw.

One of the first things I learned when I was old enough to understand where I came from was how to get out of ropes. It didn't take long to free myself once they locked me in the room. I prowled the eight-by-four-meter space but could find nothing that would serve to get me out of there. What I did find made my blood chill, sitting as it did back in the shadows.

The key turned in the lock, and an elderly man in a sweater and slacks entered the room. He seemed momentarily startled to see me up out of my seat, but he held a hand up to stop the soldier who stepped forward, weapon raised to put me back in it. He said something in a low tone of voice, and the soldier looked at me, then him, and backed out of the room. I heard the key turn in the lock again.

"Good evening, *Herr Werwolf*," he said by way of greeting.

I startled. What I was had not yet been learned by more than a handful of people, most of whom died shortly after its discovery. But he was simply referring to me by the old name the Russians had for the German partisans fighting their losing battle in the east.

He spoke to me in German. "Perhaps you would feel more comfortable in the chair?"

"Who the hell are you?" I wondered if the soldiers would make it back into the room in time to save him if I reached for him and covered my hands with blood.

He read my intentions in my crouch and expression. He laughed.

"You can, of course, attempt it." He shrugged, spreading his hands. "I'm an old man and rarely move quickly anymore."

I felt the phantom change echo in my hands and willed the nascent urge to grow into sharp nails and strong slashing strength. Like a fretful, capricious beast, it stayed lurking under the surface.

"Of course, you would immediately be killed once the guards were alerted." Dmitri motioned to the desk. "It is your choice. You can sit in the chair and talk to me, or this could get very unpleasant."

I did not sit in the chair, of course. I have never been one to do anything the easy way, and I still cherished the illusion I would be leaving the camp upright and under my own willpower. Or that I would not break when the pain began.

I found myself wrong on both counts. I was young and unpracticed, although that was no excuse when the soldiers overwhelmed me and I found myself strapped to the chair. The old man proved to have a delicate touch, knowing just where to apply the slightest volts to provoke the strongest reaction.

They eventually noticed the lack of permanent scarring, but when they started asking about that, I was too far gone to hear the question let alone whisper the answer.

———

I WOKE UP SCREAMING, the sound making me flinch. I tried to launch myself up, but something jerked me back down. Struggling, I realized my two arms were the points of resistance and that they had actually handcuffed me to the bed.

"Good morning, *Herr Werwolf.*" I jerked around to see Karen looking at me, a clipboard in her hand and an inscrutable expression on her face.

"Did I..." I began. I stopped.

She finished for me. "Scream in your sleep? Yes. A lot."

The idea of lying helpless and screaming with her looking on struck me with a deep sense of shame. And guilt. I hadn't felt those things in a very long time.

She consulted her clipboard, giving me a chance to pull it together.

I looked down at my shoulder. Once they removed the bullet, the flesh had returned to its normal color.

"Sorry I shot you." She watched me closely. I found her scrutiny a little unnerving.

"I don't blame you. I hope you'll do it again. You know, if you have to." I smiled. I was drugged. Give me a break.

She smiled back at me, treating me to sharp teeth and a matching glint in her eye. "Don't worry; I have every intention of doing so."

It didn't matter this woman scared the piss out of me. I was already in love with her.

"So, uh, can you let me out of these?" I jerked the cuffs against the bed rail and looked at her with what I hoped were puppy dog eyes. I'm not so good at those. I have more practice beating what I need out of people.

"We'll have to see what Tell says."

"What I say about what?" Tell had come in while I was distracted.

Karen nodded toward me. "What to do with him."

"I think he's the worst possible choice for this mission." Tell grimaced as if he smelled something ripe. Probably me. "But he's the best of a short list of shitty options."

"Oh, hooray, I made the team." I gave him a thumbs up with one of my shackled hands.

"Try to play ball this time." He gestured at my shoulder. "Next time, that bullet won't be aimed at your shoulder."

He nodded to Karen and left. I hated him. But as much as I hated him, I was starting to enjoy the company of the other member of the team. I didn't know if I truly wanted in on whatever big game they were going after, but returning to a solitary life of snow and beer seemed less satisfactory after even just a small taste of being back out in the field.

I grinned at her and held up my hand as best I could, attached to the bed frame as it was.

"Now, can you let me free?"

She smiled and held up another syringe. "Sure. In a minute."

That other member of the team was clearly a sadist.

10

The plane took off in an intense thunderstorm that rattled the small cabin and jostled my stomach. The small craft shuddered and clawed its way into the air until it gathered enough power beneath itself and broke out past the clouds into the bright sky above. The light pierced through the small windows and broke against the inside of my eye sockets. I pulled the shades down and reclined my seat to sleep, taking bets with myself about how long it would be until Tell started in on another interminable "planning session," as he called them.

The past month had been full of such sessions. This mission in Kazakhstan, or at least I assumed it would be Kazakhstan, involved layered cover stories, dialect training, a lot of money, and even, on my part, tattoos that hurt like a bitch given they did them realistically with a prison kit they'd lifted off some gangster who sadly was no longer with us. Eventually, my body would rid itself of the ink, but for the next month or so, I would look like a sleazy Eastern European douchebag. We were not half-assing it like we'd done the Mexico job, but there were still large gaps in the whole plan. There wouldn't be much of a safety net to cover ourselves if we happened to fall through one of those gaps.

Tell decided to make the most of being team leader, although I noticed he did not feel obliged to participate in the tattoo sessions and insisted on hanging onto the credit cards, cash, and—what did not thrill me at all—the passports. In ten years, pretty much everyone I knew where we were headed had probably died or relocated. If I got stranded, I would be up a creek on a leaky raft.

Shifting my position, I tried to get comfortable. Sleep refused to come. I used to be able to sleep anywhere, on any type of vehicle, but apparently, that was another skill lost in my years in Vermont. My teammates provided no distraction. Karen breathed regularly and deeply and was probably asleep. Tell read the contents of a folder. He seemed to have an unlimited supply of important folders with papers labeled "TOP SECRET" and "DO NOT REMOVE" stapled to the top, warning that the contents were classified. Wondering where he had removed them from, I closed my eyes and turned in my seat before he could notice I was awake and give me something else to do.

I chalked up my sleeplessness, at least in part, to the fact I felt so damn good—energetic even. I felt better than I had since they first picked me up. To be completely honest with myself—which I hated to be—I felt better than I had in a long time.

I recognized my state. I always felt this moment of clarity and energy when whatever team I currently played for finally started forward movement on an operation, and all the planning and worrying fell behind us. We were about to make things happen.

You would think by now I would be used to the pre-mission jitters, but the excitement gave me a buzz every time.

It is hard to explain. I usually don't try.

I shifted again, and this time, Tell caught me not napping.

"Can't sleep?"

"No, I'm too wired," I answered. I realized, too late, that he had asked me the question in German, and I had answered in the same language by reflex.

"Really, Keller?" He shut the folder, keeping his place with his index finger. "Four weeks of practicing a Polish cover story, and you come out speaking perfect German?"

"Go fuck yourself, Tell." I replied in Russian with just the hint of an Eastern European accent.

"You really can't help yourself, can you?"

"Nope."

"Well, think about this, asshole." He spoke low so as not to wake our third team member. "If you make that mistake on your own, the worst that could happen is someone shoots you with a regular weapon, which is pretty much useless."

"That's a fair assessment, *svoloch*." I crossed my arms and tried to settle back against the seat.

"Okay, so what happens when you screw up, and instead of you getting shot, it's me?"

I smiled, and it might have been juvenile, but they don't call it a "wolfish grin" for nothing.

Tell remained unfazed, and I let my canines settle back in my gums. "Or Karen?"

Point for Agent Tell. I scowled and consoled myself with the thought that he was still a jackass.

"Fine." I restrained the urge to let my claws out and shred all his folders. "I'll try to forget the fact that I speak German."

I shook my head. I might as well try to forget my own name. I had called myself an American for so long that I spoke, thought, and lived in English. But after all these years, I still dreamed in German.

Tell settled back, seemingly satisfied. He remained quiet, perusing his Manila files with their secret innards.

I tossed and turned and finally managed to catch some sleep, dreaming something I forgot when I woke up.

The plane landed at some anonymous Air Force base to refuel. Karen woke up the minute the plane's wheels touched the tarmac. Waking shortly before the plane touched down, I'd white-knuckled it for the entire landing.

"Stay here." Tell spoke to both of us, but mostly me. "We'll be airborne again shortly."

He disappeared down the short staircase and was gone for about an hour. He reappeared as the pilot, an Air Force lieutenant colonel with an exceptionally high security clearance, sent an announcement to take our seats and prepare for departure.

WHEN WE TOOK to the air again, Tell crowded us around a sheaf of papers he laid out across several seats.

"We have a few more hours before we pass into Kazakh airspace." Up close, Tell smelled of gun oil and something sharper, more unpleasant, that I couldn't name. "Before we land, I want to go over this one more time."

He held up a photo and showed it to us. "This man, who is he?"

"Name unknown." Karen fielded this one. "Mid-level Russian mafia operative. Possibly dabbling in drugs, but most likely a highly placed errand boy for the local syndicate."

"Yes." Tell held up another photo. "And this?"

My turn. "That's the whorehouse he prefers to visit."

"Brothel," said Tell, correcting my terminology.

"It's a house with whores." I kept my face neutral. "Whorehouse."

The plane shook with momentary turbulence, and the next couple of photos fell off the tray. I leaned down to pick them up.

The top photo showed a young girl, maybe about sixteen years old, beautiful, with fine cheekbones, thin features, and soft, curly blond hair. Her eyes were shadowed in the candid photo, which looked like it had been taken with the crappiest camera ever.

"Who is this?" I didn't know if I wanted to know.

"That's the girl he visits." Tell answered the question. "When we stopped to refuel, HQ sent these over."

He took the photo from me and handed it to Karen.

"This is our girl." He said it almost fondly. "Alia Nabieva. She'll be the one we get to the target through."

The idea left a bad taste in my mouth, tainted by memories of broken girls and sad eyes.

Tell saw something in my face. "She is important because she will deliver the target to us."

"I know." I tried not to growl. "I just don't remember MONIKER using girls to get to people." Pure bullshit—the organization had always used everything they could get their hands on to accomplish their tasks. But our memories of the past are often clouded. Mine more so than others.

Tell shrugged. "If you have an objection, take it up with corporate when we get back." He found another photograph and handed it to me. "But remember, you're here because we need you to bring the violence."

I looked at the photo. Karen looked down over my shoulder and then quickly looked away. I was staring at myself, or what the camera could capture of me, in the small room in Mexico. I crumpled the photo and tossed it on the floor.

"This isn't helping, Tell." Karen swallowed against the memories in the photo.

"I'm just trying to make a point."

"We got it." Karen frowned. "Let's move on."

It felt good to have Karen on my side, even if it was temporary, and she still did not seem to show any signs of thinking I was less of an asshole.

"So, Karen goes in, makes friends. We set up and get ready to come in after them when the target shows?" Even though we all knew the plan didn't mean I agreed with all the parts of it.

"That's the gist of it," Tell replied.

"That's an awesome plan." Sarcasm, my final retreat when I had nothing else to say and wanted to try to go back to sleep, seeped through my entire attitude.

"What's awesome about it?" Karen wasn't a fan of sarcasm, especially mine. "The fact that it wasn't your idea or that I'm the one going in?"

"Forget it." I put my hands in my pockets so Tell wouldn't hand me any more photos. "It's a good plan. We'll make it work."

Looking at both of us, Tell seemed unhappy. Karen looked unhappy, and I was unhappy. The plan would work if we functioned as a team. But I still had my doubts on that score, because we were anything but a team.

Tell picked up the crumpled photo from the floor and took back the ones we were still perusing. He put them in his folder and closed it. The stack of folders went into a thick plastic envelope he then closed with a clasp and put in his briefcase. Before he closed and locked the case, I caught a glimpse of a stack of passports, a metal cylinder, and other papers.

I was on board with the mission, but nothing would stop me from trying to plan for contingencies. He noticed me looking at the case.

"You think you want to try it?"

"Try what?" I blinked as innocently as possible.

"Focus on the mission." Tell pulled the case a little closer to his side. "There are a lot more girls where that one came from, and they all need our help."

He was right. I still didn't like him, but that didn't prevent him from being right. I shrugged, folded my arms, and leaned back in my seat. By this time, we were flying through the night. I opened my window shade and finally fell asleep to the sight of the intermittent wing lights winking against the top of the clouds.

11

The computer screen displayed an image much like a giant ball of twine. I tried to make sense of it, squinting, cocking my head, but nothing. I wanted to play with the image to get it to resolve itself and maybe tell me something, but Karen drove the controls on the equipment, so I got to sit in a corner of the van and behave myself.

We'd seen barely any traffic at the building. A pouring winter rain kept people away. Either that or there were very few tourists willing to visit Kazakhstan in the middle of winter. Not even the rich Westerners willing to pay for underage girls who were these sorts of places' stock-in-trade.

I hunkered down against the cold seeping through the windows and watched as a fat, middle-aged man levered himself out of a taxi and dashed across the street. He paused at the front of the building under a narrow awning and brushed the drops from his suit before opening the door.

"Another one." I wondered when we were going to get some lunch.

Karen did not look up from the screen. "Anyone we know?"

"Didn't recognize him." I thought I remembered a candy bar in the glove box. "Probably just another pedo looking to get laid."

Distaste showed in the sudden curl of her lips.

"What?" I recognized the grimace from the times it had been directed at me.

"Nothing." She adjusted the controls, distracted. "Except…"

I opened the glove box and rooted around but came up empty. "Except?" I prompted her.

"Except, I don't know…" She let the thought trail off into the dark.

I needed to move around a bit. I swung my legs around and shifted into a crouching position, leaning forward to look more closely at the computer.

"What is that program anyway?"

"CRIMAN." She tapped a few more keys, and the image rotated ninety degrees. It still looked like a ball of twine.

"So," I said. "What is that program anyway?"

"Sorry." She didn't look up. "Forgot you weren't read in. It's a program to analyze criminal intelligence."

"You use a computer to do that?" Doubt must have been apparent in my voice.

She leaned back from the computer to give me a closer look. "All it does is map our information. Take a look."

So I did. I used the mouse to scroll into the ball of twine. Zooming in, I saw a small, bifurcated circle, like one of the icons used to mark things on tactical maps.

I clicked on it, and the action highlighted and extracted an image of the small brothel we were surveilling. Someone had uploaded a picture of a girl and linked it in such a way that when the brothel extracted itself from the mass of twine, the girl's picture popped up as well. I recognized her as the favorite of the mid-level capo we were after. Yeah, this was the Russian mob, not the Italian, but I didn't know the currently fashionable name for lieutenants in the *vory v zakone*, or whatever they were calling it these days.

The girl's photo linked to several others, and the lines radiated outward up into the ball of twine, continuing throughout the web. I wondered just how MONIKER thought plucking one item would unravel the web and set the others loose, but maybe there were other teams in other locations looking at different areas of the map and wondering the same thing.

"Interesting." If you could understand twine.

Karen took the mouse back and zoomed out again.

"You can understand that looking at it so intensely?" I really needed something to eat.

"You can't?"

I looked back at the screen. I could no longer distinguish anything, and it actually made my head swim. I looked away and tried to swallow back bile. If she could make sense of it, she had an ability to grasp spatial geometry on the genius level.

A short knock sounded on the back of the van. Karen opened the door and let Tell in.

"All right." He closed the door behind him. "It's set."

Karen stepped back from the computer and took off her jacket, giving me my first look at her outfit. The short skirt and bodice top left little to the imagination, except to possibly imagine all the ways the laces could be put to good use.

"Don't have a heart attack." I thought she was talking to me, but the sudden acrid whiff I got from Tell let me know he was thinking the same things running through my hormones. I bit back a growl.

"Here." Tell slid some paper notes out of his pocket. I caught a glimpse of large numbers, and there were quite a few notes in the pile, but, the local economy being in the shitter, it was barely enough to buy her way in the door. Our cover story—a gift from a business associate, an addition to the local collection—would depend on Karen's ability to sell it. Literally.

She tucked the money into her pocket and opened the door at the back of the van.

"Be safe." I meant it, not a hint of my usual sarcasm. "Good hunting."

"Don't kill each other," she said and left. The silence after the door latched was, to put it mildly, uncomfortable.

Tell sat down at the console where Karen had been manning the equipment. I felt more than heard him swear under his breath and watched as he began readjusting every single dial, gauge, and reading display.

"Goddammit."

I regarded him with amusement. He wallowed in some kind of mood.

"How did you ever get into this line of work?" I watched him fiddle with the machine.

"What do you mean?" He didn't bother looking up from his adjustments.

"Unless MONIKER recruiting has changed drastically in the past decade, you seem a little different than their usual lead operative."

"Different how?"

"You're more of an asshole."

"And your excuse?" He made a series of minute adjustments to the last dial, then sat back satisfied. The video and audio feeds coming through sounded exactly the same to me. "Why did MONIKER spend all this time and money on you?"

I shrugged. "My charming personality?"

Tell snorted. Reaching into a pocket, he pulled out the pack of cigarettes he kept there. He had run out of his favorite brand a couple of days ago and been reduced to smoking something he found locally. They smelled worse and, I think, had some sort of hashish mixed in there.

"If you light that up, I'll kill you." Like I needed an excuse.

"If you don't like it, get bent." He flicked the lighter and filled the van with noxious fumes.

"I'm not joking."

Tell ignored me and turned up a dial on the equipment. "Shut it, fur boy. We've got feed coming through."

We watched the screen, and the image lightened and focused as the bouncer at the door opened it for Karen. I glanced away out the window at the door and growled under my breath as I saw her smile at him. He listened as she spoke, resting his hand on her ass. I wanted to remove his hand from her ass. With my teeth.

"Down, boy." Tell watched the screen with me. "She knows what she's doing."

Finally, they were inside, and the door closed, blocking our view. We hunkered back around the screen. The image was strictly point of view—and slightly shaking—beamed from one of the rhinestones beading the top of Karen's bodice.

The sound barely came through. The image looked kind of like a pixelated version of early silent films. A low buzz filled the mic, most likely ambient filler from the fluorescent lights lining the hallways of the cheap building. Every once in a while, there would be a *shurring* sound. At first, I could not figure out where it came from until I realized it happened every time Karen twisted her body. It was the sound of the mic rubbing against the shiny polyester fabric of her bodice.

"Can't you turn the sound up a little?"

"Nope." Tell took a drag on his cigarette and aimed the exhale in my direction. "The equipment isn't that good. If I turn it up, we'll just get noise."

"Typical." Trying not to breathe, I thought about kicking the terminal but refrained. There was nothing to be done. As per standard MONIKER operating procedure, we had purchased much of the equipment off the shelf and were stuck making what we had work for what we needed.

"If you keep running your mouth, it'll be harder to hear."

I shut up and went back to watching the screen. I'm not the best at sitting in a chair and watching television.

THE BROTHEL WAS NOT one of the higher-end models. There were no rooms of scantily clad, starving supermodels waiting to be chosen by good-looking johns. Rather, there were small rooms with doorways covered mostly by sheets and a few cheap wooden doors.

Karen turned to look in at some of them. None of the girls inside looked like they were over thirteen, and the few that did appear as if they were reaching puberty looked like they would not survive it. The men captured by Karen's screen looked pasty, old, overweight—the residue of too much good, if not necessarily clean, living.

"There she is." Tell pointed. "That's Alia."

I squinted, trying to see. On the screen, the curly-haired girl from the photo on the plane got up from a narrow bed and came to greet Karen and the bouncer escorting her. The point of view made it look like we were the ones she welcomed. I felt slightly sick.

After her initial glance, she barely acknowledged the rest of Karen's entrance, fixing the curtain to cover the doorway and returning to the bed where she curled up on the flat pillow.

The plan called for Karen to have a chance to talk to the girl before they were interrupted. If you counted all the swear words, Karen could speak fairly good, if grammatically horrifying, Russian with an accent someone could take for any of several Eastern European or Central Asian countries.

We didn't have a lot of time, thus the extremely rudimentary nature of the plan—the kindest thing you could say about it. Still, it was the best we could come up with, and like all of our plans so far, it took a nosedive almost before it even started.

The first time Karen tried to talk to the girl, she merely turned over in the bed. Faced with her back, Karen stood up and walked closer. She started to sit down on the bed, but the girl jerked up and struck out.

She spat out a string of Kazakh of which I understood not a word, but that conveyed unmistakable intent. She pushed Karen and pointed someplace off the bed.

"I'm here to help." Karen spoke in Russian. "Do you understand me? What's your name?"

The girl ignored her.

"Listen to me." Karen's voice faded in and out with the mic, which seemed to be slipping. "I have friends. They want to help you. Do you want to get out of here?"

The girl slowly turned her head to gaze impassively at Karen. For a minute, it seemed like she was looking straight at us.

"Please," she said, in very heavily accented Russian. "Leave me alone."

"I can't." Karen hadn't moved from the bed. "There are two men who want to meet you."

"They got money, they can meet me." Alia shrugged and curled back up on the bed. A harsh silence stretched out for several minutes.

In the van, I became acutely aware of the sounds of traffic outside the closed doors of the vehicle, the muffled static under the humming from the mic, and the tapping of Tell's fingernails on the plastic dashboard.

Inside the room, Karen got up, adjusted her bodice, and sat gently on the bed. This time the girl didn't move. We watched as she used her index and middle fingers to gently brush some of the girl's hair away from her face. The girl tensed, and I thought this might be the first time in a long while someone had touched her for a reason other than owning her for an hour or so.

"What's your name?" Karen tried again.

The girl spoke so softly that I barely heard her response through the noise coming through the mic. "Alia."

The next part of the conversation came through unintelligible. We saw the girl close up, giving short answers. Mostly, she nodded at whatever Karen said. She drifted closer. Finally, she came so close that her body obscured the lens.

We were blind for a time. Deaf, too. I did not like it. In fact, I thought it was time to initiate the contingency plan where I got to go in the brothel and find out what was happening. Tell did not, and so I sat in the van and started to feel sicker to my stomach with every passing moment.

Finally, the girl pulled back, and I looked up and saw her nod, eyes closed. Karen used a corner of the sheet to dab at Alia's eyes. The girl wore so much cheap makeup all Karen did was smear dark black mascara across her eyes and cheeks. I started to breathe again.

Tell looked at me and smiled, but I noticed he expelled his breath a little more forcefully than normal.

"Nervous?"

"Nope." I forced myself to calm. "Looks like she's got it locked down."

Of course, that was when the curtain rolled back, and the plan started to roll downhill.

"HEY, two for the price of one!" The man at the door was tall but not well-built, running to fat, and definitely not the guy we were looking for. "I'm not paying extra for both you bitches."

"Shit." Karen's reaction was short and profane. If our target showed up, this other man's presence might encourage him to find another girl—or scare him away. Or possibly, if our target was high enough up in the bad guy food chain, get rid of the interloper in ways that might turn unpleasant for the women. In any case, the new guy had to go.

I growled and began to stand. Tell put a hand on my arm. I shook it off.

"Just wait." Tell tensed. "Let Karen handle it."

I didn't like it. The picture on the screen had gone completely dark. The ambient sound coming through the mic had melded into an unhelpful mess of distortion and fabric scratching. I could hear someone saying something but couldn't make out the words.

"What if—" I started to ask again.

"Keller." Tell rolled his shoulders back, cracking tension out of his neck. "Let her handle it."

I hate letting other people handle things. "By the time we let her handle it—"

"Sit your ass back down, or else when she gets back here, I'll tell her how you don't think she can handle herself," Tell snapped. "I'm going to enjoy watching the hijinks that ensue."

I really wanted to choke this guy. The view on the screen finally lightened and then resolved itself. It still came through so grainy and dark we could barely see what was going on, but I could make out the outline of a body on the floor.

"Help me with him." Karen's voice came through scratchy but readable. On the screen, her shadow partially blocked the view. We watched as the two women pushed and shoved the man's body under one of the beds and pulled the sheet down over the gap to hide him from view. It looked like he was still alive. Probably.

"Everything okay in there?" Tell sent the question through the mic.

"Yeah." Karen was breathing hard but evenly. "He'll wake up with a headache, but nothing permanently damaged." She sounded regretful. "Any visual on our guy?"

"Nothing yet." Tell spared a quick view, scrolling through the van's exterior camera. "Seems like a slow night."

"Figures." Karen sat back down on the bed.

In the van, I fidgeted in my seat, wishing I could pace. The adrenaline and frustration were ramping up inside me, and I had been ready to let them loose; and although glad Karen had handled the situation and our plan hadn't gone to shit yet, I found it hard to push the need for action back down inside me.

"Look sharp, we've got company." Tell accentuated the statement by grinding out his cigarette against his boot heel and flicking it to the floor.

I turned to watch the screen.

A car pulled up and parked with the engine running. A man got out and went to the door.

"That's him?" I squinted again. I'm really bad at picking out faces on screens. "How the hell can you tell?"

Tell leaned over the front seat and looked out the window. "Yep. That's him."

"Goddammit." My leg had fallen asleep.

"You get that, Willet?" Tell asked through the speakers.

"Yeah, we're ready." Karen stood. On the screen, we watched as the room shifted and tilted upright.

"He's at the door." Tell fumbled with the controls, his fingers shaking slightly. "His driver is waiting for him. Car's still on. Looks like he's planning to hit it quick."

"We'll be ready for him."

THE THING about working in a team of three out on your lonesome is there's never any convenient backup to call when the target gets twitchy and pulls a gun on one of you. Things went well up to the point where the target entered the room and saw Karen there.

At that moment, the guy under the bed chose to wake up and pitch a fit, finding himself in the close darkness.

"What the fuck?" The target spoke in harsh, surprised Russian, and that's when the gun came out, glinting briefly in the little bit of light. The screen went black again.

"That's it, I'm going in." I jerked open the door and headed out the back of the van before Tell could get any bright ideas about stopping me.

I stumbled slightly as the cold hit me, my numb leg twisting under me briefly, but the sounds of scuffling and grunting coming through my earpiece kept me scrambling.

The driver saw me exit the van and, not being any stranger to a life of crime, knew I was probably someone he wanted to stop from going into the whorehouse. He came out of the car fast, gun up and ready, but the change rode me now, and he ended up on the ground, broken and rolling to get away. I left him there and headed for the front door.

A gun discharged inside. I felt the vibration and heard it both muffled through the front door and piercing through the earbud. I dug it out of my ear and tossed it on the ground, hoping I wouldn't be permanently deafened.

With my good ear up against the door, I tried to listen, and then sniffed experimentally. All I tasted were confusion and adrenaline. Standing back, I grasped for the change, lifted my knee, and kicked the door hard.

It splintered, and I kicked it again. This time it fell open, and I stepped over it on my way inside. One of my eardrums felt completely busted. The imbalance had me weaving like a prizefighter on the receiving end of a Joe Louis barrage. Through the dark smells of pain, I caught a faint thread of rosemary and began reeling it in.

The halls were crowded. Men and women, interrupted in whatever they were doing, milled through the hall, trying to find a way out, or trying to make their way to where the shot came from. I helped the former on their way with a swift kick in whatever area I found conveniently available. The others I dropped as quickly and permanently as I could. The flickering fluorescent lights added an extra strobing distraction.

I smelled something sick. Something rotten. It smelled of weakness, and I felt my canines respond. Saliva pooled at the back of my throat.

A man gestured toward me, lowering his gun. I heard a scream, and then it was teeth and claws and horror show shadows on the ceiling.

I painted the walls with my progress toward where Karen and the girl awaited.

Around the corner, I recognized the hallway from Karen's earlier entry. The curtain was closed, and I hoped to find everyone inside still in one piece. Or at least two of them. The curtain rustled and opened.

Karen stepped out, supporting the girl who stumbled forward on unsteady legs. Tears streamed down her face, but she made not a sound.

"He's back there." Karen nodded. "Disarmed. He was too heavy."

I didn't believe her, but I didn't stop to make a big deal out of it. Giving her a quick nod, I ran toward the room. The first man lay on his back in a rapidly spreading black pool of blood.

The target was heavier than his picture. I tried to heft him over my shoulders in a fireman's carry. The smell of borscht and gas threatened to bring me to my knees. I pulled the half-change back and stepped into the corridor, closing my senses against the different smells speeding around me.

A man with a gun tripped over a girl who had run into the hallway. He pushed her roughly to the side and raised the weapon. It was large, of a caliber that would probably pass through me and into the target. In the interest of mission success, I dumped the target and leapt for the man with the gun.

It would have felt good to sink my teeth into him, but I tore myself away. There was no time to stop for a snack. I stayed on two legs and hefted the businessman back onto my shoulders.

I emerged from the brothel, firing a few rounds back into the doorway with the automatic weapon I liberated from one of the poor saps who'd tried to stop me. I stopped short.

In front of the van, Tell and Karen faced each other. From the looks on their faces, they were in deep disagreement about something. I smelled something strange from Tell. It smelled of death and intent.

"She's not coming with us," Tell shouted. "You shouldn't have brought her."

"She's coming with us." Karen had a hand on her gun. "She'll be killed if we leave her here."

"Not our problem." Tell reached out to grab for Alia.

I growled at Tell as I dumped the target in the back of the van, kicking his legs to get him all the way in before slamming the door.

"Hey, asshole."

"What do you want, furry?" Tell demanded.

I smiled a toothy grin, and punched him in the face. Twice. He dropped like a rock.

"She's coming with." I considered punching him in the face again. "Get in the van, you two."

Picking up Tell by the scruff of his neck, I wrangled him into the back and slammed the door. Settling myself in the driver's seat, I jerked the key on and fishtailed the van as we peeled out, leaving behind the building of death and pain.

WE DIDN'T GO BACK to the hotel we were staying at, driving several hours instead to put everything behind us. At first, the girl seemed too shell-shocked to say much, but the farther we got from the brothel, the more agitated she became.

After about an hour, Tell stirred. I don't think my fist knocked him out that long. He was just tired. Also, every time he stirred, I kicked him in the head until he stopped. Juvenile—yet fulfilling.

I angled my foot back to kick him again, hovering my left foot over the brake. The sound of the hammer on my own .38 cocking back stopped me. I looked over my shoulder and down the barrel. Tell looked really pissed.

"Stop the van," he said.

I slammed my foot on the brake. We skidded off onto the shoulder. The engine sputtered and died.

"Get out." Tell motioned with my gun.

I opened the door and got out of the van. He scrambled out after me, keeping the gun trained.

"You know those bullets aren't even going to slow me down?"

"Shut the hell up." His finger rested in the trigger well. "If I shoot you in the face, it will slow you down."

I shrugged. "You can try."

He raised the weapon, but I was no longer there. I launched myself upward, my jaws gaping open to snap down on his neck.

"Stop!" The silver bullet lodged in my side, catching me in mid-leap. I fell to the ground, whimpering, and stared back up at Karen, clutching the hole in my side. Luckily, she was using a small caliber, and the round had exited after leaving only a shallow channel under the skin.

"Fuck." I rolled over. The half-change had left my shirt in tatters, and the bullet finally finished the damage. "Why is it every time he acts like an asshole, I'm the one who gets shot?"

"Shut it." No sympathy. "Get in the van. Both of you. We need to get these two someplace safe."

We got back in the van. This time, Tell hopped into the driver's seat, and I got to ride in the back with the target. Our fearless leader drove worse than I did, and I found myself flailing in the back without the benefit of seatbelts. The man had gotten sick somewhere along the ride, and I spent much of the next hour while my side tried to heal attempting to avoid rolling in the borscht-hued pile of vomit.

The girl looked at me, then at Tell.

"What is going on?" she spoke again in poorly accented Russian.

"Don't worry about it; you're okay," I replied in the same language.

"Your friend shot you." She didn't look reassured.

"Not my friend." I tried to smile, but she flinched. I closed my mouth and tried to look harmless. Not my best look. "And we'll take care of it when we get to the—" I stopped. I said in English, "Hey, where the hell are we going?"

"There's a safe house set up shortly over the border," Karen replied. "We'll stop there."

"Don't worry." I didn't bother smiling again, but somehow she seemed more reassured by that. "We'll take care of you." I might have been making promises I couldn't keep. But I'd be damned if I would let Tell drop her off in the middle of nowhere with no friends, papers, or money.

12

Getting over the border turned out to be not so fun. We stopped a few miles short, pulling off to the side of the road. Most of the electronics and suspicious gear could be easily fitted into boxes and stacked on the floor. Rolling the floor rug over them turned the van into just another crappy old jalopy with a bunch of junk in the back.

We immediately ran up against a problem. The only papers prepared were enough for the team and the target. Short of dumping the girl on the road to make her way over the border, we were stuck. By this time, the man had started to stir and come around. We let him scream and yell for a short time before Karen stuck him in the neck with something, sending him quickly back to dream land. He sank back into the back of the van with a goofy smile on his face.

I had moved off a bit away from the van to take a leak—and check my pants for embarrassing tears I might have missed.

"Keller!" I turned to see Karen waving at me.

"Be right there." I zipped up and headed back to see what they had come up with.

I wiped my hands on my pants as I walked up. "We figure something out?"

"Yeah." Tell smiled. "You're not going to like it."

"What is he talking about?" I directed the question to Karen.

"This." She nodded. Alia came out from around the back of the van. I could see why they thought I was going to be pissed. She wore my change of pants and my only other shirt. My Yankees cap covered her head, hiding her curls and androgenizing her features. She wasn't a perfect match for the fuzzy passport photo carrying my name, but with the right amount of financial grease, she would pass.

"Okay," I said. "So she takes my paperwork, and I take what? A really long walk?"

"You've got two choices." Tell's grin really unnerved me. "You make your own way over the border." He smiled even wider. "Or my favorite, you come along as the family Fido."

"Damn it, Tell, the change is not—" I choked off what I was going to say. I did not want to have this conversation. Not here, not now. Maybe not ever.

"What's wrong?" Alia asked in Russian.

"Nothing." I shook my head. "Don't be worried; my friends will take care of you." I smiled as convincingly as I could. "Go ahead, hop back in the van. They'll make sure you get across safely."

I waited until she headed back into the van and started pulling off my shoes and pants. I looked straight at Tell. "Don't even think of trying to dump her, or I will let her see me."

"Whatever." Tell shrugged. "Just get on with it."

I growled at him and reached inside of myself. The change came reluctantly, curling further in on itself. It felt weird standing there naked, trying to bring it on in broad daylight without the strength of emotion or pull of the moon to coax it out. I shook myself and grasped harder, twisting my insides and finally finding that click inside me that signaled getting through the barrier of civilization and skin. Ripping it away from my consciousness should not have been so hard. I gritted my back teeth against the stubborn pain and pushed through.

I shook myself, getting the kinks out of my spine. I felt a click on my neck and lunged forward only to be jerked back on my feet. I backed up, trying to wriggle the collar chain off of my head, but it was laced with silver, and Tell simply jerked it and hauled me into the van. I would kill him eventually. It was only a matter of how soon after this mission ended.

───────

THE PLAN SUCKED, at least for me, curled up in the back, tied like a dog to one of the metal seats' supports. The border guards were snoopy and suspicious, but they liked the smell of the euros Tell slipped them in the folded paperwork. They flirted with Karen, still dressed in her hooker best, laughed at the man passed out in the back seat with the empty vodka bottle cradled in his arms, and ignored Alia. We did our best to appear like a van full of men returning from a really good time.

I closed my eyes and pretended to be a good dog. It worked, and we soon put several miles behind us.

───────

THE SAFE HOUSE turned out to be an old farmstead that had seen much better days. The electricity hadn't worked in years, if ever, and the heat came from an actual fireplace. Water came from a pump that drew up more sludge than water. I couldn't find much to like about it, but at least it would be temporary. Tell had made the arrangements, much like everything else on this trip. Twenty years ago, I would have been able to do the same. Except I probably would have been able to find someplace with indoor plumbing.

I lit a piece of kindling, stoking the fire as Karen brought in a pail of water and Tell brought in the lump of a businessman. We had stopped at a small store when we got gas, and Alia busied herself with sandwiches and a bottle of vodka.

"Keller." Karen's voice held an uncharacteristically hesitant note under her normal innate confidence.

"What is it?" I pushed the burning embers closer to one another, using an old newspaper to fan the small flames.

"We need to figure out what to do with Alia," she said.

"Yeah." I kept stirring the fire, not wanting to deal with our problem at the moment. "Knock her out and dump her in the van's probably not going to work."

"Can you be serious for five minutes?"

"Sure." I left off messing about with the fire to give her a wiseass grin. "About twenty years ago. You missed it."

"Jesus Christ, Keller."

A spark leapt out of the fireplace and landed on the top of my hand. I swore and brushed it off.

"Sorry." I stood up, slapping my hands on my pants. "I get cranky when people put a leash and collar on me without first asking for a safe word."

"I didn't know he was going to do that." She sounded almost apologetic.

"Forget it." I didn't want an apology from her. "We've got bigger problems."

Alia looked up at us from across the room. I tried to smile reassuringly at her. I don't think she believed me.

"I couldn't leave her," Karen said in German.

"I know," I replied in the same language. "But she does complicate things."

The object of our conversation guessed we were talking about her and frowned, pausing in the sandwich making. I tried smiling again. This time I think I scared her.

"What do you suggest?"

"I have no idea." I really didn't, but I took a stab at it. "Try to keep Tell from dumping her, find out where she came from, and try to get her back there?"

WE WOULD HAVE to question Alia to find out the best thing to do with her, but the immediate concern came from her boyfriend, who Tell was tying into a chair in the other room. Tell and Karen had agreed he would take the lead on the investigation, with Karen playing the good cop and me being the backup furry muscle—and the Russian, if Karen's Berlitz course failed her when it came to asking tough gangster questions.

Karen took first crack at him. She found a rag and poured some cold water into a bowl. Soaking the rag, she squeezed it out and wiped his forehead. He started to come around, at first slowly, then jerking his head back from her grasp when it dawned on him he was alive and also not where he had fallen asleep.

"Shhh." Karen tried to calm him. "Try to relax."

He struggled against the ropes, but Tell was good at knots, and the man did not make it anywhere. "Where am I?" He added a few Russian curse words I don't think Tell caught.

"Don't worry about that." Tell stood back, blurred by the shadows. "Just answer the fucking questions."

"What's your name?" Karen tried again.

His accent reminded me of the short time I had spent in Moscow.

"Mikhail." He looked around, but I don't think he saw me. He let his gaze return to Karen. "What do you want with me?"

She smiled. "Just some information."

He looked confused. "Who are you?"

"Keep asking questions instead of answering them, and we'll let our friend play with you for a little while."

This was my cue. I growled at him from the shadows, but my heart wasn't really in it, and I'm not sure if I scared him at all.

"Mikhail," Karen said. "By now, people are going to realize you are the one we took out of the brothel. You could answer some questions, and we could slip you back wherever you like with no one the wiser. Or, you can not answer some questions, and not only will you feel a good deal of pain, but we will make sure you are returned in the most suspicious way possible." If she was the good cop, I was a toaster strudel.

"Look at him." Tell sneered. "He doesn't know anything. We might as well pop him right now and dump him out back." So, maybe she was the good cop.

I know I was supposed to be the scary bystander, but I was getting impatient. I stalked forward.

"What are you doing?" Karen turned her attention to me.

"Moving things along."

I gently pushed her out of the way and straddled the chair. He felt soft under his clothes. I could hear his heart beating against his ribs like a bat caught in a floodlight. "Look at him." I laughed. It sounded like an echo in the room.

I grabbed his shirt and tore it, ripping it and exposing his upper body under the ropes.

"What the hell are you doing?"

"Nice tattoos." I laughed. "How many of these did you actually earn?"

"Who are you?" I sensed confusion and rank fear. "Where are you from?"

My accent returned. He stared at me with a panic he had not yet shown.

"Don't ask me any questions," I said. "If you ask one more question, I will kill you."

"What—" He choked his own words off. "I—"

"What about this one?" I pointed to the scarred patterns immediately below his collarbone. "Did you give yourself this one?"

I slapped him across the face. "Are you going to answer me?"

"No." He gritted his teeth, preparing himself for the pain he expected to come.

"You are a pathetic little john." I laughed and jumped off him. "Were you in that brothel because you like girls? Or because you like boys, and you don't want anyone to know?"

"Fuck you." He spat at me.

I slapped him again, right across the face. "Don't do that again."

"Or what?" His voice shook only slightly, braver than it should have been by the lack of significant violence so far.

"Or I will take you apart with a rusty pair of pliers, starting with your balls and ending with your teeth." I smiled, and this time I meant it.

"Rick." Tell spoke.

I ignored him. I kept eye contact with the man, raised my hand, and allowed him to watch the first moments of the change. His eyes widened, and he tried to lean back from me.

"What are you?"

"That was a question," I pointed out. "Do you want to die, my fake gangster friend?"

He maintained control of his face, but a spreading stain on his slacks betrayed his discomfiture.

"That is what I thought." I stepped toward him again, suddenly, filling his field of vision with teeth, fangs, violence. "Answer the question, or after I take you apart, I will eat you."

I pushed him to the side, chair scraping and sliding across the floor, and left the room. I heard a moment of silence.

"What is your name?" Karen asked again.

I did not hear his reply. My right ear still rang from the previous night. I closed my nose against the sharp scent of the uric acid following me from the room. Alia looked up, gazing at me with wide-open eyes. I tried to remember if I had swallowed the change, but it sat on the surface, waiting to be let loose.

"Don't go in there," I said to her, keeping away from the fire. "Just stay out here, and you'll be safe."

More promises I didn't know if I could keep. But I needed to leave the house, and so I stumbled out the front door, leaving my clothes and the rest of my civilization on the front porch, stretching my legs as I bounded out into the cold Russian night.

MY RUN LASTED ALL NIGHT. My breath drew in sharp and cold in my lungs, the snow drifting against my body where I plunged through the drifts. There were a few lights in the distance, and I directed my steps away from them.

The moon shone bright, almost full, and her light followed me under the trees. I found a clearing and sat back on my haunches, howling my pleasure at the freedom. Spent, I threw myself on my back and rolled back and forth, reveling in the cold and the energy that the night sent through me. Sated, I rolled myself back to my feet. I shook the snow from my fur and continued on my path.

I made it back to the house as the moon set and the first hints of nautical twilight began to seep through the woods, resolving the general outlines of the trees and boulders in the gloom. I wanted to be back inside and away from inquiring eyes before civil twilight hit and things became clearly distinguishable. Getting shot will not kill me, but a hide full of buckshot sucks balls.

I came back into the house. From Alia's look and Karen's expression, I realized I had forgotten an important part of my post-change routine. I backed out, retrieved my clothes from the porch, and dressed. They were damp and wet, which was uncomfortable, but since Alia still wore my spare change of fashion, they would have to do.

I tried again with the entrance, and this time they ignored me. The team was eating, and my stomach growled.

"So?" I picked up a piece of bread and looked from one to another. "Any luck?"

"Some," Tell said.

"Meaning?"

"Meaning that we got some leads," Karen said.

"And?" I prompted again, starting to feel like I was the one trying to pull an interrogation session out of my ass.

"And we've got a really long drive ahead of us," Tell replied. "So eat your fucking bread and get in the van."

On that note, he stomped out of the house.

"Come on, Alia." Karen stood, holding her hand out to the girl. "Let's go."

"Wait." I crammed the remainder of the bread in my mouth and grabbed the rest of the bag. "What about Mikhail?"

Karen looked at the door after Tell, then back at me. She shook her head. "Come on." She took Alia by the hand and led her outside.

I finished chewing and swallowed. Briefly, I debated going back into the room. I sniffed the air, just a shallow test, but the scent of violent death told me all I needed to know about what had happened in there.

They'd left nothing important in the house, so I went out the door and got into the van.

13

The ride this time involved switching vehicles three times, crossing borders twice, and catching a ride on a boat Tell insisted was seaworthy, but I preferred to think of as a floating death trap. We ended up on an anonymous island off the coast of Greece, the shore beckoning under the night sky.

"MONIKER pulled some strings out from under some rocks and got back to us with the names and locations of a few of the local recipients of girls from Central Asia and Eastern Europe."

I jumped. Standing at the bow, watching the shore, I'd missed Karen's approach. My mind was miles away, somewhere up past the shoreline.

"They send word about Alia?" I took a minute to bask in her standing nearby, with no Tell or Alia to interrupt. The smell of rosemary mingled with the salt.

"I'm sorry, Rick," she said. "No word yet."

"Which means they're not going to help her." I wondered when I became so invested in the girl's future.

"Probably not."

I appreciated her honesty, but I didn't like the answer. I shook my head. "Typical. Don't know why I expected anything different."

"Don't worry." She stood close to me, elbows on the rail, looking out over the dark sea. "We'll help her. We'll just have to do it unofficially."

A noise behind me caused us both to turn. Alia was coming up the stairs. She had started sharing a cabin with Tell shortly after we boarded after Karen and I had both turned her down. I hadn't been interested in taking advantage of a kid who'd just been through the crap she'd been through. At the time, I could scent that Karen had been physically interested but far too professional and honorable to let on. I wasn't surprised. Her grandmother had been the same way. Hell, so were half the women in the O.S.S. Whatever she was looking for, I didn't think Agent Tell was going to make it happen for her, and that didn't prove anything except that he was an asshole. And I already knew that.

She made it to the top of the stairs and looked at us both.

"Hey, honey." Karen didn't smile. "How are you doing?"

She shrugged.

"You want to come up here?" I secretly hoped she would stay downstairs. The smell of her sweat was doing things to me I had spent a long time repressing. She looked nervous, but anxious, like she didn't understand her own reaction.

"I make coffee." She barely spoke broken English, but a few phrases came through. "You want?"

"Yes, please." I wanted her to go before I embarrassed myself. "Karen?"

She shook her head. "No, thanks."

"Okay." Alia hesitated as if there were something she wanted to say but couldn't find the words. "Bye."

She turned and went back below. She left the hatch open, and the warm light from beneath the deck streamed out to accent the dark.

I looked over at Karen. Standing at the rail, her face profiled in chiaroscuro from the artificial light, she looked suddenly familiar and alien at the same time. It was uncanny how closely she resembled her grandmother. For a moment, I was standing on another deck in another sea more than sixty years ago.

"Keller?" Her voice snapped me back to the present. "You there?"

"Yeah." I tried to shake it off. "Sorry. It's just, for a second, you reminded me of..."

We stood in silence for a while. Finally, Karen opened her mouth to say more but was interrupted by Alia coming back up the stairs. She balanced two coffee mugs, one in each hand.

When she reached the deck, a slow but sudden wave rocked the boat. Alia put a foot wrong, and I reached out to keep her from falling. The touch of her, sudden and still burning from her time below, was overwritten with a black sadness that threatened to suck me in as I stood there. I swallowed the bitterness rising to the back of my throat and let go of her.

"You like?" She held out both mugs. One contained black coffee, and the other mug was white with cream. "You choose?"

I normally take cream in my coffee, but I reached for the black. "Thanks, Alia."

She smiled and offered the other mug to Karen. "You want?"

Karen reached out and took it. "Thanks."

She gave us both a quick smile and then turned to go.

"Alia," I said. She paused at the top of the stairs. "If you could—" I stopped and began again in Russian. "Where do you want to go?"

"I must leave?" She answered in the same language, which she spoke much better. I wondered why she kept trying to speak English. Maybe because Tell wouldn't speak anything else.

"No—yes. We just want to know what you want to do next, so we can help you." I felt like a condescending jackass. "Do you—your family. Do you want us to send you back to them?"

She looked at me like I was the most naïve son of a bitch she'd ever met. She shook her head.

"America." She said it with deep reverence, the sort of longing for my adopted country I'd seen before.

I remembered feeling like that. I remembered the promise one simple word could hold. Shaking myself, I shoved those feelings back down deep, because that sort of stupid sentimentality could get you killed, or, as my present circumstance held proof enough, convince you to volunteer for things you had no business sniffing out. I shook my head and opened my mouth to ask another question, but Karen beat me to it.

"Are you sure?" Karen prodded. "You wouldn't rather be with your people?"

Alia shook her head. She looked at me like she wanted to say more but instead shrugged and walked back down the stairs, closing the door and cutting off the light behind her.

I caught my breath against the blackness I'd felt when I touched her and leaned against the rail again. We were caught up in the same predicament many people before us faced when dealing with the victims of human trafficking.

Most of them had been trying to escape extreme poverty, family abuse, repressive governments, and any number of bad situations normal people sitting comfortably around their televisions and reality shows could not even comprehend. The girls, and when it came to forced labor, the men as well, were stuck—they could not return home. There were few countries—even ones with such an ostensibly big dream as the United States—that welcomed them and their problems to their shores. I shook my head.

"Keller?" Karen spoke softly. "I might know some people who could maybe help."

"That's great," I said. "Help when? After Tell decides he's tired of the free sex?"

"You're not being fair." She frowned. "She can do what she wants."

"She doesn't know what she wants." I tried to avoid sarcasm and ended up sounding more bitter than I wanted. "And you should know that."

Her face betrayed her thoughts, but I already knew she thought I was an asshole. Still, I sensed something else there. The anger and loathing, I thought—I felt—was directed inward. It stemmed from more than one lost little girl.

"Karen—what did you do with the target back at the safe house?"

She did not answer.

"Karen?"

"What do you think?" She turned, glaring at me. "He's dead."

"Huh." I avoided making eye contact, watching instead the patterns of light streaking across the water. "An asset like that, and he's suddenly just dead?" My heart wasn't really in it, but I said it anyway.

"We got the information we needed," she said. "What more would he give us?"

I stared at her. MONIKER had changed in thirty years. Scratch that, MONIKER appeared to be the same as ever. But something went wrong somewhere if Margaret's granddaughter was telling me torturing an asset to death was the way things were done now.

"Don't be so damn naïve." Karen broke yet another awkward silence. "And fuck you, by the way. At least we didn't rip out his guts and eat them on the floor."

I felt the change stir in response to the image in my head. This time it didn't come physically, at least not in the normal sense. Rather, the energy of the change with the sounds that started below combined to send the night rushing through me again. I clamped my hands more tightly around the cup of coffee, now going slowly cold.

"Do you want me to apologize for who I am?" I poured the coffee out over the rail. "Should I say I'm sorry that after all these years, your organization suddenly decided they couldn't live without me, kidnapped me, and pumped me so full of silver I'm still having trouble controlling what I'm doing?"

"No, Keller." She looked suddenly tired. "I'm saying that I know you are what you are. But you've been hiding from the world so long you forgot what it's like. And what's necessary to do our job." She kept her voice from shaking, but her words were hollow and lacked conviction.

She stood back from the rail. "I'm going below. We'll be docking tomorrow."

I hesitated. "Karen—"

"Yeah?"

"I'm sorry." I tried to find the right words but didn't even come close. "You're a good operative."

She paused at the top of the stairs and looked back at me. Once again, I thought I saw someone else standing there, half hidden in the shadow. "Forget it." I thought she might have half smiled at me, but that could just have been the memory riding me.

I FELL in love with Margaret, but she was married and faithful to some man who worked in an office on Madison Avenue. She carried a picture of him in her wallet, even when it would have been safer to leave all personal mementos behind like everybody else did—especially a photo of a bona fide American war hero in his aviator jacket standing next to the first plane to get shot down from under him. After the second and then the third time that happened, the powers that be decided the fourth time might not be the charm and discharged him back to civilian life where he continued his heroic do-gooder habits by making radio commercials selling Victory Bonds.

The smell of her hair drove me insane, but an absent war hero meant more to her than the war criminal she shared a foxhole with, and even though I knew people sometimes gossiped about the two of us, I was sad to say they were not even close to guessing what actually went on. Or didn't, as the case happened to be.

Margaret reminded me of winter when I was growing up in Bavaria. Later, after the time we spent together running with the partisans in Eastern Europe, living in northern New Jersey, I remembered stark sepia trees against grave mounds of silver, snow threaded by steel, the gray veins of rural roads, and the muted sounds of traffic passing in the snow. I had wanted to tell her all of this, but she was a smart woman, and every time I gathered my courage and forged ahead with my intentions to come clean, she redirected the conversation.

She was fierce and kind, and like her granddaughter, she thought I was an asshole. Unlike her granddaughter, she also thought I could be saved. And I desperately wanted to prove her right.

WE DOCKED the next day at a small port and did the old passport switch up again. I resumed my furry disguise, and the others made excuses for me to Alia, which, judging by the acute way she stared at me, she did not half believe. We waited at the dock while Tell haggled with a short, dark man who forked over cash for the boat. He used the money to rent a car, a small, black unflashy thing that mostly fit all of us. Given two of us had no luggage, there turned out to be enough room in the trunk for the small amount of Tell's gadgets we had been able to retrieve from the van.

I "met up" with them a short way down the road in the next village. They stopped to fill up with petrol. I trotted away on all fours and returned in the clothing Karen unobtrusively left for me behind the station. The countryside was beautiful, even in the winter, and even though we had not yet made our way north, the soil beneath my feet felt familiar and comforting.

Getting back into the car, we headed north, striking a path for southern Germany. We were keeping a low profile, just four friends from Eastern Europe saving their rubles for a tour through the territory of their richer, Western cousins. I knew we had larger things to worry about, such as the fact we were heading to find the boss of the man we had killed in cold blood in a Russian farmhouse, but the small things made me happy. Real coffee, pastries without a ton of processed sugar, and the feel of ancient soil when I went for my nightly run. I was returning home, and even though I had left for all the right reasons, it felt so damn good to be going back.

THE TRIP TOOK a little longer than expected. Or at least longer than Tell expected. I had not been in the area for years, and everything remained unfamiliar to my sense of direction. Only when we crossed the border into Bavaria, back into a place so ingrained in my genes I would never scrub it out, did I feel I had come home.

Tell stopped right before the border at a small roadside rest stop. There was a little café, and the women and I indulged in some strong coffee, which affected me more intensely than usual. The proximity to my former home and the first night of the full moon crept under my skin and made my blood race. Tonight, I would definitely not be staying in my room. I would need to run outside, chasing the *Blutschuld* of the Green Man, until my paws bled.

I hoped Tell would find some time to arrange some papers for Alia or at least come up with some sort of identity better than the one they originally put together for me. I thought he might have warmed to her, but he said nothing as we went.

I looked at the two women talking to each other. Karen had made an effort to engage Alia more since the time on the boat. The two of them were holding a strange conversation, Karen speaking in Russian, Alia practicing English, at which she continued to improve. They could not talk about much more than the weather or the coffee, but they had found something to laugh about.

Women's laughter usually sets my teeth on edge. This is not a sexist thing, although I have been accused of that. It's just that I can hear the textures of fakery within the smile, the underlying false notes admitting, "I don't find this funny at all, but I'm laughing because it's expected."

This was the first time I heard Karen laugh—the first full moment of honesty I had experienced in a while.

Alia's laughter came more hesitantly, like she had forgotten what the muscles did and what they were there for. I noticed she would smile somewhat, then smile wider, and at the first hint of a laughing sound, would immediately close her mouth and hide her face in her shoulder.

I sat at the table, putting the second round of espressos in front of everyone.

"What's so funny?"

"I'm trying to explain that reality show about the kids at the beach," Karen said.

I looked at her, then Alia, then back, not sure if they were laughing at me or at their shared joke.

"Well, don't look at me." I shrugged. "I don't have a television."

That set them off again, although Alia didn't laugh as strongly. I repeated myself in Russian, and she smiled wider, her eyes glistening. She cut herself off abruptly, lowering her eyelids as her eyes dulled again. I looked behind me and saw Tell approaching.

He sat down at the table and picked up Alia's coffee. He sipped it and set it down in front of him.

"We've got the go-ahead from higher."

"Which means?" I wished he would go away again.

"Which means that once we get up to Nuremberg, we've got confirmation to move on our target." He finished the coffee and stood. "Come on, we've got to go."

I finished my coffee.

"You want mine?" Karen asked Alia, who shook her head. Karen left the cup cooling on the table.

We got back into the car and drove into the night. The highway led us to small roads wending through the hills. I wanted Tell to stop so I could run alongside the car, so I could run into the woods and be lost in the mountains. But I could not, so I leaned my head against the window and watched the countryside fade, catching glimpses into windows and yards where tall, gray women moved against the evening.

14

I noticed Karen rarely smiled. But then, she rarely did anything that wasn't one hundred percent honest. Even when assuming a cover, she found the kernel of truth that resonated within her and went with it. When she put her makeup on in the mirror, I saw a glimpse of the club girl she might have been a few years ago if MONIKER hadn't snatched her up. Watching her apply her eye cosmetics left me feeling like I intruded on a private moment.

Alia had managed to dig up some kind of party clothes. I thought they made her look like a combination between a prostitute and a teenager trying to pull off sexy but missing the mark and ending up jailbait. I didn't know how I felt about it, but standing next to Tell in his leather pants and mesh shirt, they looked like they matched.

"She's coming with us?" I had elected to forego the leather and goth trance togs and just wore slacks and a collared shirt with a leather motorcycle jacket. I somehow managed to look like a yuppie on vacation.

Karen straightened up and put the rest of her stuff in a small purse. She wore a simple black dress that let her body speak for itself.

"We can't leave her here." She smoothed the fabric against her sides.

"Why not?" I wasn't thrilled about bringing Alia back into the same kind of situation we had taken her out of in the brothel. Also, I didn't think bringing a civilian along on a contact run would end up being such a great idea.

"She's coming with us." Tell's tone indicated he didn't intend to entertain any argument.

I growled at him. The change was running close to the skin tonight. I felt it jolt under me and pass through my pores, curling around, playful and tempting.

"What are you going to do with her?" This time I asked in German to keep the words from Alia. "She can't just join the team for the rest of the mission."

He looked at me and did not answer. I cursed and turned to leave, knowing whatever Alia had tried to offer hadn't been enough.

"Where are you going?" Karen directed her question at me.

"I'll meet you downstairs in half an hour." I needed to get out of the room.

"Keller."

"What?"

Tell put his arm around Alia. "Don't be late."

Something under his voice sent warning bells ringing through my skull. I looked at him and the girl and wondered briefly if he realized he was happily swimming in the same waters as plenty of men before him who saw human beings as something to buy and sell on the open market. The air in the room suddenly smelled dirty, and I headed out as quickly as I could.

WE WERE STAYING in a youth hostel in Nuremberg—nothing too fancy or too much of a dive, just cheap lodging catering to students and some older people who wished they still were students, touring Europe on the cheap. The lobby was nearly empty. Everyone who had something to do appeared to be out doing it. Or upstairs doing it.

I stepped outside. The air hung cold and heavy with the impending snow. The city had put up lights in honor of the impending holiday. As I walked down the block, they seemed to glow, reflecting in the water that puddled the streets and slicked the sidewalks.

There were a bunch of people out tonight—tourists, locals, some speaking German and some English. I felt the cold somewhat as it whipped through the ancient buildings, turning the slush to ice and causing people to turn their heads from it.

I welcomed the wind. It smelled of exhaust and leather and something sweet, like cider or mulled wine. I paused right there on the sidewalk to take it in.

"Excuse me?" The words were English, the voice female.

I turned to see a woman in jeans and a sweater with a reindeer on it. She smelled American. I shrugged and held my palms out, indicating lack of understanding.

"*Entschuldigung?*" She persisted, trying out what from the accent sounded to be high school German, learned and forgotten several years before.

"Sorry, I speak only Russian," I told her in German.

She looked at me. I couldn't tell if she was disappointed or embarrassed. She turned without a word and began walking away.

"Making friends, I see." Tell and the women had come up behind me while I was talking with the American.

"Go fuck yourself." We were, as previously agreed, speaking Russian. It was easier to maintain as a cover. People saw Russian men as gangsters and Russian women as something to be exploited. So we were going to go with that.

I thought Karen might say something, but she just shook her head. She took my arm, Alia took Tell's, and we began walking down the street, two couples heading out to a club for the night. We seemed normal and harmless, and I busied myself on the way trying to think how to make the mission happen while extricating Alia from the same situation I found myself in way too often.

As we passed through the streets, I couldn't help but look around. It had been a while since I had been in Europe, especially in this city. I stood here decades ago, giving up the words that helped seal the fate of dozens of my former comrades in arms. I knew I had done the right thing—once a man takes the path down into the evil they had wallowed in, he relinquishes ties and obligations to any former brotherhood. But I had felt doubly the traitor and the criminal, and I had never been back since.

I noticed Alia doing the same thing as we walked along. I had not particularly thought of it, but this might have been the first time for her seeing a city, at least more than a few glimpses of it through the window of the place they had kept her. She took it in, smiling, even occasionally clutching Tell's arm and pointing something out. For the most part, he ignored her. Every once in a while, Karen smiled and said something to her.

I wished that she could be seeing the city for the first time with someone to whom she meant something, who would take her through the Altstadt and out to someplace nice. Maybe to a movie or something an ordinary teenage girl would enjoy.

I realized I couldn't be sure what, exactly, that might be. I had been in the woods for a really long time, and there'd been a good reason for going there in the first place. MONIKER had chosen this particular mission to lure me back into the fold, and they had known exactly which one would be effective at doing so. I swallowed bile in disgust at having been so easily persuaded.

The streets were pretty dark, but something caught Alia's eye. I turned to follow her gaze. Through the buildings, one street down, I saw the lights of tents and activity. I had forgotten the *Kristkindlmarkt*; in fact, I had almost forgotten the Christmas holiday approached.

As we passed the hint of the *Kristkindlmarkt*, Alia looked over, stunned. I don't think she had ever seen anything like it before. We turned and looked toward the lights, only a few blocks away now from the club.

"Forget it." Tell sensed something amiss. "We don't have time."

"Don't be an asshole." I tensed. "Nobody said anything."

He said nothing but gripped Alia's arm until she winced.

We got closer to the market. Close enough to see a few of the vendors and their wares spilling out under soft, muted light. A choir nearby sang early German Christmas carols, and the sudden smell of manure assaulted my senses. A bored-looking horse pulling a white carriage trotted by.

Another smell of cloves and red wine underlay the holly and cinnamon. The press of people was much larger here, tourists and natives alike perusing the merchandise, enjoying the music, in time with the season. I looked at Tell and Alia and then made a decision.

I leaned over and whispered to Karen. "I'll meet you there. Don't worry."

I dropped Karen's arm and reached out to Tell's elbow. Finding the pressure point, I pinched down hard. Nerveless, his arm flopped to his side. I stomped my foot into his knee.

"What the fuck?" He stumbled and fell to the ground. He tried to push himself up, but his knee wouldn't cooperate.

Grabbing Alia's hand, I took her in suddenly, darting into a gap in the crowd. Tell, back on his feet, started to follow us, and I turned and hauled off with a heavy straight right in the face. He stumbled back, sitting down hard. Karen stepped to the side to let him go down, looking after me with not so much shock as resignation. I didn't spare another thought, just grabbed Alia and took off.

Then we were into the rows and out of reach. I felt bad hurrying her past the sights and sounds, but she bent her head and ducked into me. I murmured in Russian, trying to reassure her, but mostly she just clung to me without a word, accepting me as just one more person with control over her.

By now, the change was rustling under my skin. The control I had to exert over the physical aspect of it burned near the surface. Alia leaned in closer to the warmth. The market was our maze, and we shuffled our way through it.

As we walked through, I kept looking back to see if we had lost the others. I knew they would go on without us, and Karen, at least, would trust my word that I would be there. I knew they would be pissed, but on the other hand, they'd shot me, silvered me, and stuck me in a cage without even the benefit of a fair warning. Not to mention I had yet to hear one word about whether this new mission included a contract with a paycheck instead of just a directive. Until they were paying me, I did not feel completely obligated to be a good boy and play along.

Up to this point, I hadn't made a big deal about the fact they wanted me essentially doing something I had taken a personal vow never to do again, and I was doing it—not from a conviction of purpose, or for money, but rather to get these people to leave me the hell alone.

We hurried our steps. By this time, I felt sure they weren't following us, but figured they might have circled around to try to catch us when we went to leave. I tried the air, but so much chaos floated in the ether, all I got for my efforts was a contact high from the mulled wine they were selling three stalls down.

I finally took Alia back out the way we came in, walking slowly so as not to grab attention, mixing in with a group of loud tourists all speaking excitedly in English, some football club. They were wearing dark shirts and matching scarves, and we laughed and joked until they turned the corner. Or at least I laughed, and Alia kept her face hidden in my shoulder.

We left the group and hurried down the street. It had been a very long time since I had felt cobblestones beneath my feet, and below them the ancient stone and soil my ancestors had trod. I basked in the feeling of being home, of seeing people who looked like me, of hearing the press of the crowds speaking German. Even though I left with no regrets, I did have a lot of memories. I bit down against them, promising myself I would get time to revisit them later. Right now, I had to focus.

Tell had kept the money and papers for himself, doling them out grudgingly, dealing with whomever circumstances called for when we needed something. I had not minded—much. He was the team leader, and my various scouting guises did not always lend themselves to keeping important papers safe on my person. It did not make me distrust him any less, nor did it keep me in check as well as it might have done.

No, I did not have any money or my passport. In the last ten years, most of my contacts had either died or faded from public view. Even ten years ago, some of them might have called it a toss-up between welcoming my business or shooting me on sight. But this was my home turf, and family blood ran deep in the territory. My great-grandfathers had worshipped the Green Man under the free sky long past the time civilization had begun encroaching on the *Schwarzwald*, chasing us to modern society and forcing us to adapt or become extinct.

I shook my head. I had no business heading down memory lane when I needed to keep my head in the game. Because if I did not pay attention, we would be sailing up shit creek, sans paddle. Yes, I mix my metaphors. Shoot me.

"*Gaspadin* Keller?" Alia interrupted my nostalgia. She stumbled for a moment, her tall, sharp heels becoming momentarily entangled in the uneven cobbles.

"What is it, Alia?" I stopped to hold her arm, waiting for her to extricate herself.

"How much farther?"

"Couple more streets." I helped her steady herself. "Don't worry. It's going to be all right."

I sincerely meant it.

WE FINALLY CAME to a thick door made of dark, heavy wood. A bronze head in the shape of a grinning gargoyle adorned the antique knocker. I looked around but did not see a doorbell. The man who I hoped still lived inside eschewed such modern conveniences, and it gave me hope he still kept to tradition.

I grasped the knocker and rapped several times. The knock echoed more loudly than I expected. The metal glowed hot until I realized my hand didn't burn—the full moon had finally risen above the clouds, and I was reacting to the need to change—to not only scrape the surface of the change but to embrace the full transformation. I bit it back, almost choking. I couldn't change with a refugee in tow.

The door opened, and a shuffly little man peered out from behind the sill. Seeing him came both as a relief and a sharp, hard punch to the guts.

"*Gruess Gott.*" I hoped like hell he would let me in.

"Herr Wolf."

"Dmitri." I swallowed back the moment of terror. "Are my favors still worth something with you?"

He smiled, the grin of a shark scenting blood in the water. "*Kommt herein.*"

The inside of the small German apartment was sparse and neat. The antique furniture and well-stocked bookshelves lined with not a single paperback, only leather and good bindings, bespoke a quiet, ordered existence. The most modern appliance in sight was a refrigerator, visible in the kitchen from the hallway. It looked like Dmitri had purchased it when electric refrigerators were first invented. Maybe he had.

"So, Herr Wolf, what can I do for you?" His accent wasn't quite German, wasn't quite Russian.

I nodded to Alia. "I need papers for her." I switched to Russian to keep her in the conversation.

"What is your name?" He asked the question in the same language.

"Alia."

"That's a lovely name." He turned, gesturing for her to lead the way into his study. "And what have you always wanted to be called?"

His demeanor remained friendly enough, but she stopped in her tracks and turned to me.

"Go ahead." I nodded.

She whispered something very low and indistinguishable.

"I'm sorry, I'm old, and my hearing doesn't work so well." Dmitri smiled at her—not the most reassuring sight in the world.

"Karen," Alia said and ducked her head back down.

"Ah, so." Dmitri finally shepherded her into the study and sat her on a short, leather couch. "So, you will be wanting some papers for Miss Karen Wolf, eh?"

I shrugged. It was as good a name as any. "Papers and a ticket to the States." I remained standing, not coming any closer than the door to the hall. "And your phone to call someone to pick her up from the airport."

"Hm." Dmitri sat at his desk. "An expensive proposition."

"You know I'm good for it." The bottom dropped from my stomach when he nodded.

"Yes, you are." Dmitri looked down, shuffling papers. "But I have nothing right now that needs your attention."

I was beginning to sweat, and not just from the conversation. The transformation was coming, and the urgency put me at a disadvantage in the whole bargaining process.

"Will you take an IOU?" I could feel desperation breaking down the wall between me and the change.

"You still owe me forty marks." Dmitri referred to the standing bet we'd had regarding how long the Berlin Wall would last. I had low-balled the figure—he'd guessed it almost exactly. On the other hand, he had stayed connected to the Soviet government at the highest level, so I still thought he was a damn cheater.

"There are no more marks; they switched to the euro, asshole." I scratched at the neck of my T-shirt.

"No need for that, Herr Wolf." Dmitri found the sheaf of papers he needed. "Of course, I will help you, but I'm going to need certain assurances."

"MONIKER has no idea I'm here." I shuffled from foot to foot with the effort to bite back the impending transformation.

"Yes, I heard you're running with that pack again." Dmitri smiled again as if sensing my physical unease and need.

"For a short time, yes," I said. "But if I could trust them, I would not be here right now."

"And here you are." Dmitri's smile faded. "Two of us, old soldiers."

"Yes, here I am." I snorted. "But more like a general and his pawn."

"It's all the same, *bratuschka*." Dmitri winked.

"I'm not fighting any war." Even as I spoke the words, I couldn't escape the lie. "I'm done with that."

Dmitri made no reply, just kept up that soul-stabbing gaze, and I wondered what he knew that didn't. I shook myself. That was a broad category of knowledge, much of which I didn't care to find out, and besides, I was running out of time. The change started making itself known. A sharp pain in my abdomen buckled me over.

"You're pushing it close," he said.

I used one hand to support myself against the wall.

"What's wrong?" Alia's forehead creased, worried.

"Will you help us?" I didn't know what I would do if he turned me down.

He did not immediately answer me. Instead, he turned to Alia. "Go in the kitchen, girl. There is a teapot, and perhaps we could boil some water for tea before I get started."

She nodded and looked at me, worried, but here was a man more certain and confident about telling her what to do, and she went.

As she disappeared into the kitchen, the change came again. I fell to my knees in the hallway, my hands holding me up, barely, my vision streamlining in the blacks and whites of the night.

Dmitri bent down as far as he could, being younger than I, but without the benefits of the monthly rejuvenation that changed the clocks back.

"I will help you." He gently assisted me as I tore at my shirt, at the loose-fitting pants. "And sometime soon, you will help me."

I nodded, unable anymore to speak.

"Now, go." He picked up the clothes and opened the front door. "I'll have everything ready by the morning."

I didn't bother to acknowledge him, but instead stumbled out the front door, body changing and twisting, the relief from the pressure so intense it became pure pain. I hit the ground running, legs stretching and pounding, drawing the shadows around me to cover my tracks in the December night.

I ran until the streets faded into the industrial yards and tunnels of the outskirts. I sensed prey in the dark—small and furtive, faster than

I was used to. There were people, but I kept wide of them, instinct remembering where I was and what must be avoided, even if my conscious brain no longer functioned at a higher level.

The full moon lit the paths before me, highlighting them neon white like flashing signs in the ancient walls of the city.

15

The only thing saving me from spending the entire night furry proved to be the erratic cloud cover. It finally shrouded the moon behind a blanket so thick it concealed every hint of nimbus to call the change. I paused, my half-forgotten obligations abruptly resurfacing like a broken clock that suddenly starts ticking again of its own accord. My path bisected the urgent calling between what I longed to do and what I must do. I doubled back my steps, heading for the next part of our mission.

The club was tucked away in a corner of the industrial district. There were no cobblestones here, only the stark energy of the German manufacturing complex. The area was dark, and I caught little movement, save the one or two small cars that pulled up and left at random intervals. I hoped they had remembered to add me to the list at the door. This was not the sort of place you randomly went to on your own. Rather, I smelled drugs, and the mob, and money, and I sincerely hoped they were not playing techno at top volume, though I would probably be deaf and blind from the disco effects by the end of the night.

I trotted past the club on the opposite side of the street, the few lights casting a massive shadow behind me, on the lookout for some person, unawares, who would be my ticket in. Around the corner, I found it.

Down the street, some hipster stumbled along, oblivious to the world, looking for someplace to relieve himself of the effects of a night of hard partying. I chuffed, the only version of laughter I had at the moment. The hour struck barely nine, and this guy was done for the night. He smelled like an American, and I wondered if he had friends inside who had not yet realized he'd left the club and who might recognize his outfit. But I would take that chance. If this was his condition, they were probably not far behind.

I worried I would have to knock him out, but the sight of me rising up onto two legs in pretty much my natural state caused his brain to short circuit, and he passed out in front of me.

He wore tight-fitting blue jeans, black canvas shoes, a white T-shirt, and a leather jacket with a scarf. It glittered. A pair of glasses with thick, black plastic frames completed the ensemble. I took the jeans, the jacket, and shoes, patting the St. Jude medal around my neck as much for good luck as to make sure it was still there. The T-shirt was wet with something I did not want to think about, and the glasses were prescription and made my eyes go blurry. I threw away the scarf, too. I'm not much of one for glitter.

MY NAME TURNED out to be on the list not as Rick Keller, but as Peter T. Wolf. Tell's idea of being an asshole. Or possibly his idea of a joke. The rather large bouncer looked at me, looked at the list, then looked at me again, and I wondered if he had a problem with me or my outfit. I realized I completely misread the situation when he slipped me his number as he opened the rope for me. I felt his hand on my ass as I went inside. I blamed it on the clothes.

The stairs from the door led down into a basement of what looked like it used to be a large factory floor. There were three bars, one on each side of the room opposite the entrance. The place was packed with sweaty, hungry, desperate people dancing to a frenetic beat that amplified the light pulsing from multiple points of the room. There were the obligatory platforms and women dancing, some dancing with themselves, with men, with other women, trying to melt into each other.

The scents and sounds were almost overwhelming, but the change still rode me, and I had Karen in my senses now. I closed my eyes and opened my sight. I followed her impression until I caught up with them near the dance floor, at a table with a view of the upper levels where the modern-day Tsars looked down on the people.

"Where the fuck is the girl?" I didn't think Tell saw me approach, but he turned and spoke as I came up behind him.

"With a friend." My hearing was already shot. I leaned in closer than I wanted. He smelled like cigarette smoke and bile.

"You don't have any friends here."

"I'm sorry, I can't hear you," I shouted over the noise of the club.

"Don't fuck with me, Keller; I know you can hear me." Tell pounded his fist on the table. The gesture went unnoticed in the commotion. "What the fuck did you think you were doing?"

I noted with satisfaction that the right side of his face sported an angry swollen mark the size of my fist, highlighted every time the trancing lights paused on a bright white floodlight. The piercing beam illuminated the dance floor and turned everything to day before winking out into total blackness to begin again the fade in a pattern of light and energy.

I shrugged. "Is that our target?"

Karen followed my glance, one of her hands wrapped around the stem of a cocktail glass with a clear liquid inside. The scent of olives and very expensive vodka drifted past as she lifted it to her lips. She pretended to take a sip. Or maybe she did. I believed it.

"That's Pulty." She rolled her eyes. "Don't know where the nick-name came from; his full name is Vlad Raskilnov, and yes, he is the target."

The man was tall and so thin as to be almost skeletal. Crudely complex ink tattoos—this time the one hundred percent genuine mob boss thing—protruded on his wrists and hands past the sleeves of his expensive Italian cut suit jacket. As I watched, he leaned over and said something to the girl sitting at his side. Without changing expression, she pulled her hair to the side and got down on her knees in front of him. Although the angle of the balcony hid her from sight, there could be no doubt what she was doing. The expressions of the men in the room did not change, but even from the floor, I could tell they were affected.

For a second, I thought the girl looked like Alia. But that was only my own subconscious, fueled by the sudden hatred I felt for this man who used his power so casually yet in such a profligate manner.

"How long has he been up there?" I breathed shallowly, trying to calm myself, not wanting any more pollution in my lungs.

"About an hour," Karen answered. Tell fumed.

"Do we have a plan?" A rhetorical question.

"Tell sent up his calling card about an hour ago." Karen took another maybe-pretend sip of her drink.

"And?" I prompted.

"He'll send someone down when he's ready," Tell said. "He doesn't want to seem too eager."

A man like Raskilnov would not be eager to do business with someone he did not know. "What did you send up to him?"

"A souvenir from the brothel in Kazakhstan." Tell said it as dispassionately as he might discuss a used car deal.

He'd played a tricky move. Something too far to the excessive side would tip Raskilnov over the edge, and he would invite us up there to shoot us in plain view of his domain. Something too weak, and we would never make it past the very large man guarding the door. It never occurred to me to ask what he had sent up.

"So for the past couple of hours, you've just been sitting here waiting?"

"Yes." Karen radiated anger. She hid it well, but it scratched under the surface.

I shrugged. "Whatever. I'm having a drink."

"Where's the girl?" Tell wouldn't let it drop.

"She's not going to be with us anymore," I said. "Don't worry about her."

Tell bristled but subsided as a large man dressed in black came out of the side door by the farther bar and headed our way. With her spare hand, Karen reached and squeezed my hand briefly. Startled, I jerked away.

"Thank you." She mouthed the words when Tell wasn't looking, and I thought maybe I had done something right, finally.

"Are you John Tell?" The large man came up to the table. He spoke in Russian.

"Yes."

"Okay. You can come upstairs." He jerked his fingers at Karen and me. "Your whore and your driver can stay down here, okay?"

Tell shrugged. "They go where I go."

The man glared at us. He looked up at the booth and caught Raskilnov's eye. Raskilnov inclined his head, barely.

"Okay," the man repeated. I think the phrase constituted his entire grasp of the English language. "You can come, too. But we pat you down for weapons, okay?" He kept repeating that one English word. It had a slightly absurd comedic effect, and I choked back a laugh.

He led us past the door. Behind it stood a man with an AK-47, insurance against any partygoers lost on their way to the bathroom or looking for a quiet place to fuck each other in public.

Another man stopped us and subjected us to a very thorough pat-down. They found Karen's thin wallet, strapped to the inside of her thigh, with her Russian papers and a few rubles. They found out I hadn't stolen the hipster's underwear when I took the rest of his clothes. They looked pretty disappointed. Sorry, fellas.

"Satisfied?" Tell pulled out of the pat-down a beat early, showing them he wouldn't be intimidated. "My people are clean. Mostly." He directed that last bit at me. I felt a little hurt at the lack of effort he put into the insult.

The big man shrugged. "Okay, it's only business, you know? Everyone wants to see the big guy, okay, but some of them aren't so nice."

"Okay!" I said, with way more enthusiasm than the situation called for, and smiled brightly at the dirty look Tell threw my way. I stepped back and gestured for him to go first. "After you, boss man!"

We headed up the stairs behind him, Karen between us. I knew it was inappropriate, and a distraction, and sexist, but the night and the change and the energy were still clinging to me, and I could not help but notice the way her dress clung to her. I swallowed hard and ducked my head. The man behind me laughed.

"Got a thing for the boss's girl, huh?"

It would take too much energy to embark on a denial, and besides, we were already at the top of the stairs.

The windows were soundproofed, but they must have done it on the cheap because the glass muted the music just enough for us to hold a conversation without shouting at each other. My head had begun to pound, and I prayed for any kind of lessening of the barrage of noise. The large man gestured Tell toward Raskilnov, keeping Karen and me at his side with a subtle gesture.

Aside from the man who had escorted us up to the private level, there were two men standing behind Raskilnov, ostensibly bodyguards, bulging with muscles and firearms strapped under their jackets. The man himself appeared confident. Or maybe his men were very good.

Karen averted her eyes from Raskilnov, watching out the window as the girl began finishing her work. I stared at the back of Tell's head. He looked down at the girl, face impassive. I wondered what sort of test this was and if we were passing. I bit the inside of my cheek, hard, trying to focus on the pain instead of the scents flooding through me, and the energy that followed, staining me inside very slightly. I was both charged up and sickened at the same time.

The girl finished and wiped away the residue with the hem of her very tight shirt. I tried not to gag from the smell. I felt the change prickling again, and I swallowed it firmly down. This was no place to lose control.

"Get out of here." Raskilnov spoke in Russian. At first, I thought he meant us, but the girl stood, smoothing her shirt back down, and walked past us. I breathed out as she went past, trying not to smell her.

"So," Raskilnov began, adjusting himself. "What is it you want?"

"We are here with a proposal." Tell took the lead. No one else wanted it.

"And, what is it you want?" Raskilnov seemed bored, staring out across the crowd, watching the waves of humanity breaking against the walls of his club.

I suddenly realized why the girl smelled familiar. When Tell had said he sent up a souvenir from the brothel, he meant he had sent one of the girls. Sometimes I'm really not that quick on the draw. Likely, he had planned on using Alia. The sudden realization almost tipped me right over the edge.

"Well?" Raskilnov grew impatient. "What?"

The thorough pat-downs we had received hadn't been thorough enough.

Tell pulled his piece from the small of his back and put two rounds neatly through each bodyguard's head. I turned and leapt, and by the time I reached Mr. Okay, I had changed just enough to take him down with teeth and claws.

"Keller!" Karen's voice rang loud and close. "Don't even think about it."

I looked up from the body and growled. She didn't need to worry —this time, I hadn't even split my pants.

"We don't have the time." Karen pointed her weapon at Raskilnov, but her words were meant for me. "We need to leave now."

Raskilnov ignored her gun pointed at his face. He stared at me, stricken. I let him watch as I slowly returned to a form that would allow me to walk out without someone filming me and putting me on YouTube. I pulled myself together and smiled at the man who had grown pale as the moon I still felt call to me.

"Listen to me." Tell pulled the man to his feet. "We are going to walk slowly out of here."

Raskilnov nodded.

"You are not going to make a sound; you are not going to alert anyone," Tell said. "If you do, my friend here will know. Understand?"

Raskilnov nodded again. I grinned at him. The blood from his man still painted my face. I could feel it in my teeth and wished briefly there was time to indulge the more carnivorous side of my personality.

"Walk ahead of us down the stairs." Tell pushed and prodded the man, who five minutes before used to run one of the largest criminal networks in Central Europe. "Nice and casual. You're just going out to another party with three friends."

"Fuck you." Raskilnov finally found his voice.

Tell hit him across the face with the fist holding the pistol. To his credit, he barely flinched. A small drop of blood beaded in the corner of his mouth, but he did not bother wiping it away.

"Go."

AMAZINGLY, our entourage made it out the door without incident. Tell's bluff, that I would somehow know if Raskilnov tried to play us, seemed to work. Or maybe, seeing what he saw had momentarily fazed him out of reality, and it would take a moment to get back. The man with the AK-47 had been reluctant to let his boss go, even with Raskilnov's lack of resistance, and I left him bleeding on the floor. Too bad for him, but at least he had made his own choice of employer.

Once outside, we walked a short way to another building. Tell produced a key, and we went inside. The building turned out to be another large warehouse, this one a maze of hallways, storage, offices, and doors leading to stairs and other buildings. I trusted Tell knew where he was going, not because I trusted him, but because even with the change on me, I would have been lost. Or at least slightly distracted.

We entered a final building, one I hoped lay far enough away from any real estate Raskilnov's little corner of the mafia had oversight of. Tell led the way to a small room with a metal chair and a door that locked from the outside. I shuddered involuntarily. I hated small rooms with doors that locked from the outside.

Tell sat him down and cuffed him to the chair.

"Move, and we'll kill you."

"You're going to kill me anyway." Raskilnov glared, perhaps wondering how he'd let us walk into his club and then walk right back out with him.

"Let's just say we don't want to go there just yet." Tell straightened, slipping the key into his pocket. "There's still some room for negotiation."

"Fuck you." Raskilnov sneered. "I've been cut on by the best. You're nothing but a little punk."

"A little punk with a violent friend." Tell stepped to the side so he could see me, leaning against the doorjamb. I smiled. Raskilnov gave me the compliment of paling even further in the ambient gray light.

"What do you want?"

"All in good time," Tell answered.

He gestured me out of the room and followed me, closing the door and locking it behind us.

I stepped away. Morning would roll in on us soon enough, and I had to get back to Alia. Besides, I could feel the adrenaline welling up in Tell, and he either wanted to ream me out for leaving them earlier or spray me with some more of his special weaponized silver. You could count me out for either of those options.

"Where are you going?"

"Nowhere." I shrugged, not about to answer any of Tell's annoying questions. "I thought you wanted me here for the interrogation?"

"I wanted you here, period."

Karen looked at the two of us. She'd been quiet all night. I found it hard to tell what she was thinking. "Tell, he's just trying to do what he thinks is right."

"Helping some slut disappear is not what's right in this situation," he said.

"That's unnecessary," I said calmly. "If you want to insult someone, do it to my face."

A loud crash came from inside the room.

"Fuck!" Tell put his hand on the doorknob and twisted it. "You. Stay here. I'll deal with you when I see what this asshole is trying to pull."

He closed the door behind him. I took off my borrowed jacket and shoes.

"What are you doing?" Karen didn't sound happy about me leaving, but she didn't move to stop me.

"Not staying here." I paused in unbuttoning my pants, suddenly uncharacteristically shy.

"Tell's going to be pissed." She didn't sound too angry about it. I thought maybe I detected a little concern and more than a little resentment at the third member of our so-called team.

"What's he going to do, shoot me with silver and lock me in a cage?" I threw her a grin, although voicing that option made me realize it wasn't actually out of the realm of possibility.

"Good luck." She turned, giving me a bit of privacy.

I grinned, stripped, and changed, heading back into the night to find an old Russian spy with a young Kazakh girl.

16

I made it back to Dmitri's flat as the clouds began to lighten with the nautical twilight. He had left the back door open, and I slipped inside to find my clothes neatly folded behind the door. I sniffed them cautiously. Someone, probably Alia, had washed and folded them. They smelled of detergent and her. I rubbed my cheek on them, wishing I could drop them to the floor and roll the scent all over me. But time, like friends, wasn't something I had in great supply. I dressed quickly and padded down to the kitchen in my socks. I wasn't sure if Dmitri would be awake, and I didn't want to rouse him if he were asleep.

I should have known he would be up. I found him at the kitchen table, reading a newspaper covered in Cyrillic text. He nodded at me as I came in.

"How was hunting?" He asked the question in German.

"Very good," I replied. "The quarry was slow, and the chase was swift."

He chuckled. "You Germans could always spin a good metaphor."

"I always thought we were a very literal people." I enjoyed speaking the language again.

"Sometimes," said Dmitri. "And sometimes you are the very souls of the poetical."

I stared at him.

"Never mind." He waved my concern away. "I see this morning we are all business."

"Where's Alia?" Suspicion rose on me, just for a moment.

"Your friend is asleep." Dmitri might have sensed my unease. "She is inside on the couch. She was worn out."

"And her papers?"

"A full set." Dmitri put down his paper. "She is now Karen Wolf, eighteen years of age, a resident of New York City on a student visa from Prague."

He got up from the table with only a little difficulty, creaking with age and a very long night. Atop the ancient refrigerator lay a sheaf of papers. He took them down and began shuffling through them. He handed me a passport showing citizenship in the Czech Republic, a student identification card, a visa, and a bank book with a sheaf of notes inserted in it. I looked carefully—he had inserted a stack of euros in there.

"I still can't pay you except on credit." I shuddered as I said it.

"I know." Dmitri kept his face neutral. "I know you will owe me very much indeed in the future."

I did not like the look on his face, but I had little choice in the matter. I settled for voicing my doubts. "Are you sure these papers will make it through customs?" I took them from him and looked them over once again. "It's almost harder to get into the United States than it was to break out of the gulag."

Dmitri's eyes glinted. "Pfah."

I raised my eyebrow. "These are that good?"

"Nothing is one hundred percent secure." He waved his hand again as if dismissing the entire Transportation Security Administration. "Security? Customs? An illusion."

"Thanks so much for the philosophy lesson, Dmitri." I held up the papers. "All I want to know is if these will get her into the States."

"Of course." He looked offended at my doubt. "The more rules people make for their protection, the easier it becomes to fool the system."

"I don't understand." Actually, I did. But he always enjoyed lecturing me, and I let him go on.

He laughed. "If you have all these systems in place, all these rules, all these scans, you start to think you have all your bases covered." He sat back at the table. "And even if you want to look over your shoulder to see if something's sneaking up on you, you can't because there's too much else you have to look at."

He picked up his newspaper again. "While you're running through your ten-page checklist, somebody is watching you check them out and finding out what you're missing."

I shrugged. "If you say so."

"I do say so." He nodded sharply for emphasis. "People think they thought of everything until their enemy thinks of something new."

"Interesting perspective."

He rested his finger along his nose and winked. "Trust a man who's spent his life in the business, son."

Although I feared and respected this man, I did not like him, and the memories I had of him went back to a very bad place, but he did know what he was talking about.

"Mr. Keller?" Alia had woken up and stood at the door to the kitchen. "Is everything okay?"

"Everything is great, Miss Wolf." I switched to Russian for her, holding out the papers to her. She took them eagerly, almost as if she couldn't believe it and wanted to grab them quickly before one of us changed our mind and took them back from her—but at the same time she held them gently in case they crumbled beneath her fingers.

She looked up at Dmitri. "Thank you."

He shrugged. She pulled a sweater close around her. I had noticed the faint scent of him on her, and I hoped it came from the sweater.

"We've got to get going," I told her. "I have to get back to the others."

"I'm ready." I realized she didn't have any possessions other than what she wore on her back. One thing we had in common.

"Good luck." Dmitri almost sounded like he meant it.

"Luck will be the least of what we need," I said.

"Then stay alive." He switched back to German. "You owe me some huge favors."

"How should I get in touch?" Not that I had any intention of doing so.

"Don't worry about it."

"I live pretty remotely," I said. "And I'm planning on changing my address when I get home."

"Ah yes, MONIKER found you, didn't they?" He chuckled. "And who do you think they came to when you needed finding?"

A sudden wave of pure paranoia swept over me, hitting all my panic buttons.

"Please be calm, my old friend," he said again in German. "You will scare your young lady friend."

"Thank you." I clamped down hard and reached for the calm. "And now we are really going."

The cold air on my face as we walked out into the sunny morning proved a much-needed remedy for the darkness that threatened to swallow me from the past I kept trying to move beyond.

I took Alia to the airport via bus and *Strassenbahn*. She was awkward and hopeful, excited in a way that still held some reserve. She regarded me as I bought the ticket, negotiating in German with the agent to explain the circumstances. She was a student on a visa, I said, and she needed to get back before classes started in order to do a work study. The agent did not buy it completely, but she sold me a ticket taking Alia, or Karen, as I tried to remind myself, straight into LaGuardia, and I would try to have someone meet her there.

Every time Alia/Karen tried to step closer to me, I shifted my weight in the opposite direction. I could sense a concern, as if she read in my intentional distance that I was not someone she had to offer herself to for what I was doing. But it had been a long time since that had been the case. I could see she did not trust what I was trying to tell her without a long, obvious explanation that would be embarrassing for both of us. I wanted her to understand and to maybe see, if there were one person she could trust, then she might open up to the next one. But maybe I was just as manipulative an asshole as the next person because I wanted to help her to prove something as much as to kick dirt in Tell's eye.

I also needed to do something to piss off MONIKER and remind them I was no longer their bitch. Even if it wasn't true. I don't know what I wanted to do, just hoped to get points for good intentions.

Alia took the ticket and tucked it in with her papers. I walked her to the entrance, where the security personnel began their screening.

"When you get off the plane, I will have my friend look for you," I told her. "She'll have a sign with your name on it—your real one. That way you'll know you can trust her. She's about six feet tall, short blond hair, and she might have her baby girl with her. She speaks some Russian, but not that much. All right?"

"Rick?" She hesitated.

"What is it?" I almost didn't want to know.

"What did you promise that man?" She eyed me steadily, halfway between suspicion and understanding.

"I don't understand." Pity isn't something that exists in my world; it took a minute to recognize it.

She smiled sadly. "I know how things work. You didn't give him any money, so it must have been something else."

I shrugged. "You do what you have to."

Alia looked at me, then took her papers and began walking away. I watched as she handed the boarding pass to the gatekeeper, who waved her through. She paused momentarily to look back and then started walking again, disappearing into the crowd of travelers. I crossed my fingers and wished her an uneventful journey.

I found a phone and placed a collect call. The voice on the other end let out a few choice curse words when she found out the collect call came from me, currently standing in Germany, but she took the call anyway.

"What the fuck are you calling me from Germany for?" My neighbor's voice came over the line, fuzzy from something, maybe stress or lack of caffeine.

"Because that's where I am."

"What the hell are you doing there?" She coughed, a deep hacking cough. I guessed her current attempt to quit smoking wasn't going so well.

"It's a long story." I checked the time on the large wall clock. "Listen, I'll make this quick. Are you still working with that agency in New York?"

"The Refuge Society?" The line crackled somewhat, and I wondered if someone was recording this call and if I were putting my neighbor in a dangerous situation. On the other hand, it was an international call from a pay phone, so I pushed the thought out of my mind.

"I've got a girl landing at La Guardia tomorrow at five in the afternoon," I answered. "She's got papers but not much else."

"What the hell are you talking about?"

"Listen, Victoria, I'm completely serious." I tried to be as quick as I could—if I didn't get back soon, Tell would implode, and I wouldn't be there to see it. "I told you I used to work for some shady people?"

"I thought that was the ouzo talking." Her voice sounded a little clearer now.

"It was, sort of." I hedged, trying to remember my part of that boozy conversation. "But part of what I do was true, and this girl until one week ago was working in a brothel in Central Asia. I need somewhere safe for her to go."

"You're not drunk, are you." It came out more of a statement than a question. My neighbor, a former Marine, had worked with female engagement teams in Iraq and Afghanistan and, when she got out of the service, returned to work with agencies helping the victims of human trafficking. I knew she would be pissed, and we were not so close that I felt comfortable dumping this on her, but she was the only one I could count on to do the right thing first and kick my ass later.

"All right," she finally continued. "What's the flight, and what's her name?"

"Lufthansa, Flight 1175," I replied. "Her papers say Karen Wolf, but her real name is Alia. A-L-I-A. I told her you would have a sign with her real name on it; that's how she would know you."

"A little presumptuous of you."

"Not presumption, desperation."

"Don't worry, Keller," Victoria said. "I got her. She'll be safe."

"Thanks." I tried not to let out my breath too heavily. "And Vic...be careful." I winced, anticipating her reaction. "There might be...complications."

"When aren't there?" I could almost see her shaking her head, palm to forehead. "You owe me big time, asshole."

"I know," I said, but she had already disconnected. I shook my head. Ten years of minding my own business, and I already owed favors to everyone still speaking to me. At least only one of them was a psychotic Russian.

―――――

It was past lunchtime by the time I made it back to the warehouse, and part of me hoped they had ordered something to eat. The other part of me wondered if Raskilnov would be fair game after they finished with him. I would even be willing to let him have a head start through the maze before running him down. My stomach growled, but then I thought of Karen and her reaction to what I thought was simply a natural function of the change, and decided I hoped they had found a pizza joint somewhere in Bavaria that delivered. Or Chinese. I'm not picky.

I got to the building in time to see several large men bundle a thin, hooded figure into the back of a plain white van with German plates. The hooded man was bound with his wrists behind him, and I saw blood flecks speckling his once fashionable suit.

Upstairs, Karen and Tell were wiping down the room. Other than a small puddle of blood left on the floor, there was no trace of what had happened there the night before.

"You guys finished with Raskilnov?" I didn't bother to announce my arrival. "I noticed him out the back. Cleaning team picked him up?"

"We got what we needed." Karen didn't look up.

"Where to next?" I sniffed again, the blood putting an edge on my already enormous appetite.

"Where next?" Tell stood, turning to point his finger at me. "Where next is going to be a small cage and a short leash until you fucking quit disappearing on us."

"Fuck you, Tell." I hate people pointing their fingers at me. I took a step toward him, not backing down. "I was taking care of something important."

"Something important is staying on mission," he said. "Not running after some little slut trying to be her hero."

I made it across the room faster than I could think about it, knocking Karen to the side, and driving a hard right at Tell's face.

"Hey!" Karen shouted. "Stop it!" I ignored her.

She dodged out of the way as Tell blocked my fist with his forearm, tangling my straight and responding with a right hook that drove into my temple and rang my bell.

I pushed away from him, lifting my hands to protect my face, then tried to move in again, to catch him in the clinch. He blocked my strike. I backed away. As I stepped back, I threw a jab at his face. It connected but did not faze him.

He launched himself at me, tackling me with a shoulder to the stomach, reaching around my thighs to sweep my legs out from under me. He winded me and took me down.

I rolled with it. He tried to scramble, but I moved with him. My blood was up. I could hear it rushing in my ears.

We wrestled, jockeying for position. Every time I thought I had him pinned, he would roll out of it. I tried to throw a few punches. They landed, but I was out of position, and he shrugged them off. The change pulsed through me, tempting me with visions of teeth and blood.

I came at his side. He tried to roll away, but I kicked at his ribs. He changed direction. This time, though, he gave me his back. I threaded my elbow under his neck. He twisted and kicked, but I had him in a classic rear naked choke, and the more he pushed away from me, the tighter I clasped my arms around his neck and head.

Finally, his eyes began to flutter. His face flushed darkly.

"Keller." Karen spoke behind me. I ignored her again. "Keller! God damn it, you're going to kill him if you don't let up. He's out already."

But I was too far gone, and I simply squeezed harder.

The silver-laced spray hit me in the face—some sort of oleoresin capsicum derivative. I received the full effects of both pepper spray and silver at the same time. My body seized and choked. Letting go of Tell, I rolled away, trying to wipe at the misery consuming my entire existence. I tried to breathe, but the air would not come. I crouched on all fours, heaving around my collapsing lungs, trying not to puke and trying to breathe all at the same time.

Gradually I became aware of someone patting my face. Karen had a wet towel and was pouring water from a bottle down my face. It flushed some of the effects away; although the sensitive membranes around my eyes and nose still felt like they were on fire, I could at least open my eyes and trickle some air into my lungs.

"Holy shit, what was that for?" I choked out.

"If you kill him, you'll be lucky to spend the rest of your very short life in a cage," Karen answered. "More likely, they would shoot on sight, and I think you have a lot more to offer us."

I breathed a little more deeply as an experiment. The air seared through the tissues in my lungs. I hawked and spit, regretting that decision as all it did was spread the pain around my throat and mouth.

"That stuff should be outlawed," I said. "I'm pretty sure it counts as chemical warfare."

She laughed. "And what would you call using a cannibalistic biomorph whose existence is so classified even the government has forgotten he exists?"

I stared at her. "Cannibalistic biomorph?"

"It fits." She shrugged.

I grimaced. "Yeah, it just sounds so John-Carpenter-horror-movie."

Tell stirred, coming around. Karen knelt down next to him.

"Careful." She held out her hand. "Don't try to stand up too quickly."

"Holy crap, what was that?" He shrugged off her help.

"The two of you decided to indulge your inner juvenile delinquents." She didn't actually throw her hands in the air, but she did toss the towel at me.

Tell looked over at me. Tears and snot were still leaking down my face. I used the towel, but the dampness of the fabric just smeared the fire around some more.

"Holy fuck." I shook myself, trying to get rid of the burn. "That shit sucks. What is it with fucking MONIKER and its fucking werewolf science projects?"

Tell caught my eye. I was still having trouble breathing. He started to laugh. That started me off.

"What the hell is wrong with you two?" Karen demanded.

That set us off even harder. I could not catch my breath to answer her question. Tell just fell back, laughing.

"Men." Karen rolled her eyes. "Sheesh."

Yeah, we beat the shit out of each other and found it funny. But it was either laugh or give in to tears. Pepper spray is no fucking joke.

"Come on." Tell rubbed his neck. "Let's get out of here. I could use a drink. We'll tell you what we found out on the way."

17

It's a stereotype, but it's true. Sometimes when you have some dick you just can't get along with, all you need to do is beat the shit out of each other to show the other guy what you can dish out and what you can take. Mutual respect is established, and you can move on to more bonding activities such as getting obliterated on expensive vodka and hitting on Eastern European prostitutes.

We were going posh this time, booking a place to stay under yet another cover, paying cash for three rooms in a nice hotel with a bar on the first floor populated by rich businessmen who make a lot of money and spend even more.

We talked on the way over. There was a sharing of information, although it degenerated into a semi-friendly exchange of insults when I refused to tell them where I had been, and threats when Tell tried to get me to tell them. But with Dmitri and Victoria, I'd exhausted pretty much all of the aces I held up my sleeve, and they hadn't even been sure things. Like I said, I had been out of the game for a long time. By now, I wasn't even sure what the rules were anymore.

From what Tell and Karen told me about how the interrogation went, I gathered Raskilnov hadn't been as tough as he thought he was. A lot of the little men are like that. They get a tiny bit of absolute power in their own private realm and start to believe their own press. They get a couple of tattoos without crying, and then they think they are the toughest thing since Charles Bronson in that movie where he plays an old boxer who goes after the mob single-handedly. The trouble is, the old-time mafia forgot to pass on their balls to the younger generation. Most of the organized crime bosses got their start after the war when the violence and retributions weeded out the weak from the ones who could be utterly ruthless and fearless.

At the risk of starting to sound like I wallowed, lamenting the good old days, I could say that one of the reasons I decided to hang up the old spurs was that the new crop of assholes didn't impress me at all, and I figured MONIKER could take care of them.

By now, I had started to doubt their entire line of reasoning for pulling me out of retirement in the first place. So far, all I'd contributed was scaring a few people who probably would have pissed their pants the first time Tell held a little electricity to their balls. They would have spilled their guts for far less than the song and dance we gave them. But someone was expending a lot of energy and time to put me back in the game. I just wasn't sure anymore exactly why they were doing it.

I shook off those thoughts, not liking where they were heading, and concentrated instead on the mission. Raskilnov had given up the location of the working establishment feeding most of the prostitution in the area, which was itself fed by the trains coming in from the shipments landing in Greece.

Tell explained this to me in terms so cold and remote, I wondered if he were some kind of machine. I thought it possible he might actually be a clinical sociopath—MONIKER wasn't picky, just look at me. Whatever the problem, there was something wrong with his wiring.

We sat at the bar in the hotel, Tell and me on one side, Karen at the far end flirting with a dark-haired woman in a low-cut shirt. The woman's heightened scent, sharp and crisp like fresh apples, showed her interest. But there was something stale and hesitant under there, and Karen wasn't putting her whole heart into the flirtation, as if she, too, could sense something wasn't working.

I drank vodka, straight and cold. Tell elected to go for a Pilsner served in copious quantities. The residual effects of the OC spray were still making themselves felt, but the vodka was making it better.

"What is the next move?" I asked him. "Are we going after the…" I was going to say whorehouse, then discarded that word in favor of discretion, considered "brothel" and finally went with, "…working establishment?"

Tell shook his head. "We've sent that information to the local authorities. Sometime tomorrow, when we're hitting the railyard, they'll be raiding the…working establishment." He finished his beer and signaled the bartender for another one. "That way, we keep our noses clean and out of it, and the organization assumes the *Polizei* are also the ones that interdict the shipment at the yards."

I finished my drink. "Sounds good." I slammed the glass down on the bar with a little more force than I intended.

"What, no smartass remarks?"

"Nah." I shrugged and thought about ordering another shot. "It's a plan. Sounds good to me. How many people are we expecting to be guarding the tracks?"

"No more than fifteen."

"Nice odds."

"It helps to have someone with your special…talents." Tell spoke with the barest hint of a slur in his voice. I stared at him. That was the closest he had come to admitting my presence on the team wasn't the biggest mistake MONIKER ever made.

"We can take them," I said. "And after that?"

"And after that, you're done." Tell made a flicking motion with his fingers. "Finished. If this is the shipment we expect, we'll have enough proof to get larger organizations involved." The bartender set another Pilsner in front of him. He paused for a moment to take a sip. "Our mission was to disrupt the traffic coming from the Kazakhstan node, interdict the girls, and save the day. Everyone is happy, and we all go home heroes."

I regarded him with surprise. The last couple of sentences came out with unexpected bitterness.

He looked at me and laughed. "I'm drunk, Keller. Don't take anything I say too seriously."

I shrugged. "It happens." The bartender looked at me, raising an eyebrow in inquiry. I shook my head. "I'm going to bed."

Tell ignored me, turning to the bar and the small television showing some European football game.

I thought I remembered a bottle of Scotch in his room when we arrived and wondered how hard it would be to pop the lock on his door.

"You coming up soon?"

Tell and I turned to see Karen standing next to us at the bar. Very sneaky.

"Yeah, we're almost done." Tell tipped his glass in a half salute.

"What happened to your girlfriend?" I nodded at the empty space where the woman had been.

"Turns out she had a girlfriend." Karen shrugged and yawned. "I'm out. It's going to be an early day. My contact has what we need, but we need to pick it up before the sun comes up."

I groaned. Tell grinned. "We'll be there."

"Good night, then." Karen turned to go. "Try not to kill each other."

Tell watched her leave, then turned to watch me watch her leave.

"She's something, don't you think?"

"She's a hell of an operative." I didn't like what he was getting at.

He smirked at me—back to the familiar mocking grin—raised his glass and drained it. "Well, I'm out of here." He threw some bills on the bar. "I'm going to see what I can find down the road." He gave a mock salute. "See you in the morning."

I finished my drink and my inner debate. The elevator ride was interminable, but the moments before I knocked on her door seemed even longer and heavier.

She answered the door in sweatpants and a Dropkick Murphys T-shirt. I smelled rosemary and Pinot Grigio. My nostrils flared. My body grew warmer.

"Can I come in?"

She looked past me. "Sure, I'll be up for a little while."

Her room was nice. But then, all our rooms were nice. They had nice paintings on the walls, and they smelled clean, neat, and orderly. I sat in an easy chair. She sat on the bed. She was drinking white wine from one of the paper cups that came with the little coffeemaker. The hotel definitely catered to Americans. I found a list of takeout places that listed pizza and Chinese food.

"I've been wanting to ask you a question," Karen began.

"Shoot."

"How old are you?" She crossed her legs under her. "For real. Your files go way back, but there isn't really any information before the fifties."

There was a reason for that. I look the age I was when I began this life—thirty-five. The age when you finally realize that your mistakes are not as easily remedied with a smile and a youthful exuberant apology like when you were twenty-five. The wrong person you married is not getting any righter. The money you spent before you earned it is still gone, and you still don't have it. And those friends you made before you knew the meaning of the word, they do indeed lead you down the wrong path, far past the reach of salvation.

Then one day, the country you thought you believed in puts a uniform on you and trades you a rifle for your soul. When I was younger and thought about the future, I thought there were mysteries and marvels, and there are. But I finally found out they are merely the gilding on the same old human pestilence that haunts our species.

"I was born before your grandmother, Margaret." Saying her name, even now, still stung a little.

"Really?" She looked doubtful.

"Really." I thought of the Scotch in Tell's room and wished I'd made it upstairs first.

"And were you really a Nazi?" She kept her gaze on me, not looking away.

We were treading uncomfortable territory. There was a lot of truth I wanted to tell her, to hold her and try to explain, to see if she could find the sort of forgiveness I'd always hoped I would one day see in Margaret's eyes. But there was a lot of transgression in my past, and I held tight to these things because they were the only things I could sometimes remember through the pain.

"I was a German soldier," I finally answered. "And after that, I was a partisan."

"A partisan?" She finished her wine and poured another cup. "Like an insurgent."

"A guerrilla," I said.

The Americans called them "werewolves," after the name they claimed for themselves with typical Teutonic dramatics. They'd been around before the Nazis claimed them for their grand Third Reich, and they were around long after, only under a different name. That had been how MONIKER had reached me. I had been drowning, and the organization had thrown me the only lifeline around. I didn't know whether I was grateful or bitter after all these years.

The *Werwolf*. They had looked to the mythos of the German *Geist* and *Kunst* for their desperate heroics in support of a man who had retreated to his bunker and punched his own ticket. They might have claimed the name, but they still crunched soft and sweet between the jaws. I almost called them patriots, fueled by misguided loyalty to a long-lost cause, and I felt I knew a little something about that. But I killed them anyway.

I thought all these things, but I could not say them. I was falling in love with this woman, and I still couldn't be sure I saw her as herself or as the ghost of the woman I remembered from those early years when I first grasped toward redemption.

I snapped out of it to see Karen regarding me over the lip of her glass.

"It must be strange to live like that," Karen said thoughtfully. She was halfway through the bottle of Pinot but had yet to show any effects.

I shrugged. "It works for me."

"The movies always show how hard it is, moving around so people don't notice you don't age."

"That's one advantage to living out in the country." I grabbed the bottle and a cup and poured some of the wine for myself. I dumped a few ice cubes in it—otherwise, dry white wine gives me heartburn. "Eighty-five percent of the population is tourists, and the other fifteen percent are good people who mind their own business."

I picked an ice cube out of my glass and crunched down.

"You never had anyone ask about you?" Karen regarded me doubtfully. "Not even once?"

"Never," I answered. "Never once have I felt compelled to share with someone my deep, dark secret." I smiled at her, the smile I reserved for a beautiful woman when I was sharing a drink with her. "All I ever did was switch my bank account to an online service."

"It all seems somewhat prosaic and boring when you put it that way," she said.

"That's me," I said. "Sorry, but if you wanted romance and adventure, you met me a couple decades too late for that."

"Damn." She grinned. "And here I was thinking I knew you from what my grandmother wrote about you."

"Wrote about me?" I might have gone pale.

Her smile—no, it was too sardonic an expression to be called that —turned teasing. "In her journal."

"What did she write?" I sounded worried and wasn't faking it, either—there were things about me I didn't want Karen to know.

"Uh uh." She wagged her finger at me, a highly uncharacteristic gesture for her. I abruptly realized she was flirting with me—and a little tipsy. "That would be telling."

"That's not fair." I felt the heat in the wine, even cooled by the ice. "You definitely have me at a disadvantage."

"And that is just where I prefer my men," she replied. "Come here." She patted the bed next to her.

I gingerly sat down next to her. She placed her hand on my shoulder and turned me to look her in the eye. She gazed at me for a long time, then put her hand on my cheek and left it there.

I did not move, worried that the slightest wrong step would derail where I thought this might be going.

"I don't know," she said.

I pulled back slightly and took her wrist in my hand, gently taking it away from my face. She looked at me, and I caught her gaze like a lifeline.

"If you want me to, I'll leave."

"No." She shook her head. "I don't want you to do that." She leaned toward me and rested her cheek on mine. When she brushed her lips across mine, I tasted summer and salt.

I kissed her back, and she put her arms around me, one hand in my hair, the other splayed across the muscles of my lower back. I closed my eyes against memory, losing myself in the need I had for her. She drew away, and I opened my eyes.

I felt the change stretch inside me, comfortable to lie under the surface. She might have caught a glimpse of it because she reached for her glass of wine, although she didn't move from my side. I held my breath again as she leaned against me. I put my arm around her, and we sat that way for a while.

We were both exhausted from the evening and on edge about the day to come. We ended up making love before sleeping, quickly and quietly, with hardly more motion than simply clinging to each other. When I moved in her, and she arched to meet me, Karen wasn't Margaret, and I wasn't whoever she saw when she closed her eyes. We left the lights on and fell asleep with them still burning.

18

The package Karen arranged for from her contact turned out to be a Dragonov sniper rifle with a scope that would give any shooter a serious hard-on. The shooter in question being Karen, I figured she would skip that step and head straight to bringing the pain. Her face lit up when she opened the case. She put the weapon through its paces with a delight only genuine marksmen and gun enthusiasts exhibit when holding a truly awesome piece of weaponry in their hands. I did not understand it myself, but I enjoyed her reaction.

Tell guessed what we'd been up to the night before. He didn't say anything, and I don't know if Karen noticed, but his reaction to the two of us when we stumbled down the stairs at four in the morning was enough to tell me he knew.

I had asked Karen the night before, as we were drifting off, what his story was. She told me Tell used to be a cop, NYPD, and a great one until the day MONIKER set its sights on his skills. Now he worked for the organization, leading teams. She'd worked with him and another woman for the longest time. I didn't ask what happened to the other woman. From the undertones threading her voice when speaking of it, I could guess.

Tell found us a car, and I didn't ask too many questions about where he got it. I don't often get the chance to ride in a BMW, and it was a really nice car. The trunk was spacious and could conveniently hold a body and a Dragonov sniper rifle.

I was feeling expansive, healthy, and even a little close to happy, watching a beautiful woman do what she enjoyed best, watching her body as I remembered it under me.

She paused for a moment in disassembling the weapon and looked straight at me, as if to say, I can guess what you're thinking. I smiled as innocently as possible, a grin that elicited a sort of half-smile in return.

Tell shook his head in disgust and lit up one of the most foul-smelling cigarettes he'd found to date.

"Come on, you two." He shook out the match and tossed it to the ground. "Let's get a move on."

WE STILL HAD some ways to go. The car's GPS highlighted a route that took us on a direct path over highways and around cities until we reached the railyards near a small district on the outskirts of Cologne. We were taking the easy way until Tell decided we were being too predictable and directed Karen, who was driving, to take the next exit. We ended up lost in the middle of the East German countryside with the GPS squawking at us in a voice that sounded remarkably like my mother when she got to her most frustrated with me. Thinking of my mother made me sick to my stomach.

"Can you turn that off?" I slumped in the back seat, nursing a headache. My blood sugar was dropping. I had skipped breakfast and hadn't eaten much of a dinner. I needed to eat something or else deal with the throbbing head pain that came from my body not getting enough fuel.

"I can't figure it out." Karen glared at the machine. "Why don't you try fiddling with it?"

"I don't have much luck with modern technology." I don't. Things with electronics tended to implode around me.

I caught her eye in the rearview mirror. She grinned.

"Jesus Christ." Tell leaned over and punched something on the touchscreen. The map remained, but the angry voice stopped yelling at us.

He sat back and pulled out yet another file from a thin portfolio in his bag. "We didn't get a chance to go over this back at the hotel, so here's the transcript from our interview with Raskilnov." He handed me a sheaf of papers.

"What does it say?" I took them and gave them a quick shuffle. "'Ow, quit hitting me?'"

"Shut up and read the file." Tell wore sunglasses with polarization too thick for me to see his eyes. From the smell of old alcohol, stale sweat, and cigar smoke emanating from his pores under a thin layer of hotel shampoo, I thought his hangover was maybe worse than mine. I grinned and took the file.

There wasn't much new information in there. Raskilnov had given up a few names and places. Two of them were brothels conducting actual transactions. Another was a time and date for a shipment. As Tell said, they were going to tip the *Polizei* to the warehouse. It did seem logical the local authorities would be the best ones to handle the evidence, the women, and the established gangsters with ties to the community.

We would be taking down the shipment as it rolled in, interdicting it, and hopefully finding out where they were coming from and where they were going. I re-read the file to see if I could find a hint of anything else coming in on the train. Arms? Drugs? Black-market piñatas? The details were hazy.

"Wait." I flipped through the pages again.

"What is it?" Tell sounded grouchy. I tried to pick out any smells underneath to see if he had gotten laid last night. I caught a faint hint of cheap perfume and potato vodka. Maybe that was why he was more charming than usual. I decided not to mention it, a feat of remarkable self-control on my part.

"I thought you said the police would be raiding one house while we interdict the shipment?" Something hovered on the edge of my thoughts, sniffing out a scent that just didn't belong.

"Correct." Tell held out a hand for the file.

"Shit!" Karen swore. "I just missed the damn exit."

Tell looked at the GPS screen. "You can turn around up ahead in about two klicks." He waited. Then, to me: "Well? What did you want to ask?"

"Raskilnov talked about two locations they were prostituting the girls from." I closed the folder and handed it back. "If you tipped the police about the one in Nuernberg, and we're hitting the Cologne shipment, what about the one outside Aachen?"

"We wait on that one," Tell replied.

"What do you mean, wait?" I couldn't bite back the growl that welled up.

"Quit growling at me, furry," Tell snapped. I could hear actual pain in his voice, but I can't say I cared too much.

"These aren't just targets on a map," I said. "These are people we're talking about."

I tried to catch Karen's eyes in the rearview mirror again, but she kept looking straight ahead. I didn't know if she was avoiding my glance or simply trying to find the turn.

"We need a contingency plan," Tell said. "It sucks, yeah, I know, but if everything goes to hell at the interdiction, we'll need another lead. And we won't have one if the police roll it up." He leaned his seat back. I'm a short guy, and there wasn't much room in the backseat to begin with, luxury automobile notwithstanding. The chair pressed against my knees. "If it makes you feel better, we can call them afterward and leave another anonymous tip. Now, if you can put a lid on the wiseass remarks and you," he said to Karen, "can figure out how to drive, I'm going to try to fucking sleep."

He crossed his arms over his chest, leaned his head back on the seat rest, and was asleep. I felt jealous.

I wanted to say something to Karen, but she was driving angry, her face hard. She wasn't happy. I held on to the door handle as she went fast and swerved around a hairpin U-turn, and started heading back the way we came. The energy in the car had shifted. I rested my head on the window and watched the view through the fog my breath left on the glass. Every time the team seemed about to cohere, we just couldn't seem to keep it together. My stomach clenched in a knot. I was hungry and worried about how this would go down. You could even say I had a really bad feeling about this.

I MUST HAVE SLEPT for a little while because when I woke up it was late afternoon and we had stopped at a café in a little village. I stepped out of the car into dirty slush up to my ankles. If we didn't get some kind of food, I was going to faint. By now, I felt ready to eat a small household pet.

The cold air tasted delicious, and I felt it all the way down in the bottom of my lungs when I took a breath. I coughed, and my throat felt like I swallowed a drawer full of knives.

"How far out are we?" I looked around. Nothing smelled familiar. Tell had gotten out of the vehicle. Karen stayed in to keep the engine running and the car warm. We headed into the café.

"We've got about another twenty minutes." Tell seemed a little less grouchy.

"Sounds good." I stretched. I felt rested after my nap but in a cramped, joint-popping way. The back of the car was a lot smaller than those things looked in the commercials. I almost would have preferred riding in the trunk with the sniper rifle.

Walking into the store, a wave of aromas washed over me, and I almost peed myself. I was so happy to be near food. Imagine walking into your favorite bakery and being hit with the scent of things baking and how hungry it makes you feel. Now, multiply that feeling by a hundred, and you'll get some idea of how ready I was to pick up the nearest package of whatever and chow down without even waiting to unwrap it.

"Control yourself, Keller." Tell spoke softly. "You're going to get us noticed."

"You're the one with the money," I said. "Either buy me something to eat, or I change right now and snack on you."

"Fuck off." So he wasn't less grouchy, just less sleepy.

He handed me a couple of euros. I picked the first thing off the shelves as I headed to the cashier, a younger girl in her late teens with straight blond hair and light eyes. She smiled at me and might have said something about change, but I was too busy fumbling with the wrapper, trying to get whatever it was I had bought into my stomach.

She stared as I simply stuffed the corner of the food into my mouth and began chewing around the paper and plastic. Her eyes widened.

"Don't mind my friend." Tell came up behind me, arms full of sandwiches and soft drinks. "He's a little uncivilized." I noticed his German had a hint of a British accent to it.

I still couldn't smell anything over food. Whatever I had just eaten wasn't even enough to take off the edge. I took another sandwich out of Tell's hands, ripped the wrapper off, and started chowing down some more. Tell shook his head, paid for the food and drinks, and grabbed my arm to lead me out of the store. I shook him off.

"Wait a minute." My stomach growled again. The scent of food started to abate, although my saliva glands hadn't stopped activating. I wiped my mouth. Something picked at the back of my brain. I sniffed the air again. This time, I could smell the residual tang in the cashier's hair from the joint she'd smoked on her lunch break. I could smell the cleaning solution they used on the floor last night and picked out the scent of Old Spice and Cuban cigars. At first, I thought it came from Tell, but the personal scent didn't seem right.

I looked around the small café. It was more like a convenience store with shelves of snacks, coolers with drinks, and a couple of tables with chairs. The cashier wore an apron, and she probably doubled as the waitress. We were the only ones in there—at least, that's what I thought until I heard the toilet flush and the bathroom door opened with a flood of other scents.

The guy coming out of the toilet, wiping his hands on his slacks to pretend like he'd washed his hands, seemed really familiar.

"What is it?" Tell turned, halfway to the door, food in his hands. "Rick—we need to go."

"Shut it, boss man." I shoved the last bit of sandwich in my mouth, talking around the morsel. "This guy smells wrong."

We spoke in English. The cashier looked at us, looked at the guy, and then dove for cover as I launched myself at him without pausing to chew.

The man threw his hands up, trying to catch me in mid-leap. I thought the momentum from the attack would take him down, but apparently, he had studied some sort of martial art, and he went with the flow, flipping me over his hip. I landed on the ground on my face and rolled over to see him reach into his suit jacket.

I kicked his knee, setting him off balance, and swept his leg out from under him. He fell toward me, and I scrambled to get out of his way in the narrow hallway.

There wasn't anywhere to go. I found myself grappling, struggling, and trying to get closer to him.

The guy inched away from me on his back, hands up, using his feet to keep me from getting closer to him.

"Keller! Don't do it, I swear to God—" Tell stood back from the hallway. I wasn't going to change. Or at least I hadn't been meaning to.

The momentary distraction gave the guy on the ground an opening. In one motion, he turned, got to his knees, and sprinted for the back of the hall. I took off after him, feet slipping against the tile.

He banged out the back exit, and I got a face full of metal door on well-greased hinges. The delay gave him a few seconds' lead, but there was no place for him to go in the open field behind the café, and when he paused to look where he should run, I caught up to him. I tackled him around the legs and drove him to the ground, ending up on top with his neck in my hands.

My stomach growled again, and I gathered my will power to keep it together. Changing and eating some random stalker in an open field was no way to preserve operational security.

"Who are you?" I demanded in German, smacking his head into the soft ground for emphasis. The slush muted the effect. "Why are you following us?" He groaned.

I shifted my weight, grabbed his ankle, and manipulated his leg to put an incredibly painful amount of pressure on the knee I had taken out before. He paled and tried to swat at me, but the half-hearted blows were ineffective. I felt the cold snow soak through the legs of my pants where they lay against the ground.

"Why are you following us?" I asked again.

"I'm—" was all he got out before Tell hit me across the head with a two-by-four he picked up from a trash pile of wood outside the back door. It bowled me over, and I came up angry.

Tell raised the board with one hand, the other straying at his waist where I knew he kept the small gun with the silver bullets. I stepped back, raising my hands.

"Fine, you ask him," I growled. "Ask him what he was doing back at the hotel and what he's doing here now."

"I don't know what the fuck your crazy friend is talking about." The man spit blood. He rolled to his side, but it took him a second to get up. His knee refused to cooperate. He shivered in the cold.

Tell extended his hand and helped the man up. Standing, he towered over Tell, thin and lanky. Tell backed up, putting his hand on my arm as if to hold me back. "Excuse my friend," Tell said in his crisply accented German. "He served a little too long in Afghanistan, if you know what I mean."

I shook him off, but he immediately grabbed my arm again, this time squeezing harder. "I recognize him," I said. "He was at the hotel."

Tell glared. "Go get in the car, Keller."

"But—" I couldn't figure out why Tell wasn't listening.

"Get. In." Tell dropped his hand to his pistol for effect. "*The car.*"

I knew the man. I could feel Tell on edge, shimmering in the knife's edge vibrations I picked up from him. Why he didn't let me beat the snot out of the man on the ground until he told us why he was following us, I didn't know—or why Tell would kill me to keep me from doing so.

I was still hungry, and the signals I was receiving—the physical and the others—were confusing the hell out of me. It was cold. I gave up.

"Fine." I left the two of them alone in the snow-covered field.

***

"YOU LOOK LIKE SHIT, by the way." Karen stared at my disheveled state. I had several large wet patches on my clothes and a trail of dirt and gravel from my hair down my cheek.

I wasn't in the mood. Growling something under my breath, I got into the backseat, trying to ignore the actual worry in her eyes.

"You okay?" She looked around for Tell. "I thought you two were getting food."

"Your boy tried to start World War Three with a random stranger." Tell opened the door and got in the passenger side. "Nice way to keep our presence low-key."

"He was following us." I knew it and wasn't about to let it go. Karen glanced at me in the rearview mirror as she started the car. I felt like a stray dog caught misbehaving yet again. So, I ate the last four sandwiches. We sat in awkward silence as she pulled out and accelerated down the highway. A sleeting mix of rain and snow began to fall, and the heater felt good.

"He wasn't following us." Tell broke the silence once we had gotten down the road a way.

"I don't believe in coincidences." I was still pissed.

"Maybe you were mistaken," Karen offered.

I gave up. It wasn't worth arguing about. In any case, whoever the guy was, he wasn't going to be following us any time soon with his knee in that condition. I sprawled out across the backseat and pulled my Yankees cap down over my eyes. "Wake me up when we get there."

***

THE AWKWARDNESS DID NOT ABATE as we ate up the last miles into the city of Cologne. I don't often think of myself as a superstitious man, although I guess I have the same bad habit of believing in luck or fate as most people who spend their lives in dicey places. I drifted in and out of sleep on the ride. Every time I came up, I touched my St. Jude medal out of reflex before I could catch myself.

There was something wrong about all this, and it lingered at the edges of our circumstances, a scent I couldn't quite recognize. I couldn't discern where it started or where it would lead—it gave me nothing to grab onto. Even if I couldn't really smell it, I knew something smelled rotten, and I would eventually find myself rolling in it up to my haunches.

For one thing, I couldn't figure out what the hell was up with Tell and the man from the hotel. As we drove, I started to second-guess myself, wondering if I really smelled what I thought I'd smelled. Then I would remember the other thing I got from him, the live wire of adrenaline and hatred and something else I couldn't quite define, and I would go back to wracking my brain trying to figure out why Tell wouldn't let me at him. Maybe he didn't believe me, and that was the only reason he stopped me from talking to the guy. But I doubted it.

Worse, the longer we drove, the more unease I sensed coming off of Karen, most of it directed at me. I could taste her regret, a palpably bitter aftertaste in the back of my throat. That regret, tied up in self-doubt and loathing, left me feeling like I'd failed her again. I'd used her to try to make amends with my past. I should have known. That never works.

My other inner voice, the smart one, kept telling me this op was a bust and what I should really be doing was planning on how to get the hell out of Dodge before the silver bullets started flying. But now that we were this close to our objective, it seemed dumb to suddenly try to jump out of the car. I really didn't want to face the look on Karen's face if I tried.

I felt one more time under my shirt for the little scrap of metal and fell against the seat as the car rolled to a stop. I scrambled to a sitting position in the backseat and pushed up my ballcap. My pistol had shifted in its holster on my waistband, and I adjusted it back to a more comfortable position as I tried to peer out into the gloom.

We were not at the central railroad station in Cologne, a big gleaming *Hauptbahnhof* nestled against the Gothic spires of the Cologne Cathedral. We were instead at the Huerth-Kalscheuren freight switching station. It was still busy this early in the night; we pulled up as a train slowly picked up speed, the big gray beast piercing through the sleet as it slowly gained momentum down the tracks. The ambient light from the city and the glow from the lines of strobing, fluorescent signaling lamps lit up the night, leaving hardly a shadow through which a lone *Werwolf* could slink.

The yards were not interminably huge, but it was still a lot of distance for the three of us to cover.

"You ready?" Even Tell seemed uncertain.

19

The little station was south of the Cologne Eifeltor container yards, connected by a short stretch of track running up under the highway and along a small area with a few shops and other buildings. Our first thought had been to put Karen on the overpass with her rifle, but now it became apparent that the bridge over the tracks sat too low and too far away to serve as an adequate overwatch point.

We got out of the car, parked on the side of a little road that came off the traffic circle, and followed the highway a short distance, disappearing under the bridge. Tell had propped the car's hood open and started fiddling with the engine. It looked like he was connecting and disconnecting various tubes, but the car's guts were brand new and run by a computer, and I couldn't make sense of them. I caught a whiff of rosemary as Karen came back down.

She had the Dragonov encased in a black canvas bag slung over her shoulder. She shook her head as she came up to us.

"It's not going to work."

"Shit." Tell stood up, wiping his hands. "What time is it?"

I looked at him blankly. "I have no idea." I never wear a watch.

"We're pushing midnight," Karen told him.

"The container should be there now," Tell said. "We've got about a three-hour window before it gets picked up."

"We need eyes on." I liked this plan less and less.

"I've got an idea." Karen stood slightly to the side, eyes scanning the area. "It might work. You have the map?" This last she directed to Tell, who nodded and went to retrieve some papers out of the back-seat of the car.

He opened yet another Manila folder and grabbed a printout showing an overhead view of the railhead, freight yards, and surrounding area. Karen pulled out a flashlight with a dark filter over the lens and shined it down.

"Here." She pointed. "We can make our way down the tracks and to this first line of containers."

I followed the path she traced down the page.

"If you look here, this line of containers is pretty much unbroken on the north to south axis," she said. "I can cover you from up here. You two can take the flanks, and we can pretty much scout this place out in a straight line until we find what we're looking for."

She turned the light off. We were parked in the bridge's shadow, but I could feel the adrenaline poised beneath her skin. It was a good plan. Tell frowned but nodded.

"Let's do it." Tell closed the folder and stuck it in the car, under the driver's seat. "Keller, I want you to stay upright on this one. Go furry if you have to, but I'd hate to have to explain a naked werewolf to a container full of panicked women."

I couldn't think of anything clever to say. I went with: "I'm ready, boss man."

THE WALK down the tracks was just dark enough to obscure the details of the rails in the snow but not dark enough to hide our approach from anyone who might have been watching. As we got nearer the yards, they grew larger, seemingly interminable. Feeling uneasy to begin with, I grew twitchier as we got closer. We had a lot of space to cover, a little more than half a klick. There were a lot of shadows to hide any manner of unexpected adversaries.

We were approaching in a triangle formation with me in the lead, Karen to my four, and Tell to my seven. If anyone saw us, we would be hard-pressed to explain what we were doing there, and I tried to think up a plausible cover story all the way to where the rails terminated at the yard. I couldn't think of a single one.

Then we were at the first line of cars. Tell braced his back against the container and offered his hand to Karen. Using his knee and shoulder, she vaulted herself up, caught the edge of the top, and pulled herself up and over. She disappeared momentarily but then poked her head back over the edge.

"It looks like we're clear." She pitched her voice low. Sounds carried in the cold night air. "Toss me the rifle."

I reached the bag up to her. She snatched for the handle, missed, then grabbed it and pulled it up over the side with her.

"Keller, you getting anything?" Tell directed the question at me as Karen unpacked her weapon and slung it around her neck. She knelt, sniper rifle at the ready.

I drew a deep breath. I got snow, diesel, grease, and electricity running in big, bold currents through the winter night. I closed my eyes and opened my awareness. There was something deeper there. Some black undercurrents of despair and fear. In the bushes, a small animal scampered away from my questing consciousness. I salivated unexpectedly.

"Well?"

Tell's question broke my concentration, and whatever I felt faded quickly. I couldn't be sure it was even there to begin with.

"I'm picking something up about one hundred meters ahead." I wiped the corner of my mouth. "Can't be sure it's the target, but it's on our way."

"Right, okay." Tell shifted his stance, weapon at the ready. "Let's go. I'll take left flank. You take right."

"Roger. I'll cover you." Karen disappeared over the side of the container.

I threw him a mock salute, but my heart wasn't really in it.

We set out, moving silently through the night. I listened for Karen's footsteps on the roofs of the containers, but she was very good at what she did. The most I caught was the very faint scuff of rubber soles when she leapt from container to container and, from time to time, the odd whiff of rosemary. Unless there was another werewolf in the container yard, she would be undetectable.

I couldn't see Tell. On the ground, surrounded by the containers, I could barely see anything past the mute steel walls of various shades of gray. I wasn't sure if I was keeping pace with the others but counted on Karen in my ear to let me know if anything came our way.

The floodlights in the yard illuminated much of the area, but there were deep shadows along the edges of the walls as I slowly made my way. I paused every couple of steps to sniff the air again or to rest my ear against the walls of the containers. I debated trying to stop and see what I could sense again, but we had to keep moving.

Then, I smelled it. The unmistakable aroma of human beings packed too tightly together. Beneath the dirt smells, I could taste the sharp, strong scent of fear, adrenaline, and underlying them, the stale, cold taste of resignation.

"I think I have something."

"Wait one." Karen's voice was clear. I looked up to see her, a predatory shadow crouched atop the container wall.

"What have you got?" Tell's voice came through the earpiece.

"I'm not sure," I said. "It feels like..." I thought for a moment. "It's not quite..."

"Jesus Christ, Keller, what is it?" Tell demanded.

"It's a couple rows to the north." I couldn't miss it.

A short pause over the speaker, then Tell said: "I'll swing around and come in on your left flank. Karen, you cover us."

"Roger." Her silhouette moved off.

Using the shadows for concealment, as best I could with the bright floodlights coming down everywhere, I found a break in the container wall and slipped through. I found myself along sets of tracks, one of which was currently occupied by a short train consisting of three cars and an engine. I stopped.

"It's not coming from a container." I ducked into the shadow on the side of the train opposite the floodlights.

"What do you mean?"

"It's not a container," I repeated. "The shipment is already loaded. I'm looking at the car now." I shifted uneasily. The energy coming from the car beside which I crouched sickened me. Underneath it all, I felt the faint sweet scent of decay, like not everyone in the shipment had made it.

"Wait for us," Tell directed over the mic. "I'm almost at your position."

"No problem." I hadn't the slightest inclination to try anything heroic by myself. I looked back up at Karen. "You see anything up there?"

"Nothing." Her voice crackled in my ear. I found the familiar sound comforting through the overwhelming cacophony of smells emanating from the car.

"We're going to need you on the ground." This time I heard Tell both through the earpiece and across the yard. He emerged from the container wall about fifty meters down from my position. He crouched and ran toward the train, taking up a position on the same side as me, facing me.

"You want me to come down?" Karen's voice held more disbelief than I think she meant.

"We're going to need an extra set of hands down here," Tell whispered. "And it might help if the first friendly face these people see is another woman." He nodded to me, and we exchanged places. We sat alongside the train, backs to each other.

There was a long pause over the wire. The feeling of something being wrong returned full force. I tensed, but then Karen's voice came again.

"I'm on my way to your position," she said. "Watch for me on your six."

A few seconds later, she drifted up like a ghost from behind the ranks of the yards.

"What have we got?" She slid in behind me, keeping her eyes and rifle trained to the rear of our position to inhibit the chances of anyone trying to come up on us from behind.

Like the two men smelling of beef and potato vodka currently creeping along the siding.

I noticed them about two seconds before Karen put her hand on my arm, leaned back, and, without taking her eyes off of them, whispered, "Coming up on our three."

"I see them." They were unmistakable.

"Where?" Tell's position blocked his view.

"They're at the front of the train," I replied. "I smell gun oil and rust. I think I can take them."

I took off, bounding forward. I sensed Karen behind me, but Tell's presence faded slightly. He stayed with the car, silent in my ear.

The first man didn't see me before I was on him. A knee to the rib cage and an elbow to the temple, and he was out. The other man had enough time to think about putting up a fight and did the best he could, but Karen had my back and pointed her weapon at him. He stopped in mid-lunge. I smiled at him, and the smile held more than a hint of the change.

"Good boy." I took his gun, reversed it, and hit him as gently as I could at the base of his skull. He collapsed like a jack-in-the-box when the music runs out.

I leaned forward to see if he was all right, and someone rudely jerked me back. I twisted away, but the same someone held me tight. I thought Karen was overreacting, but Tell had come up, grasped me at the shoulder and the waistband, and was now pulling me away from the man.

"Calm down, Tell." I pushed him off me, snarling. "He's fine; I just put him to sleep."

He let go and backed away, tucking his shirt back into his pants where it had pulled out in the scuffle.

"Reasonable mistake, Keller." He kept his voice low. "I just don't want you to eat them for doing their job."

I flipped him the bird.

"Back to business, gentlemen." Karen turned and led the way back down the dark train with her rifle.

THE LOCK on the car door was easy to pick, but the padlock turned out to be a redundant system, and we ran up against another internal lock that I didn't have much luck with. Tell pushed me away and pulled something out of his pocket.

"Keep a lookout." He bent to the lock. "This might get a little noisy."

The something turned out to be a minute amount of plastic explosive, and while it was indeed slightly noisy, it was also pretty effective. The lock mechanism melted, and the car door slid easily open. Tell stepped aside.

"Karen." He gestured for her to take the lead up the steps.

Darkness shrouded the interior of the car, although little points of movement disturbed the velvet blackness hiding the girls from our view. The smell washing out of the car overwhelmed my senses, numbing them. I wrinkled my nose against fear and adrenaline, but it was the empty kind that had nothing to fuel it except more fear.

Karen slung her rifle on her back and grabbed the handle next to the open door. With her other hand, she pulled out a small flashlight and flipped it on. The dimmer-than-usual beam, filtered by the lens she put over it, was good for staying tactical but not so good at picking out individual people from a pile of over a dozen. The light reflected briefly in the open eyes of some of the women, giving them the appearance of a boxcar full of abused puppies blinking against the night.

"That the shipment?"

"Yeah," Karen replied. She sounded tired. "I count about sixteen."

"That's it?" Not the right question, as I could tell from her sudden surge of anger.

"How many—" She cut herself off. I could hear the knives in her voice when she spoke again. "I'm going to need your help up here."

"Coming up." I grasped the same handle she'd used and stepped up on the first rail under the door.

I was about to swing myself into the car when a too-bright light flooded the boxcar, and a man with a gun stepped out of the shadows. In that instant, I realized I had lost Tell's scent in the mix coming from the car.

I froze halfway between the door of the rail car and the ground. The object staring blankly at me was familiar but not at all comforting.

"Come down from there." I recognized the man. I had first seen him in Vermont—he was one of the men who had come for me there. Three men joined him, weapons pointed in our direction, and I squinted against the glare. I couldn't see anyone else, but once I realized they were there, I couldn't smell anything from them except the sharp, bitter piercing tang of silver. There could be more. I couldn't tell.

I dropped down, crouching, but there was no place to run. I watched as he cracked the cylinder of my .38. I could smell the silver casings. I wanted to change; I wanted to fight, but the thought of stray bullets bouncing around the car full of women kept me from jumping down and wreaking havoc.

"This is a nice piece." The man loaded the weapon slowly, pausing to look up at me for effect. "It will make a nice souvenir of this night."

Hot anger short-circuited my brain, and my hands twitched. The change clawed the surface. That weapon was one of the last pieces of my life to stay with me. It stayed longer than any woman or country had ever stayed loyal, and as ridiculous as it might have been to need the piece, I did.

I'd never loaded silver into the weapon. This man was polluting the last sure thing in my life. He closed the cylinder and spun the barrel. Cocking the hammer back, he raised my weapon at me and pulled the trigger.

The last coherent thought I had as the silver began to spread and the curtains started coming down was that MONIKER had finally cut the last thread binding me to their sad, sorry intrigue of an organization. If I woke up, I would find some way to return the favor.

But I wasn't down yet. The pain almost made me wish the silver would finish me off, but that wasn't their intention.

"Come out of there." The man waved the piece for emphasis.

I fell to the ground, slush soaking through the seat of my pants, my hand against the hole in my shoulder. It wasn't gushing blood, but the steady warm seep from under my palm let me know I was in trouble.

I tried to concentrate on what they were saying, but all I could think of was Tell pulling me back from the guard, his hand at my waist, then his movements as he tucked my pistol into his waistband. I couldn't understand why. I could barely understand *what* had happened, and my mind kept circling around that moment like water in a drain.

"Tell, what the fuck?" Karen stood, framed in the door, her hands raised. There had been no time for her to go for her weapons.

Tell stood to the side of the group of men, weapon pointed at the ground. I growled and started trying to rise, but there was no point. Whatever they had loaded into my gun was more than silver and spread through me pretty quickly.

"The girls are yours, Dobroyev." He nodded at a man dressed in a black leather jacket and black wool cap. "As for you," he said to me, "the highest bidder will be here to collect soon."

I tried to shake my head to clear it, but I was rapidly sinking back into a drowning pool of thick black nothing. I felt Karen drop to the ground and heard an exchange of words between her and Tell as the men began to unload the women off the car. I couldn't hear exactly what they said. The roaring in my ears gave me the feeling of being trapped in whitewater rapids, unable to hear or move, caught up against the current dashing me against the rocks. I could make out anger and betrayal and thought to myself as I started to slip away how often I had tasted both on my tongue and paid for them with my blood.

The gunshot brought me back to the surface.

Karen stumbled, and I realized she had tried to make a play, and one of the men had shot at her.

Adrenaline cleared the decks for just enough of a moment. I surged to my feet. She fell back against the car but struggled back up, and as she went for the men again, I grabbed her hand and took off.

Karen slipped on the slush, awkward from not wanting to follow and the sudden movement.

"Run," I said, or thought I did, but she took the hint, and then we were running for our lives through the snow and shadows. She was fast, and I changed as we went, but the silver in me slowed us down. I panted, tongue lolling. The men's footsteps grew louder.

With her hands now free, Karen wrestled the rifle to her front. I galloped alongside her. We weren't slow, but we were not going to be fast enough. Without missing a stride, she racked the bolt, twisted, and fired a shot back at the pursuers. Through luck or skill, she dropped one. I heard a cry and the footsteps behind us stopped. I guessed they decided we were not as easy prey as they would have liked.

As we disappeared back into the container jungle, I looked behind me. In the split-second gaze, I saw Tell, framed against the light, his face a block of stone as he watched us go. At the last moment, he might have smiled, but that could have been a trick of the light.

Karen and I ran without knowing where to go. We retraced our steps down the long railroad, painfully exposed and expecting any moment to be overtaken and shot or, in my case, something else. I couldn't think around the pain, but some deep-seated fear kept my four legs fumbling forward. We made it back to the car, and I couldn't take another step. I collapsed against the wheel of the rear passenger's side.

"Rick, don't give up on me now." Karen huddled by the side of the car, rifle propped on the roof, checking to see if anyone followed behind us. She popped off another shot and then one more for good measure.

I might have whined, but everything was hazy. I saw her at the door of the vehicle, and then she somehow opened it and was half-lifting, half-pushing me into the back seat.

"God, you stink, wolf." When she straightened, I saw a long, dark streak on her jacket that hadn't been there before. It glistened in the ambient light as she moved, and I realized I hadn't stopped bleeding. Another faint movement, and then she sat in the front seat, wrenching the key in the ignition. The engine started, and as we moved, I felt a great black nothing.

20

Tell kept this entire operation pretty close to his chest, and I'd just been lazy about seeking out the details I didn't know. Karen hadn't told me, but she had done some extracurricular research, and so she knew about the MONIKER safe house a few towns away. It turned out to be a small apartment on a quiet street, and when we rolled up in the early morning hours, there were no good people of the village to mark our coming.

I drifted in and out, fading from black to white to gray. There were monsters preying on my vision from the corners of my mind. Karen glanced back over her shoulder, and her face sported a fluorescent death's mask grin.

"Can you make it?" She looked doubtful. "We've got a flight of stairs to go."

I lifted my head, whined, and set it back down. She cursed, a sharp guttural sound in another language I didn't recognize. The mixture in the bullet spurred some bad effects, and now I saw her as a giant skeletal being with a bird's head. I whimpered because I thought she was going to eat me. Then we were inside, and someone carried me, someone who cursed every time I struggled against the arms holding me.

"You are one heavy bastard." Karen picked the lock, and we made it inside the apartment before she dropped me on the floor. I yelped and shook and changed and then sprawled naked and bleeding on the floor.

"Dammit." She closed her eyes for a moment. "Shit."

The change cleared my head somewhat. At least I wasn't hallucinating anymore. Or thought I wasn't hallucinating. I wasn't quite sure. I lay on the floor next to a couch but didn't have the energy to get up onto it or even try to pull myself up into a sitting position.

Karen came back around the corner with a white box with a thick cross on it and a pair of shorts. She knelt by my side and put the box on the floor. Grabbing me under the armpits, she wrestled me to a sitting position, then pulled the pair of shorts on and helped me get them over my hips. They were loose, but I wasn't about to hit the court to shoot some hoops. Once they were on, she shifted her attention to my shoulder and probed the skin around the gunshot. I whined again.

"Shut it, Rick." Florence Nightingale, she was not. "We're going to have to do something about your shoulder, and I don't want to hear it."

She seemed really angry, but I couldn't think of anything I had done, so maybe she wasn't angry at me.

I tried smiling at her, but it came out as a grimace as she doused a cotton gauze pad with disinfectant and swabbed the entry wound. With one hand, she held the pad against my shoulder, and with the other, she pulled me forward to look at my back. She stiffened, and I didn't like her reaction to seeing what happened back there. Sometimes, with minor injuries, the shifting of muscle and bone from the change can heal them up. Other times, it makes them worse. This seemed to be one of the latter times.

My face was in her shirt, and I smelled sweat and rosemary. I was in love and told her so. She leaned me back against the couch, took my hand, and put it over the gauze pad.

"Hold that there, Keller." She ignored whatever I was blathering on about. "I've got to make a phone call."

If I had been one hundred percent, or even maybe seventy-five percent, I would have asked a few questions. Like, how did Karen know about the safe house when I didn't? What the hell did Tell mean when he referred to the "highest bidder," and if Karen knew about things I didn't know, why didn't she know about that? Or, why had we not been pursued more determinedly back at the site of the failed interdiction? But I don't like to ask questions when I know I'm not going to like the answers, and right then, my mind could barely gather itself enough for me to ask for a glass of water.

Karen came back into the room taking the battery out of her phone and slipping the device into her pants pocket. The battery she put into her jacket and zipped the pocket shut. She knelt beside me and took the gauze. My hand dropped to her knee. I tried to find some kind of safety in her face, but all I got was more anger.

I opened my mouth to try to say something.

"They're sending someone," Karen said. "They've got a team about an hour out. I alerted them to Tell's actions at the drop."

She put another gauze pad up against my shoulder and taped it into place. It darkened rapidly. She opened a few more and pulled me forward again, this time more gently. I felt a painful pressure as she put them against the back of the wound. Everything started going shifty and dark again when she froze.

Footsteps. It was still too dark to be the neighbors, and even as torn up as I was, I realized the curious blankness in my senses meant they were protected by silver.

I thought maybe the footsteps belonged to Tell, but he wasn't the one who showed up. Karen pulled a pistol, but the men who burst through the door were prepared with heavy Kevlar vests and plenty of ammunition and hate. I was in no shape to struggle, and Karen could only take down so many before she fell under their fists.

Someone snapped a silver-laced collar around my neck, then bound my hands with silver behind my back. I convulsed with pain and the effort to change, but the silver kept me human. My vision darkened around the edges as they dragged me toward the door, head bumping against the floor. I tried to find Karen, but then my vision went completely black for about the third time that night.

I DRIFTED DEEP DOWN AGAIN, buried in the remnants of memory, the silver settling in my veins and thickening my blood. I passed in and out of consciousness through a bumpy ride in the back of some vehicle, a less-than-gentle drag down some interminable corridor stinking of propane and rat feces, and finally a small dark hole of a room that tasted of death and, for some reason, cinnamon. They had taken Karen, too, and one of the men took off her handcuffs before closing the door, but they left the silver on me. I couldn't form a coherent sentence, and she didn't have anything to say, so we simply waited in the dark.

The overhead light in the room turned on before the door opened. Karen's face was swollen with angry dark marks, a prelude to developing bruises. Abrasions covered her cheek and neck. I growled, but there wasn't a lot of strength behind the anger.

"*Herr Keller.*" The man speaking was tall, thin, blond, and wearing a white coat with a pocket protector. "My name is Dr. Gratuszcak."

I wasn't sure what to say to that, so I didn't say anything.

Karen did. "What the hell are we doing here?"

"He is here because we paid good money for him." Gratuszcak's hair was just long enough to fall over his eyes, and he pushed it back with a gesture that looked habitual. "You're here to make sure he behaves himself." He smiled at me. "I'm sure we understand each other."

Karen stood up. "Who are you?"

"Sit down, Dr. Willet." The harsh words contrasted with his previous tone. She sat down. He gestured behind him, and two men came into the small room. They picked me up, one on each arm.

Karen tried again. "Where are you taking him?"

"We need to get the bullet out." The doctor might have even smiled at her. "Don't worry. We need him in good shape."

"For what?"

Gratuszcak, ignoring her, turned and left. The men hauled me after, one of them closing and securing the door behind us.

THE ROOM WAS WHITE, and the hum from the lights set my teeth on edge. The main smell was of disinfectant over stale blood. The two men lugged me to the bed situated in the center of the room and wrestled me up onto it. They unfastened the handcuffs from my hands and then cuffed me to the rail of the bed. I fell down against the paper covering before they could push me down. The ceiling was made of white tile, and there was a corner missing from the tile directly above my head.

I blinked as a face came into view, and my eyes refocused. It wasn't Dr. Gratuszcak but someone else. I couldn't get a hold of his features; they kept slipping in and around and away from me.

The face disappeared as the man straightened. He probed my arm and found a vein. I clenched my fist, but I wasn't going anywhere. He reached over out of the range of my vision and came back with a needle. I shrank away, but he simply grabbed my arm, pinched a nerve in the elbow, and slid the plunger home effortlessly.

Whatever he slid into my veins, it hurt like hell. I started to scream, but it only lasted a second before my brain imploded on myself, and I was out again. I think I dreamed. But it could have been memory.

I WOKE up in another room, this one completely white and devoid of furniture, and I had it all to myself. Duran Duran's "Hungry Like the Wolf" came over the loudspeakers at a volume so loud I thought my ears might bleed. I couldn't hear myself think, let alone ask out loud if anyone was there. The song was just about to end, and as it spooled down, I got a momentary pause before it started up again. Someone had a sick sense of humor—and a crappy stereo system.

193

I tried to reach out with my senses, but the silver collar still fastened around my neck effectively blocked my efforts to learn more about my environment. I tried to sniff the air, but all that burned through my nose and throat was the smell of bleach. I found myself blind in more ways than one.

My shoulder wasn't hurting as much. I tried to crane my neck to get a better look at it, but all I could see was the white bandage swathing the front and back of my upper body.

The silver-laced anesthetic they knocked me out with still lingered in my system, but at least now I wasn't seeing little mutant bird creatures. My collar itched against my skin. I started to fiddle with it, turning it around my neck, probing to see if I could pick the latch.

"I wouldn't do that if I were you." The words echoed in the sudden silence.

I jumped and turned. Apparently, I was as blind as I thought because I hadn't seen Dr. Gratuszcak come in, flanked by two men with serious-looking weaponry. One of them trained his weapon at me while the other set down a metal folding chair in the middle of the room.

"Please." Dr. Gratuszcak motioned to the chair. "Have a seat."

I stayed on the ground. "Why wouldn't you?"

"Because the minute you take that off, my colleague will shoot you in the head with a silver bullet." He carried a file, which he opened. Licking his index finger, he began to page through its contents. I was unnerved and angry to see that it was similar to—hell, it was exactly the same as—the "TOP SECRET" labeled folders much beloved of Agent John Tell.

"MONIKER's record-keeping is quite thorough," he said. "It seems you've taken a lot of damage in your career, but I don't see any record of that sort of head trauma." His voice was very smooth, almost devoid of accent, and I couldn't smell anything from him—at all. It set my skin creeping. He closed the folder and clasped it behind his back in folded hands. The posture gave him the attitude of a college professor about to embark on a long lecture on an obscure topic. "Although I'm sure it would be a fascinating study, we couldn't be sure you would survive it, so perhaps we'll save that for later."

I stared at him. "What the fuck?"

"We have some questions," he continued. "How you answer them will determine a number of things."

"Like what?"

"Like when the next time you see food might be." He flicked his eyes to the men flanking him. "Or the amount of pain to which your colleague downstairs is subjected."

"You've got my life's story right there," I growled. "What the hell else you want to know?"

Dr. Gratuszcak snapped his fingers, and one of the men handed him a tablet. He slid something on the touchscreen and held it up for me to see. It was the video feed from Karen's cell. She sat on the bed. She looked pissed.

"As you can see, she is currently unharmed," he said. "Keep asking questions, and I promise you that will change."

I came up off the floor at him but abruptly stopped against the two barrels the guards pointed at my chest. I growled and reached for the change, but I came up empty. The silver in my system and around my neck had tucked it away. The temperature in the room stayed cold, but sweat glistened on my skin. Someone told these people, whoever they were, a lot about me. I had a feeling that person was an asshole who answered to the name John Tell.

I sat back down on the chair.

"Good." The doctor nodded. "Let's continue."

He remained standing but began pacing back and forth. He reminded me of a giant cat at the zoo, stalking its prey, but this time I was the one on the wrong side of the bars.

"First question, and you can feel free to estimate this one, when were you born and where?"

"A long time ago." I couldn't help myself. "In a galaxy far, far away."

He didn't react visibly. He simply pulled his phone from his pocket, made a call, and then held the tablet up for me to see.

On the screen, Karen stood up as two large men entered her cell. They didn't do anything, just stood there. I saw her body tense, and anger once again flooded through me. With it came a slight clearing of the blurriness around my brain, and I felt the change in my grasp for just a second, but then it retreated back over the border just enough to leave me stuck.

"I'll ask you again," Gratuszcak continued, holding the tablet so I could see the screen. "When and where?"

"Early nineteenth-century Bavaria." Close enough to not be a lie.

Gratuszcak nodded. The screen on the tablet darkened, but he didn't bother to wake it back up. Instead, he simply handed the device back to one of the men and resumed his pacing.

"MONIKER's records of you don't begin until the last year of the war," he stated. "What did you do before then?"

I stared at him. It wasn't that I didn't intend to answer the question. At this point, I couldn't see a reason not to, especially with Karen downstairs and not a lot of options anywhere else. It's just that I had no idea where to start.

"Start wherever you need to." I jumped. That was an eerie trick, to pull a question out of my head and feed me the answer. Although maybe he was just good at interrogation.

"I was a soldier for a long time." That was the truth. I had been for more than sixty years before the war.

The Germans used to have a saying for what we were: *Das Wolfhaut getraegt.* To put on the wolf skin. Folktales tried to explain the few tracks we left by claiming we were men wearing magical skins of wolves. But then, myth has always attempted to explain away what some otherwise rational people wanted to believe in.

My service didn't begin in the 1920s, but it was the beginning of the end. I took off the uniform at the end of the Great War, but no matter what else I tried to do, by then, I didn't know what else to be but a soldier. I never believed in the promises of leaders—I'd been at war for more than half my life and seen what comes of listening too closely to what our masters tried to sell. But I did love my country, and I was prideful enough to be flattered when they came to cajole me back into the fold.

Then came the attacks, the assaults on the people I'd sheltered with, the destruction of the Institute in Berlin where, for a time, I'd found a home.

That was the night I went missing, the start of several nights of death seeking those who wore the symbol that polluted the streets of my homeland. As they burned people and books and knowledge, I lost myself in high mountain garrisons and the tunnels and bunkers of the SS, and I would like to give some justification or expiation for those deeds. But there was none. At the time, I simply followed my nature. I have no remaining feelings of guilt, or so I'd like to think, only memories of blood on snow.

I had never tried to explain any of this to anyone, and I wasn't about to start now. I shrugged.

"What else do you want to know?" I picked my teeth with my pinky fingernail.

Dr. Gratuszcak was one of those rare humans who didn't want to punch me in the face ten minutes after meeting me. In fact, I wasn't getting any emotion off him at all. It could have been the crappy reception my senses were currently getting, but I began to suspect there was little there to be sensed in the first place. He nodded to his two men, and they each took a side. One kicked my legs out from under me, and the two held me down on the ground.

The good doctor left the room and returned with a little rolling table, the kind actual medical doctors sometimes use. On the table lay a tray with assorted implements and syringes. Apparently, they had more than one interrogation tactic at hand.

He picked up the syringe and I lost it, bucking up against the two men holding me down, trying to get away from whatever other poison he intended to pump into my veins. The adrenaline coursing through my body started once again to clear my system of what was already polluting it. I reached for the change, almost grasped it, teetering on the edge of it.

The plunger dashed home, and I fell back on the ground, writhing. It wasn't silver, but it still sent a wave of white pain through all of the nerve endings in my body. The pain concentrated around my joints, and I felt my body twist in ways it wasn't supposed to go, popping in and out of place. The wave passed. The two gentlemen helped me back to my chair.

"What was that?" I panted, gasping.

"A trigger." Gratuszcak frowned. "Something your organization has been working on for a while. It's not as effective as advertised."

I sensed that the trigger would have been effective if the weapon, namely me, wasn't broken. It would be typical of MONIKER to have been cooking something up in the lab even if their favorite rat had jumped the maze. Not for the first time, I wondered if my entire life in Vermont had just been me at the end of a very long leash.

The change pushed against my skin, urgent and demanding. I held it back now, the silver at my neck assisting. If these people wanted me to change, that was the last thing I wanted to do.

"No matter." Gratuszcak's forehead smoothed back into his normal, banal features. "We have plenty of time to refine that particular formula."

"Go fuck yourself." I'm always at my most witty in these situations.

He perused his instrument selection but didn't pick anything up.

"MONIKER had you for what? Fifty, sixty years?" I didn't answer, but he didn't need me to. Apparently, he'd read everything in my file.

"They had you for over half a century, and at the end of it all, you broke ranks and ran like a child who's tired of playing a game."

That wasn't the most flattering way of putting it, but he got the essentials right.

"We want you to work for us," Gratuszcak said. "Or rather, we have an interest in duplicating your special talents. You see, MONIKER was mostly interested in getting you to work for them again."

I stared at him, biting back the pain that crashed heavier and heavier against the barriers I threw up against the change. I couldn't even summon a single-syllable profanity.

He picked up another syringe. "There are several chemical compounds MONIKER was experimenting with, physiological behavior modification, psychiatric pharmaceuticals, that sort of thing. I'd go into more detail, but I'm pretty sure you wouldn't understand a word I was saying."

"I don't understand a word you're saying now," I managed. "Don't let that stop you."

He uncapped the syringe. I shrank back, but the two guys holding me in the chair weren't getting any smaller. I wasn't going anywhere.

"They had two formulas they were going to try out on you," he continued. "One to bring the change, the other one to control you. I think they had the chance to try one on you?"

I thought back to that first meeting, when Karen had destabilized the change, and then our nightly sessions at the old factory, when I struggled to keep control through the fog of the nano-silver. These people had apparently come up with some new and improved version.

"This one, though." Gratuszcak probed my arm to find a vein. "This is where we'll see how close we are to getting our money's worth out of you."

I wasn't quite sure what he meant, but the words "behavior" and "pharmaceutical" were enough to spur another fit of adrenaline and rage, and I rocked back in my chair. I snapped and snarled, squirming my arms out of reach, but the episode only lasted a few seconds before one guy had me in a chokehold with one arm twisted up around my back and the other holding out my other arm, ready for Gratuszcak's needle.

The change, fickle traitor bastard, leapt to the surface, ready and hungry to go.

Here's the secret about the change. It hurts. Even when the change is happy to come and responds to the slightest call, the pain is so deep and fierce it can't be described. That was one of the reasons I had stopped controlling it after I left the game.

It was a point of pride to be able to overcome the pain, but it had the side effect that any manmade efforts at inflicting hurt paled in comparison. I screamed out loud but kept laughing on the inside until he finally got the needle positioned over my skin and sent the particles through the needle into my bloodstream.

Then I was screaming for real and decided it was time to end this shadow show.

21

I n case you were wondering, this is the disadvantage to secret, experimental formulas. They don't always work exactly the way they're supposed to. The men waited expectantly, and if I hadn't been screaming, it would have been almost comedic. Eventually, the pain died down enough. I smiled up at Gratuszcak.

"What was that again? Some magical mind control serum?" I laughed. "You think no one ever tried that before?"

I laughed again, but the change was clawing its way up my spine, and it took every effort I had to keep it clenched down.

Gratuszcak didn't seem perturbed. He simply stepped closer and felt for my pulse. It rocketed under his index and middle fingers, and he smiled back.

"It's getting a little harder, isn't it, Herr Keller, holding back the beast?" He made a note on his pad. "I understand you are trying to maintain control, but truly, what we are interested in is your other form. So please, do not try to stop the change."

The gunshot echoed in the sterile room, and one of the men holding me slumped away, freeing my arm. I twisted away and hit the floor as another bullet found the other man. He landed beside me, sightless eyes staring at the ceiling below the gunshot wound in the middle of his forehead.

"Don't move."

The voice came so familiar and welcome I almost cried. I scrambled to my knees off the cold concrete floor. Gratuszcak grabbed for me, but I sprawled out of his reach, rolling and coming to my feet. I blinked back a moment of vertigo, and as it cleared, I saw Karen framed in the doorway, rifle at the ready. There was blood on her clothes, but none of it belonged to her.

They had brought her from the railyards thinking she was someone to keep me docile. It might have worked, but they had seriously underestimated her ability to kick ass and take names, and she was erasing a couple off her list. She had taken out the two men in the room downstairs and then mowed her way through another dozen before showing up at my door with enough extra armaments to outfit a squad of military police.

I was already in love, but this gave new meaning to the word.

"You okay?" She kept her weapon pointed at the good doctor.

"Fine," I replied, fumbling for the collar around my neck.

"You." Karen gestured at Gratuszcak with her rifle. "Help him with that." The man hesitated, and she took a step forward, raising the weapon and giving him a face full of intention. "Help him *now*," she suggested.

The doctor unbuckled the latch behind my neck. He pulled it free, and I shook my head. This time, the vertigo cleared right up. My vision sharpened, and even though the smell of bleach remained overwhelming, I started to sense other things below the bleach, things that smelled of blood and death and other promises.

"Rick, we've got to get out of here," Karen said. "I need you to stay upright because we're bringing him with us."

Another party pooper—but she was right. I could eat him later, once we were out and safe and had gotten a little more information out of him.

With him leading the way, we headed out into the corridor, locking the room behind us. The halls were empty except for the occasional body Karen had added to her count on the way up. I was impressed, and I already knew what she could do.

"As far as I can tell, we're still below the ground floor," Karen said. "I've been trying to find the exit, but all they have are more stairs."

I grabbed Gratuszcak by the scruff of his neck and shook him gently. "Where do we go?"

He didn't say anything, so I stopped, turned him to face me, and gave him a face full of teeth.

"Where?" I asked again, this time less nicely.

He shrugged. I still wasn't getting anything off of him, which was weird, but we didn't have time to get into it. "Follow me."

The doctor led us to a flight of stairs half hidden behind a bend in the corridor. I've had recurring nightmares about this sort of building: long wide rooms, narrow corridors, and no entry or exit in sight. It was with a not-quite-concealed sigh of relief that we emerged from the upper basement onto another floor. I still wasn't sure where we were, but at least we were getting somewhere. Up here, I could start to hear sounds of traffic and footsteps.

"Are we going to meet anyone we should worry about?" Karen prodded him in the back with the rifle's flash suppressor.

"No," said Gratuszcak. "It's still early."

I couldn't tell if he was lying, but I growled to let him know it would be a bad idea to do so. I expected some villainous reply, but he didn't say anything.

"Which way?" Karen prodded him again, hard enough to cause him to stumble slightly. "And not the front entrance, either."

"Follow me," Gratuszcak said again.

He led us down and around a corridor. This floor seemed to be some sort of mix between hotel lobby and corporate offices. I wasn't sure where we were, but hopefully, we would be gone soon.

We turned another corner and finally, at the end of the hall, saw two large glass-paned doors. I could see the street outside, the first rays of false dawn lightening the stones in the street and glancing off the windshield of the car parked out front. I'd never been so happy to see a street in my life, or at least in recent years.

"Walk," Karen said. I hadn't realized we had stopped until we started forward again.

I wouldn't have noticed the door. It was made of dark wood and was closed, and I didn't have much situational awareness once I focused on the exit at the end of the hall. But the faintest bit of scent stopped me in my tracks. I grabbed Gratuszcak by the shoulder, rocking him back on his heels. Karen swore softly as she almost ran into me.

"What is it?"

"Something..." I trailed off. "Hold on."

I left Gratuszcak there, not worried. Karen could handle him. I pushed the door open and stepped inside.

The room was larger than I expected. Floor-to-ceiling bookcases lined most of the walls, and where there were no bookcases, there were expensive oil paintings hanging on wood-paneled surfaces. There were two large leather armchairs facing an expansive oak desk, behind which another chair stood mute sentry. The smell of leather and oil and glue washed over me along with the curious void I was coming to associate with Gratuszcak.

"This your office?" I knew the answer but asked anyway.

He shrugged, which I took to mean yes.

The scent that had piqued my interest persisted there, somewhere. It reminded me of snow and pines. I followed it to the shelves. There were collections of books older than I mingled with newer texts. He owned quite a collection of psychology and neuroscience, from Freud and Jung to some Czech writer whose name I could barely read let alone pronounce in my head. But the scent I hunted for wasn't there.

"Keller, what the hell?" Karen prodded. "We need to get out of here. Now."

"I just need a second." I prowled closer to the desk. There the scent came even stronger. That and something else.

I opened the top right drawer of the desk. It stuck a little as if the wood had expanded, and it took a little jiggling to get it to pull free. Nestled inside, I saw my pistol. I reached down to grab it, and it burned slightly against my skin. The silver bullets were still in it.

Someone had set it in the drawer on top of a chamois, which I used to wrap the weapon and drop it in the pocket of my shorts. I would take the silver out later and hope the gun wasn't irreparably taken out of my grasp.

I pulled the drawer out farther. It responded with a reluctant screech, but there was more to be found at the back of the space. My fingertips touched leather, and I closed my hand around a thick notebook. I drew it out and held it to my nose. There, under the smell of old ink and paper, lingered the thread I had sensed. Cold and pines, vodka and baking powder. Dmitri.

I flipped open the notebook. Dmitri had recorded every session in minute, precise Cyrillic, his language clinical and unemotional. I swallowed back the change that even now threatened to unmask itself at the memory of my time within the walls of Dmitri's little kingdom.

"Is there anything in there that can help us?"

I closed the notebook gently. I needed to get out of there, needed to run, to break something, to kill something, to let the change run its course until the memories that I had become so adept at burying deep within my subconscious went back to their hiding places and left me alone.

"What does it say?" Karen asked again. The cramped, cursive Cyrillic was beyond her Russian comprehension skills.

I shook my head, the anger igniting, slowly burning away the remnants of the silver they had pumped into me. I felt the change within my grasp, and I ached for it.

"It says that MONIKER sold me out." I held myself tightly against rage. "All of this—the mission, the team, the whatever I thought you might want from me—was nothing but another line of bullshit."

"Rick..." She trailed off. There really wasn't anything to say.

"We need to get going." I shivered involuntarily. "Backup could arrive any minute, and I want to get as far away from here as possible. You think he knows anything about where they're holding the girls?"

It was a long shot. I didn't think Gratuszcak knew anything about our previous mission, didn't think the two were anyhow related, but it was worth asking.

Karen shook her head. "He doesn't know crap."

"So what do we do with him?"

"Whatever you want," she answered. "I'm tired of this bullshit. I'll find a ride and wait for you outside."

She turned on her heel and walked out of the room. Gratuszcak and I faced each other.

"You're not going to tell me anything, are you?"

"Would you like me to tell you yes?" He squinted at me, a slight tightening of the skin around his eyes.

"Not necessarily." They were the last words I spoke before my four paws landed on the expensive carpet, and I lunged for him. Even though I intended to fill the growing void in my belly with the good doctor, when my teeth closed around his throat, I tasted a strange bitterness and spat it out. Hacking and coughing, I spit again, trying to get the taste of him out of my mouth. I finally changed back, pulling on my shorts and patting the pocket to make sure my gun was still there. It wasn't immediately obvious if he was still alive, but there was enough blood soaking into the beautiful wool of the carpet to satisfy me he wouldn't be for long.

I STEPPED OUTSIDE INTO A COLD, crisp Bavarian morning. The air brought all measure of delicious aromas, and I started to salivate. The change had burned away everything in my system, and I felt good—clear-headed, no vertigo—if completely ravenous. I pressed against my shoulder with my fingers. Luckily, the hole that had taken me out the night before felt just about healed. A few more days, and it would be gone, leaving nothing but the memory of another close call.

The shorts I wore were made from someone's old cut-off battle dress uniform pants, woodland green pattern, and the cargo pockets on each leg were big enough to hold the pistol and the notebook. The pants felt even looser, and I gripped them with one hand to keep them from falling off my hips.

Karen waited outside in a small black Volkswagen. I didn't ask where she got it, just closed the door behind me quickly so we could leave before its owner came looking for it. My breath had briefly steamed in the morning air before I hopped in. She had the heater on full blast, and my entire body began to sweat. I felt a little nauseous.

"Can we turn down the heat?"

"Crack your window." She wrenched the car in gear. That was the last thing she said as she peeled out.

I didn't know where we were going until I started seeing signs for the city of Aachen.

"Why are we going there?" I asked Karen when she confirmed our destination.

"Our mission was to interdict the girls and disrupt the trafficking node," she said. "The last shipment landed in Aachen. They might have switched up the exchange site, but my bet is they're still in the city somewhere. We can make it there in an hour or two if we don't hit traffic."

At the speed she was driving, I didn't doubt it. I wore my seatbelt, and I usually don't, but it helped keep me in the seat.

"Why don't we just call the *Polizei* and let them take over?" It wasn't a serious suggestion, but I thought one of us should throw it out there. "They have a lot more resources than we do, and they're not idiots."

She looked at me briefly, and I feared for my life in the long seconds she took her eyes off the road. She turned back to the road without answering. But I understood. No way were we calling in the cops. Not yet.

We were, instead, going to crash the party and see if we could find our erstwhile teammate and get the answers we both wanted. I finally understood my part in this. Apparently, what I was had not been kept as secret as I'd thought, and my disappearance from the MONIKER fold had encouraged other groups to make a play for me. One of those groups had gotten to Agent Tell, who chose to betray his country and his partner for whatever they offered. Having been through all that once myself, I wondered what his tipping point had been, what price he had been willing to pay, and if he found it, in the end, to be worth it.

The sun rose higher as we drove, and I began to feel hungry again, but the cold window against my face settled my stomach. We made one stop to pick up sandwiches and a sweatshirt and shoes for me. I didn't have any money, and I didn't ask where Karen got the euros, but apparently, she had her own resources.

The food in my stomach and the warmth of the car knocked me out. I only woke up when Karen rolled to a stop at the rear of a youth hostel. I opened my eyes and blinked blearily.

"Where are we?"

"Someplace we won't look too out of place." She let the car idle, looking around. "From what my contacts are telling me, the girls will arrive in town sometime soon and spend the night before they head out to wherever they're selling them."

"What's the plan?" I rubbed my eyes with the palm of my hand. "Show up and wreck shop?"

"If this were the 90s." She put the car in park and turned off the engine. "You should work on your slang, hipster. Come on, let's get in."

Karen had enough money to pay for a small room convenient for its privacy. Although, like all the other rooms in the hostel, it shared a communal toilet with everyone else on the floor. I worried briefly about letting the other guests see us but figured we wouldn't be there long, so I availed myself of the facilities. Taking a shower was wonderful. Toilet paper, too, is great. I love modern conveniences.

I had no idea what we were going to do. We had a limited supply of ammunition, no money, no equipment, and I was all out of friends. Force of habit kept me thinking of myself as all alone on this one, but I wasn't. Karen had more than a couple favors of her own to call in, and she got to work.

When I came back from the shower, dressed again in my shorts and sweatshirt, she handed me another stack of euros and sent me out to pick up a few things. Since one of them was dinner, I didn't mind. If I were by myself, the entire plan would consist of a frontal assault, and probably more people than bad guys would die. Whatever Karen planned would definitely be better.

One of the men she sent me to meet handed me a heavy box that smelled of gunpowder and brass and clinked when I exchanged it for most of the money she had given me. He raised an eyebrow at the fact that I was wearing shorts in Germany in January, but he didn't ask any questions. The whole trip took me about an hour and a half, including stopping for pre-made salads, sandwiches, and sodas.

I brought all these things up to our room and showed them to Karen, who didn't say much but nodded in approval. She waited until I got distracted with food and then went outside to make the rest of her phone calls. I didn't blame her. She'd been betrayed by one member of the team already—and he had been the one she trusted. I was perfectly content to fall in line and be the toothsome violence in her well-laid plan.

22

My grandfather claimed to have fought for Peter the Great. I always thought he was full of shit, but lately, I wasn't so sure. He had told me many tales of those times, whopping great stories of the sneaking about on foreign soil that could be had by an enterprising wolf. My mother always told me I took after him too much for my own good. She was neither happy nor particularly surprised when I left home to don a soldier's uniform. Thinking about that makes me uneasy. A tale for another time.

It had been a long time since I wore a uniform, but I still enjoyed sneaking about. The building housing our targets, though located in a residential area, seemed made for such an activity. It lay nestled along a street of old houses, narrow alleyways not even large enough for a VW Bug running through the warren. This was old Germany, the former seat of the Holy Roman Emperor, the city my ancestors had run through when the nights were dark enough to hide their passage.

Through cajoling, bribery, and some pretty vicious threats, Karen narrowed the possible exchange sites to three. Two of them we struck off the list after a few nights' surveillance. Too much traffic, too much light, too few shadows. The third one was perfect—isolated, off a side street, with plenty of nooks and crannies and gables to break up the light and cover our approach.

Karen and I would be making almost the exact same play we followed running The Gauntlet back at the old mill without, of course, the benefit of someone at our backs watching to make sure we didn't fall through the holes in the stairs. The other difference was we would be coming in from the roof.

The building next door was a large house long ago converted to apartments. We waited until a couple left the building, too involved in their discussion to notice as we caught the door and let ourselves inside.

We made a queer-looking pair, me in my shorts and sweatshirt and Karen in a thigh-length trench coat conveniently concealing the many weapons stashed about her person. She also carried the notebook I lifted from Gratuszcak's office. I wasn't sure if I would get it back, but I felt the team needed some gesture of trust, and I didn't have anything else to give. She tucked it away with my pistol in one of her many pockets, buttoned securely down against any strenuous activity that might occur.

We came up onto the roof, letting ourselves out the emergency exit onto a sharply gabled surface. The alley below now seemed much less narrow than it did before. I very much did not like heights. Karen looked at me, smiled, then took a running leap and flew across the gap. She scrambled briefly on the other side, the rubber soles of her boots catching against the roofing tiles. I started breathing again only when she moved up a safe distance, holding herself on the roof by grasping the ridge. She motioned back at me.

I froze. The way down seemed really far. She frowned and gestured even harder. The setting sun flushed her deep in shadow, but I could see the expression on her face, and it wasn't pretty. I figured I should probably get over there before she came back to get me, so I gathered my nerves together, swallowed them down, and backed up a little. I ran a few steps and launched myself out into space.

I landed on my knees, and pain drove through them. It quickly faded, and I scrabbled after Karen, following her as she led the way to the emergency exit. I hugged the roof as she jimmied the lock and then followed her inside as quickly and gratefully as I could. Roofs are no place for wolves.

We paused inside the door, closing it behind us. It was dark, not pitch black, but just devoid enough of light to make it hard for Karen to see. I tried to calm my breathing, panting hard. I really, really hate heights.

"Follow me." I shrugged out of my shorts and sweatshirt, kicking them to the side of the stairs so she wouldn't trip and fall over them. I gritted my teeth against the change as I went furry. She placed one hand on my neck and followed me down.

We reached the top floor, and Karen nodded to me as we split up. We had agreed to cover more space on our own and were splitting up the place by floors. I had the evens, she had the odds—American numbering, not European—and the signal to come to the other's rescue would be a lot of gunfire and screaming.

She drifted off like a shadow in the unique way she owned. I sensed her presence receding down the hall, the scent of her drifting behind her like a wraith. My tongue lolled, and I panted, heading down the corridor. My toenails clacked against the hardwood floor, and I tried to step more gingerly.

Now that I was fully wolf, the place opened up to me like jasmine under a full moon. I could hear movements, sense aromas, and taste things on my tongue the darkness hid from mere humans. Not all the rooms were occupied. There had been a lot of traffic in and out of the building and some of the tracks were hard to make out. I put my nose to the ground to get a better feel and kept going.

The top floor gave me nothing. Maybe one room had a couple of people in it, but they didn't smell important, and from their heavy breathing, I could tell they were sleeping. I nudged the door with my shoulder, and it opened. I slunk my way in, trying to stay in the shadows. There were two men, one crashing on the couch, one on the bed. They had a couple of guns each, and I took them to be security, catching a quick nap before the shipment arrived.

I picked their weapons up by the leather of their holsters. It was awkward carrying them in my mouth, but I simply found another empty room and hid them in a closet with a conveniently open door. If they did wake up for some commotion, at least they would be coming to the party unarmed.

I padded down the stairs, pausing on the landing to suss out my partner's location. Karen crouched at the far end of the hall. I gathered she'd found as little as I had. I continued down the stairs and stopped short of the landing on the next floor.

Light spilled out from the corridor. I shrank back from the smells and people, chuffing slightly to let Karen know through the earbud I'd come up against something. I waited and watched. In the hallway before me, several men supervised the unloading of the shipment, about fifteen women between the ages of fifteen and twenty-one, dressed in various traveling outfits. The waft of decay, body odor, and cheap perfume wrinkled my nostrils, and I growled softly in spite of myself.

"You see the girls?" Her voice came through barely a whisper.

I growled again.

"I'll take that as a yes," she said. "Hold your position. I've got one more room, and then I'll be down to you."

I chuffed again and kept myself pressed against the wall. The men ushered the last of the girls into the room and then followed them in, closing the door behind them. On the one hand, we found the shipment. On the other hand, going into that room full of armed men and unarmed girls would result in the deaths of more than a few innocent bystanders.

Karen came up behind me. I felt a lot better with her rifle pointed down the corridor.

"What the fuck?"

I followed Karen's gaze to the men coming up the hallway. If I hadn't been furry, I would have echoed the sentiment. At first, I thought he was leading the way down the hall. As he stumbled and tried to catch himself, I realized his hands were tied behind his back, and one of the two men walking behind him had a weapon pointed at his spine.

Tell stumbled to a knee but managed to regain his posture by leaning on a wall. He looked in bad shape, his face in worse repair than Karen's, and I wondered what had gone wrong for him. Betrayal never goes as planned for the traitor. You could look at me for living proof of that.

I craned my neck and whined up at Karen. She took a quick glance out into the corridor. I felt her hand pat my shoulder.

"Go," she whispered.

I launched myself out into the light of the hallway, a silent, streaking presence on the men before they knew what happened. Tell saw me coming and threw himself to the ground, flattening himself onto the dusty wood surface as I hurdled his body, aiming for the throat of the man with the gun.

The second man tried to kick me, and the tips of his steel-toed boots dusted my side as I twisted out of the way, tearing the rest of the first man's throat out in the process. It took only a few more seconds of panic and claws, and then the second man lay prone on the floor, adding his blood to the rapidly growing pool.

There hadn't been time for either of them to scream. I nudged Tell up. He scrambled to his feet. I hit the backs of his knees with my nose, herding him toward the stairs where we could take a moment to regroup and figure out what to do with our erstwhile teammate. He went reluctantly, but then Karen stepped out of the shadows, pointed her rifle at him, and gestured for us to hurry up. That and the creak of the door opening behind us sped his steps, and we made it back into the concealment of the landing before the men came back out into the hall.

"Tell." Karen kept her weapon aimed at him. "If you want to live, stay here."

He looked up at her, hope warring with disbelief. I think he thought for a second we had actually come for him before the realization came full force that, of course, we wouldn't have come to rescue someone who sold us out. He shook his head.

"I'm not going anywhere." The mumbled sound betrayed the loss of at least one or more teeth.

The men in the hall reacted predictably when they saw their comrades lying on the ground. There was a lot of yelling, a lot of commotion, and eventually, all the cold, hard men who had followed the girls into the room came out of it.

Karen carried the big guns, so I stepped to the side and cowered as she started sending rounds down the hallway, wondering if my hearing would survive the night. She fired with discipline, shooting three-round bursts and adjusting fire quickly and accurately. The men in the hall dropped to the floor, confused at first as to where the rounds were coming from. The few men not bleeding from the forehead figured it out quickly and tried to return fire.

Bullets splintered the doorjamb, gouging into the wall behind us. Tell huddled against the wall, trying to evade their path. I heard sets of footsteps on the stairs, and then the men who had been sleeping on the upper floors came into my field of vision.

A sharp pain—a stray bullet from the hall—pinched my side momentarily, ruining my leap. Instead of clearing the flight of stairs, I landed awkwardly in the middle of the steps, scrambling and clawing at the slippery wood. The first of the men fell on me before I could gain my feet, and we clawed at each other as we tumbled back down.

The two of us rolled into Tell, whose head bounced off the wall, but then my teeth found my attacker's neck, and it was all over. Karen ducked back against the railing, taking cover as she continued firing at men in the hall. The angle was all wrong; I couldn't see what was going on.

Without their guns, still safely hidden on the upper floor, the last man found himself out of options. Every time he reached for me, I snapped, closing teeth around skin. He jerked back, flesh flapping from his arm. Finally, he took a page from my book and launched himself at me in a rugby tackle. He was a big guy, flattening me right to the ground. I'm strong, but I couldn't get leverage to get him off me.

Tell had been knocked loopy but not completely out. He kicked at the head of the guy who had me pinned. The man's grip around my neck and body loosened for a second, and I started to wriggle my way from his grasp. Karen's rifle rang out, and he stopped squirming.

I'd had enough of trying to claw my way out from under three hundred pounds of muscle and gear. I reached for the change, and with my human limbs, I began sorting my way out from the pile on the floor. I almost didn't recognize the quiet in the hall. My ears rang like a bell choir from all the close-quarters gunfire.

I heal quickly, and my eardrums are no exception. I heard Karen say something and shook my head to clear it. She held out a pair of shorts. I took them. We seemed to be in the clear, and I didn't want to traumatize the women any further when we walked into the room.

"Nice shooting, Willet." Tell didn't exaggerate. While I was wrestling with Mr. Rugby Tackle, Karen had finished off the men in the hall, shifted fire without pause, and shot him, a near-perfect head-shot in the dark.

We paused in the stairwell to regroup and re-survey the hall. Once my ears cleared, I couldn't hear anything except the odd shuffle and muted weeping from the room where the women were being held.

I tried to separate the various scents coming to me, but the adrenaline and death blended into a primordial soup, and I couldn't figure out what came from where. "You see anything?" I asked.

"No, we're clear." Karen checked her mag and exchanged it for a full one.

"I'll go first." I didn't ask for my weapon. I didn't want the business end of a rifle to be the first thing the women would see. "We don't want to spook them."

"Fine." She raised her rifle to cover my approach.

I wasn't much of a better sight, leading the way down the hall barefoot and in shorts, other men's blood smeared across my side and the tops of my shoulders. I picked my way around the bodies on the floor. For a moment, I felt nauseated. It was a weird feeling. I thought I was done wading through bodies.

We paused outside the door, locked on the outside with a sliding bolt. A simple yet effective way of ensuring their human cargo stayed where it was supposed to.

"What time is it?" I directed the question to Karen, who stood at my back, covering the hallway just in case we had missed someone.

"We've got about twenty minutes before the cops show up," she answered without looking at her wrist.

"Are you sure?"

"Yes." She sounded impatient. "Now poke your head in there, tell them to stay calm, and let's get Tell and get the hell out of here."

"Yes, ma'am." I didn't bother throwing a mock salute this time. I was ready to go home.

I slid the bolt back and opened the door.

A SINGLE SWINGING bulb illuminated the room. The light cast unflattering shadows. The women in the room were hungry, exhausted, and terrified. I could smell their fatigue as the door opened —their fear was steeped in adrenaline past the point human bodies could endure. They had been frightened for so long they could no longer react.

"*Dyevushki*." I held my hands out so they could see I wasn't armed. "*Spokoini*."

Their gazes focused on me, but none of them spoke.

"How many of you are there?" I asked, still in Russian. They were remaining calm, but it was the calm of unbearable stress.

"I think...fourteen?" One of the women spoke up. She spoke Russian with the accent of someone raised in one of the former Soviet satellite countries. "Who are you?"

"A friend." I meant it. "Don't worry. The police are on their way."

It wasn't the right thing to say. Several of the women started crying again.

"Can anyone tell me the names of the people who brought you here?" I tried again. "Who were they?"

No one would talk to me anymore. I had the sense there was no good to be done in that room, at least not by me.

23

I had almost gotten the girls settled down when I felt it—that curious void stinking of silver, accompanied by a strange emptiness. Something was very wrong.

I pointed to one of the girls who seemed less panic-stricken than the others, the one who had spoken to me before. "I'm going to lock this door. Don't worry. I'll come back."

She nodded and huddled with the others against the wall. I went out into the hall, closing the door behind me. Karen still stood guard, shifting her stance slightly as I came up next to her.

"What is it?" She didn't look at me as she spoke, keeping her gaze focused on any threat still alive in the house. "We've got to get out of here."

"We've got company," I told her. "I think."

The hallway went dark. Not the darkness of someone turning off the lights, but the utter pitch black, heart-racing absence of light and the ability to sense and smell. I felt wrapped in a roll of thick wool, unable to catch even a glimpse of anything. The silence roared in my ears. I couldn't even feel Karen standing next to me.

I stumbled, losing my balance in the void. I tried to catch myself, but the disorientation was complete, and I wasn't sure if I had already fallen, where the walls were, or where my partner had gotten to. A high-pitched whine started to build in my ears. I tried to shake it off, but the more I swung out wildly, the closer the darkness got.

I struck out again and again. The motion was uncoordinated, un-aimed, but as I gathered the kinetic energy around me, the black across my vision took on a curious tint. I had never seen this before. It wasn't any of the darker or lighter shades of white, black, or gray that normally comprised my vision. Rather it was what I have often imag-ined the color red to be—a bright, bloody field of anger and hate.

I reached inside, swung again, and came out wolf. The change tore through me, triumphant, burning through the fog smothering me. The red retreated to the edge of my vision, sharpening and enhancing it. An enormous surge ripped through me. I landed on four feet, snap-ping and growling...ready.

Karen lay on the floor, still and unmoving. I wasn't sure if she was dead, but at this point I was beyond caring, even for her. I searched for my enemies.

"Wolf."

The voice sounded in my head, not my ears. I reared up, trying to understand where it came from. I took off running, cornering in the narrow hallway, searching for whatever could speak to me without words or sound.

The building was old and narrow, and I received my answer as I raced past a dark wooden door. I tried to stop myself sliding on the floor, scrabbling to keep my balance.

Sniffing tentatively, I came back to the door. The silver lacing the lock mechanism burned my nose, and I backed away, whining.

A click sounded, and the door swung open. I slunk through, approaching the top of what appeared to be a long, dark stretch of stairs heading down to the basement. I growled. I really dislike long, dark basements guarded by silver doors.

As I waited, hesitating, the light below clicked on. The voice came again.

"Wolf."

The word in my head carried with it a curious compulsion, one I could sense without necessarily feeling impelled to follow. But I had too many unanswered questions in my past to pass up a chance to take care of this one, and so I started down the stairs.

THE ROOM WAS huge and blank. I pulled up short just off the last steps. The six men standing in the center of the room in a semicircle emanated the same complete void I had experienced in the presence of Dr. Gratuszcak. I couldn't smell anything from them, only sensed a faint thrum hinting at the silver in their bloodstream. Behind them stood a medical examination table, and next to that, a tray of strange instruments and bottles of liquid.

Around the outside of the room, laboratory tables lined up in cold, unyielding ranks. On each of them lay women's bodies in various states of dissection. Some were no more than a small collection of limbs. Others, like weird mannequins, lay waxy and blueish with patches of fur lining their lower extremities. Every one of them was devoid of scent except for the tangy copper taste of stale blood.

"*Dobro pozhalivat, Tovarisch* Wolf." The man in the center spoke aloud. I recognized his voice from inside my head. "My name is Pushkin."

I growled. I didn't care if he were Tolstoy reincarnated. All I wanted was to rend them into pieces and leave their bodies in separate waste bins scattered around the city.

"None of that now." Pushkin frowned. He reached out to his fellows, and they joined hands. "We are The Collective."

What the hell?

A sudden surge of raw sensation pushed through me, and the door at the top of the stairs slammed shut. I startled, whipping around to see if anyone had come in, but the stairs were empty. I turned back around in time for another blast of energy, this one aimed at me, catching me off my feet and throwing me against the wall.

It didn't hurt—just some bruising that quickly faded. I rolled to my feet, paws braced, teeth bared, snarling and growling.

Who was this guy?

"We are a group of philanthropists," Pushkin answered, "highly interested in what good you can do for us."

That made me skip a step. The surprise must have shown in my furry face.

"Would you mind rising up?" Pushkin spoke again, and I briefly wondered if any of the other men spoke, or if he pulled the questions they wanted to ask out of their heads as neatly as he seemed to be pulling from mine. "It would just make it easier for us to carry on a conversation."

I focused and considered in very vigorous, graphic detail what I thought these men could do with their conversation. To my surprise, the men actually looked somewhat offended. Curious. Apparently, the ability to pluck thoughts from my brain wasn't limited to Pushkin alone.

My body thrummed with imminent violence. As if they could sense that, too, Pushkin gathered more energy into himself and raised his hand. Their strange wave of power came crashing toward me again. I dove into it and made it a few feet before it threw me to the floor.

There were only a few more feet to go. I wasn't sure how much of that searing power they had left, but I thought it wasn't sufficient to outweigh how much I wanted to rip apart this strange, unexpected threat. I heard sounds from the floor above and spared a quick thought of concern for Karen and the other women, wondering if the police had arrived or if there were other attackers we somehow missed.

"This really would go much easier if we could just talk," Pushkin tried again, and I thought I would be damned if I let them bundle me up and strap me down to that table. I'd had enough of that in the twentieth century and wasn't about to spend the twenty-first as someone's lab rat.

The next wave of energy came as I ran the last couple of feet toward the men. With my shoulder, I bowled Pushkin over, knocking him to the ground and breaking the connection. I stood over him, my teeth on his throat. Unlike the thugs upstairs, these men weren't using guns, and I grinned, tongue lolling. This was my kind of fight.

I bit deep, finding the important parts that kept the life flowing through his body, and punctured them. I waited for the sweet taste of blood on my tongue, and then the same strange bitterness I had tasted on Gratuszcak caught in my throat. I gagged, hacking and spitting, trying to get it out of me.

The red around my sight blurred and sang across my vision. I pawed at my face, trying to get the strangeness away from me. I felt hands reaching for me, trying to catch me. I twisted away.

The taste reached down my throat, and I felt myself choking, the muscles contracting. It felt like they had tried to destabilize the change, but on this night, the weird of the old magic had the upper hand. The rage that had steadily grown since that full moon in the woods of Vermont reached out to the strange energies trying to trap me in place, brushing them aside. I gave myself over to the struggle, feeling the Old Power of the city reaching up through the layers of concrete and science to infiltrate my consciousness.

As a pup, my grandfather had whispered stories to me when he thought my mother couldn't hear—stories of old wolves from hundreds of years before who could achieve a transformation unlike any known to modern werewolves. It wasn't simply the change, but a total transformation, the *Überwechsel*. He told me of beasts—more than either man or wolf—old ones who could fight on two feet, their bodies a perfect, killing mesh of man and wolf.

I had achieved a certain kind of half-change before, but this blasted those previous attempts far and away. When I turned my back on my family and my country, I turned away from anyone who could have taught me. But here, back on my own soil, with this strange energy crackling down my bones, I found the *Überwechsel* within me, waiting as if it'd prepared a long time for my beckoning. I reached for it, and it rushed toward me.

The pain came quickly, harder than any change I had ever experienced. The bones did not merely crack but lengthened and grew powerful, the energy dancing like lightning.

I surged to my feet, and the lighting cast multiple shadows around the room, a crazy Lon Chaney mix of wolf and man against the splatters flying against the walls. I could see the color, the red, bright from the veins, darker where pieces of brain or body matter hit the paint and slid down.

The men were powerful. I could feel their energy batting against me, trying to catch a handhold on my body, but I wrenched away from the questing force, pulling and pushing, dancing a wild brawl in the blood-painted room. I became more than a wolf; I was a force of nature, akin to the old ones as they threw their bodies into the elements on the mountains of the German Alps. Around me, I felt the shadows of the pack, racing the night and winter through the old forests, chasing Green Jack on the ancient Hunt.

Finally, my teeth and claws could find no more enemy. I straightened, the film over my eyes clearing slightly. The room returned to its antiseptic brightness, the bloodstains giving it an oddly cheery cast.

Someone started a slow clap behind me. I whirled, claws extended, not ready to quit reaching for the violence I still felt within me, within this new, marvelous change-shape.

"Amazing," Dr. Gratuszcak said. "Exactly what we were hoping for."

He stepped over the bodies of his former Collective. He still reminded me of a long-winded college professor as he pointed at the ceiling. I followed his gesture. Above me hung the dark glass half-sphere of a closed-circuit camera.

I launched myself at him without thinking and found myself pinned back against the wall, writhing in agony. The energy of his acolytes had been but a brief taste of the power he could muster, and I kicked and grasped, trying to catch a foothold in midair. The power burned through me. My nerve endings were on fire.

"There is so much to learn." His normally banal expression twisted into desperate hunger. "The notes were less than incomplete." He reached for me.

A sound came like thunder—rapid-fire, thirty-eight caliber thunder. I found myself on the ground, blood singing, able once again to move under my own power. Gratuszcak steadied himself on one knee in the middle of the room. Behind him, Karen stood in a perfect Weaver stance, holding my gun in her hands, still pointed at his back. Smoke rose from the barrel. She started toward me.

"Wait." I held up a hand. She seemed as surprised as I felt to hear me speak in wolf form. Or at least growl the word out.

But that wasn't the reason for my gesture. Instead, I watched as the gaping exit wounds on the doctor's chest knitted, faded, and finally smoothed away, leaving not a sign they were ever there. From Karen's audible gasp, I figured she could see the same thing from the back.

Like a good fighter, he attacked quickly, catching us off balance while we were still trying to make sense of what we were seeing. Gratuszcak's features blurred, and he reached for me with both hands.

I slipped his attack as he came for me, circling around, trying to catch him on an angle, trying to work my way around so Karen wasn't directly across from me. The horror movie shadow I cast on the wall paled in comparison to the creature forming before me.

Limbs sly and spindly snaked out from his lab coat, the nails at the ends of his fingers growing into long, twiggy daggers that quested toward us. He moved to block me from reaching Karen, stumbling as she unloaded the other three silver rounds from the chamber into his back. The momentary stagger gave me my opening. I lunged for him, wrapping around his body in a tango dance of violence and anger. We clawed and grappled, bowed and tumbled, and his dagger nails drew blood from my throat. Where he scored me, my body forgot to heal.

The roar of a gun came again. This time Karen unloaded the magazine of her M4 into his body. The rounds weren't silver. She didn't have to worry about them affecting me. But he seemed as immune to them as I was.

We rolled on the ground. I was getting winded. The *Überwechsel* left my body incredibly strong and powerful, but I wasn't used to it, and I had started the night hungry. I could feel myself burning energy at an unhealthy rate. I stumbled, and he leapt on my back, pinning my arms, blocking my attempts to wriggle out of his bony grasp.

Gratuszcak snaked his arm around my neck, choking me with the crook of his thin, wiry elbow. It felt like I was being garroted with a length of piano wire.

"Keller!" Karen bellowed across the space. The word barely registered in my ears. I felt it more in my body, her desperation and fear. "Roll! Now!"

The red was almost gone from my vision, replaced by a thick black coming down on me like a curtain. I struggled, twisted, and finally rolled away.

I heard a sound like a steak knife sinking into flesh, and then the arms around my neck loosened. I took advantage and scrambled away and to my feet.

I turned to see Gratuszcak—tall, mean, and spindly like some nightmare creature from a medieval folktale—stumbling his way across the floor toward Karen. From his back protruded the handle of her last-ditch effort to save me—seven inches of combat knife. She fired again and again as he advanced on her.

Preparing to launch myself at him again, he casually gestured, and I found myself flying through the air once more. I hit the exam table with my side, flipping over and landing full force on the tray of instruments. I was bleeding heavily, trying to breathe, running on fumes of rage. I dug deep to see what reserves I might have left. My hand closed on the bouquet of syringes littering the floor.

I didn't know what they had been planning for me, but I knew the clear liquid in the vials spelled bad news for someone. My new size made it hard to hide behind anything, but I crouched behind the table and watched as Gratuszcak advanced on my partner.

She scrambled back from him, but his onslaught was as inexorable as an incoming wave. He closed his hand around her throat, long fingernails carefully prodding her hair and skin.

I stood up.

"Yes, Wolf." Gratuszcak's deformed muzzle added a sibilant hiss to the words. "Come, watch."

I walked toward him, trying to project reluctance. I came within one simple arm's reach when he turned around.

"This one, we can work with, I believe." He, too, was breathing hard, heaving to get the air in past his elongated teeth.

Karen's eyes rolled back in her head, and for a moment, I feared the worst, but then she squeezed them shut and kicked the good doctor squarely between the legs.

He flinched, and in that same moment, I lunged forward, sinking all five syringes into the fleshy part of his torso and depressing the plungers.

Gratuszcak screamed and dropped Karen. She scrambled away, hand to her neck. I dodged to the side and came up beside her. Gratuszcak screamed again and then doubled over.

Strange muttering growls came from his throat. His limbs twisted, lengthening and contracting. His teeth grew sharp and too long for his mouth, cutting through the skin around his lips. He dropped to all fours, his pasty skin dusted with a coat of fine, pale fur.

I suddenly realized what he was and what I had injected him with. Someone had finally tried to synthesize the change. Gratuszcak moaned through a mouth full of teeth, flinching as his body tried to settle into one shape or the other—we were looking at what had to be one of the first viable prototypes. The syringes, whatever they were, had accelerated the process too much for his body to control. I shuddered to think what part they had planned for me in all of this, what secrets they had already begun to coax from my blood.

Gratuszcak began screaming, this time a high-pitched, even, unending scream. Karen and I covered our ears in pain. I think my nose began to bleed. A pounding came on the stairs. I wanted the sound to stop. I wanted the pain to stop. I wanted to close my eyes, and when I opened them up, I wanted to be back in my woods in

Vermont. I'm sure we looked a sight, the soldier bristling in weapons and the giant werewolf cowering on the floor, but we were gone beyond caring, caught up in the pain.

The scream intensified in pitch and volume, a sudden uptick, and then it cut off. Raising my head, I caught a glimpse of twisted flesh before Gratuszcak's body settled back into its familiar shape and size. Eyes closed, his head lolled. I could sense a faint pulse of life, although I hoped like hell he was circling the drain.

We held our breath through a moment of complete silence until a loud sound broke our concentration. I realized Karen and I had both taken a deep breath at the same time.

We both jumped as someone pounded on the door again.

"Police." Karen checked her watch.

"Yeah."

"You should change back."

"Yeah." The words came out fuzzy; I didn't want to let go of this new form. "Let me see what I can do."

I reached for the change, and there was a fast moment of panic when I couldn't find it and pictured myself stuck as SuperWolf for the rest of my life. I backed off of it, then turned and brushed up against it, inviting it instead of pursuing it. With a sigh, my body untwisted itself, settling back into the familiar lines of my human frame. I felt a momentary and crushing sense of loss.

I sat there for a minute. Karen moved over to one of the bodies. With clinical detachment, she pulled off a pair of men's pants and handed them to me. I put them on. They were loose, but they would do until I could go shopping. I picked up my gun from the floor and tucked it into the pocket. I still felt traces of silver, but it didn't burn me like it had before. Interesting.

A glint of metal caught my eye. My St. Jude medal had broken off during the change, the chain unable to fit around the *Überwechsel*. I picked it up and slipped it into my pocket next to my gun.

The pounding on the door came again.

"Is there another way out of here?"

"How the hell should I know?"

"Sorry," I said, and I meant it. "Wasn't thinking."

Karen shook her head. "Forget it. Help me with the doctor. We can't leave him for these guys to find."

I picked him up under the shoulders, and she grabbed his feet. Together, we looked around the basement for another exit. We were in luck. There was a chute of some sort that afforded us the space of a small tunnel to squeeze our way out of the underground cell we found ourselves trapped in.

I went up first, an easy fit. I hoisted myself out of the opening, keeping an eye open to see if anyone lurked about. The chute emerged into the small alley at the back of the building. I could see the flashing lights from the emergency vehicles reflected against the brick but didn't sense anyone else in the vicinity. The red had faded away, and I was back to seeing the world in shades of black and gray.

"Rick, hurry up; they're about to bust through down here," Karen called up.

I turned and bent down. She stuffed Gratuszcak up through the chute. He almost didn't fit, but I was able to get my hands under his armpits and pull him up the rest of the way. I maneuvered him up to the street, dumping him onto the sidewalk, and then bent down again to help Karen through the opening.

Once we got out on the street, our plan was simple: go to the place where the police weren't. We hoisted Gratuszcak between us, draping his arms over our shoulders, playing the "taking the drunk home" scenario. It served to get us out of the alley and through the shadows, away from the lights and sounds of the police raid on the building. I turned around briefly to see the police officers escorting the women out of the building. I truly hoped they would be able to find some peace, that we had accomplished something more in this building than finding someone else who wanted to stick needles in me. The thought of the mission made me think of something else.

"Wait." I stopped short.

"What?" Karen took advantage of the pause to readjust her grip on the good doctor.

"What about Tell?"

"Fuck him," she said. "Let's go."

We got the hell out of there, carrying the doctor with us, following Karen's plan. We found someplace safe to hide until we could return to the States and take the good doctor with us. MONIKER was going to want to ask him a few questions.

24

Ken Ramirez hadn't lost his taste for flannel, but at least this time, we were able to dispense with the PowerPoint. We were back in the corporate conference room, the guards with the automatic rifles and silver bullets once again stationed at the door. A small video camera on a tripod caught everything in its beady little gaze. After six hours, I hoped someone would order a pizza. Or a beer. Or really any food that wasn't an MRE, which was all I'd had to eat since we left Europe.

MONIKER had chartered us a flight out of Germany. It wasn't some swanky private jet, but a battered, nondescript military cargo plane that meandered its slow, turbulence-ridden way across Europe, stopping every half hour it seemed to take on or load off some mysterious boxes of MONIKER crap before trundling its weary path across the North Atlantic. We had Gratuszcak on a steady drip of something that kept him in dreamland. I tried to sleep, too, but spent most of the flight simultaneously airsick and ravenous.

Also, every time I closed my eyes, I saw—not the strange creature Gratuszcak had become, but the room we found as we were leaving the building. It had only been a glimpse, but in the flood of scent that waved over me, it told the whole story. Why the doctor's organization had been trafficking in young women, why those same women disappeared without a trace. MONIKER had had me to experiment on at will. This organization had not, and the women had paid the price.

We were met at the airport by a special committee. They brought several different flavors of weapons but no fruit basket. Not even a Danish. None of them cracked a smile when I asked if they had any Grey Poupon, just loaded us into two black SUVs, and drove us straight to MONIKER headquarters. I was half-expecting to be thrown into another cage, but they treated Karen and me like a real team—or at least two-thirds of one—and brought us together straight to the conference room. We sat for six hours answering questions we didn't know the answers to.

"And you say you didn't recognize this man who called himself Doctor...Gratchik?" Ramirez led the interrogation. I mean debriefing.

"Gratuszcak," I replied again. "And, no."

"And you have no idea how he found out about you?" It was the tenth time he had asked me the question. I kept score, jotting little hash marks down on a piece of notepaper.

I hadn't mentioned the notebook, and Karen hadn't dropped the dime on me yet. She had handed the journal off to me without a word somewhere over Greenland.

"No." The emotion that surged to the surface of the word betrayed the fact that I was lying, but I banked on the hope that they wouldn't bother trying to torture the truth out of me. After all, we had brought them this tasty new object of scientific curiosity on which to try out all their techniques. They might eventually pull the source of his knowledge from his screaming lips, but I wanted to be far away and out of the range of questions when they did.

On the other hand, MONIKER being MONIKER, it was entirely possible they were going to float money, equipment, and pretty much everything Gratuszcak's little iceberg of a weird-tasting heart could want, simply to have him come work for the organization, teach them the secret of his science-induced transformation, the powers he had coaxed from his chemically saturated brain. They had done more for less. Just one more reason for me to get the hell away from there and back to my woods.

"Do you have anything to add?" Ramirez sounded tired.

Karen shook her head. "No."

"Fine." Ramirez shuffled his notes together and toggled a switch on the video camera. "Here's the deal."

"I can't wait," I said.

"Shut up, Keller." He picked up the paperwork and folded it in half. "Dr. Willet, we've decided to give you a break from fieldwork for six months. You'll be on probation, down in the lab with the science bubbas, helping them work with whatever you two brought in."

"Seriously?" Karen's voice sounded strangled. "A lab rat?"

"You're lucky you're not on permanent unpaid leave, otherwise known as separation from the organization," Ramirez said. "Believe me, I had to pull quite a few strings, some of them attached to your grandmother's legacy, to even get that."

"That's beyond unfair, Ramirez," I said. "I'd be dead, and your organization wouldn't even know about Tell and Gratuszcak and whatever else was going on if it hadn't been for her."

"Rick." Karen shook her head. "Don't try to help me."

She didn't sound angry, only resigned. I can't say I was surprised. MONIKER had started out as an end-run around stifling military bureaucracy and had apparently come full circle to embrace the mind-numbing illogic of its parent.

"As for you," Ramirez began.

"What about me?" I decided to push the envelope. "Do you have a nice comfy lab assistant position down in your dungeons for me too?"

The retort was too long-winded to be punchy and clever. Ramirez shook his head.

"Against my better judgment, we're keeping you on as a field agent," he said. "Enough of my colleagues agree that it's a mistake to let you walk away again. Welcome back, Agent Keller."

I stared at him.

"Dr. Willet will show you to Personnel, finish up the rest of the paperwork," he said, folding the camera tripod and tucking it under his arm. "Karen, take him to the fifth floor, get him settled with one of the geobachelor rooms; we'll talk after the weekend."

I didn't bother to get up when he left. I don't think he expected me to.

FINALLY, it was just Karen and me, staring at each other across the table. She stood up, and I followed suit. I followed her to the door, but she paused, hand on the handle. She turned back to me, and we were standing face to face.

I fought back the urge to brush her hair back over her ear. Our moment had passed.

"I hate to ask," I said, "but where is the bathroom in this place now that I'm not being held in a werewolf-proof cage?"

For some reason, that struck her as funny, and she laughed a short harsh chuckle. She sobered up.

"Down the hall and to the right. It's the little figure that doesn't have pants."

"They're overrated." I smiled, trying not to give anything away. "Always get in the way of a good change."

We paused at the same time. The silence grew awkward.

"Are you—?" Karen raised an eyebrow.

"Yeah, yeah. I'm leaving." I stopped smiling. "Be right back." I stood up and started to leave.

"Hey—Rick?"

"Yeah?"

"The lone wolf act is really convincing." Karen held my gaze in the steady way she did. "You weren't the only one there that night in the hotel."

I slammed the shutters down against the surge of hope.

"We took Gratuszcak down together," Karen continued. "Don't you even want to find out what he is?"

"I know what he is," I answered. "He's what you get when a century of scientists get bored studying a thing and try to create a monster of their very own. Thanks, but I don't think that's something I want to know about or be involved in. I've had just about enough of my past trying to kill me."

"Doesn't it concern you that there are obviously people out there who know about you and want you for their own purposes?"

"And whose fault is that?" I demanded. "I didn't put an ad out on Radio Free Europe."

She ignored my outdated reference. Not that I have any current ones. "We're going to protect you. MONIKER has a lot of resources."

"Yeah, sure." I nodded, not sure if she saw what I was planning or if she was just that good at getting inside my head. "I've seen how they use some of those resources firsthand. What about Tell?"

"What about him?" she asked. "We'll find him. Eventually. You can't tell me you don't want to be a part of that."

"I've had enough vengeance to know that's a dead end." I only half meant it. I stuck out my hand, and when she took it, I folded her into an actual hug. She hesitated, then returned it. Finally, after the moment had gotten completely awkward, I dropped my arms and stepped back. "I gotta take a piss."

"Rick…"

"It's okay, Karen."

She opened her mouth to say something, but nothing came out.

DITCHING MONIKER wasn't as hard as I thought. The toughest part was walking away from Karen, knowing she would take the brunt of whatever displeasure Ramirez felt at me disappearing. But I had been happily retired, and I saw no reason to jump back in the fold of the same agency who hadn't had enough oversight of its own agents to keep them from selling me on the black market.

I had no doubt that MONIKER would blame Karen for me fucking off out of there—twice over when they realized I used her building access card to get the hell out of the building. There were a few hundred dollars in her wallet as well that I grabbed when I lifted it mid-hug; I still needed to make my way out of the city without leaving a trail. The phone number I slipped into the wallet before leaving it on the counter in the ladies' bathroom would give her a chance to call me on it.

I hoped she'd take her time.

Outside, the sun was starting to set, and the wind was picking up. I'd been in and out of the building a few times by now, but never any time that I was conscious enough to remember. I'd come out around midtown, not too far from the Port Authority. From there, I could grab something that would get me north, away from the teeming mass of people that surrounded me.

Still, a crowd was as good a place as any to start to disappear.

EPILOGUE

The outskirts of the little village consisted of long fields covered with the deep January snow. The night was clear, the moon only a dull glint in the sky. A dog howled, the noise echoing uneasily through the village.

At the edge of the cluster of tumbledown outbuildings, the remains of some old farm, a light showed under the door. The man outside shifted from side to side uneasily, trying to keep warm. His breath frosted, the steam mingling with the smoke from his knockoff Marlboro.

Inside the shed, two men stood below the solitary light. One man, dressed in jeans and a heavy sweater and overcoat, fed logs into a wood-burning stove that cast little warmth into the cold room. The other, dressed in an expensive suit and trench coat, stood in front of a chair on which sat a bound, solitary figure.

The man's bare feet rested on the stark concrete, red with the chafing cold. He slumped against the ropes binding him to the chair. Marks of previous interrogations shone dark black and blue against his body.

John Tell lifted his head, trying to see past eyes nearly swollen shut.

"It's your turn to talk now." The man in the suit picked his teeth with a long, sharp nail, spitting out whatever he found in there. "I'd like you to tell me about Herr Richard Keller."

THE END

ACKNOWLEDGEMENTS

In 2011, two friends sat down to pursue the victory of NaNoWriMo. One of those friends won NaNo and went on to run IronMan triathlons around the world, attend graduate school for mechanical engineering, and then leave the Army to be a badass firefighter.

The other one wrote this book.

Thanks, Liz, for being my writing partner. Thank you also to Trey and Jim for your comments and edits and encouragement. A word of thanks is also due my spouse, Rob, who puts up with a lot, including his wife wandering around the house and muttering to herself when the characters start misbehaving.

ABOUT THE AUTHOR

As a military journalist, Rachel A. Brune wrote and photographed the Army and its soldiers for five years. When she moved on, she didn't quit writing stories with soldiers in them, just added werewolves, sorcerers, a couple evil mad scientists, and a Fae or two. Now a full-time author and writing coach living in North Carolina, Rachel enjoys poking around old military posts and listening for the ghosts of old soldiers ... or writing them into her latest short story. She lives with her spouse, two daughters, one reticent cat, and two flatulent rescue dogs.

ALSO BY RACHEL A. BRUNE

Side Roads: A Dark Fiction Collection

FRIENDS OF FALSTAFF

Thank You to All our Falstaff Books Patrons, who get extra digital content each month! To be featured here and see what other great rewards we offer, go to www.patreon.com/falstaffbooks.

PATRONS

Dino Hicks
John Hooks
John Kilgallon
Larissa Lichty
Travis & Casey Schilling
Staci-Leigh Santore
Sheryl R. Hayes
Scott Norris
Samuel Montgomery-Blinn
Junkle